To
Danielle —
and to the start
of a beautiful
friendship!
Best, Holly Carter

D0860788

Cape May

a novel

Holly Caster

TDC
publishing

Email correspondence to: capemayanovel@gmail.com.

First published in the USA by TDC Publishing, Nyack, New York.

ISBN: 978-0-99664-890-5

COVER DESIGN BY SARAH FITZGERALD
INTERIOR DESIGN BY SUSAN B. GLATTSTEIN
AUTHOR PHOTOGRAPH © DARRYL FOSSA

Dedication

I'd like to thank, in order of appearance: my sister Wendy, who, among so many other things (enough to fill another book), gave me her front row seat for the final performance of *The Light in the Piazza*; Tom, my husband of 26 years—we were engaged after knowing each other three months and I don't know why we waited so long; and my children Charles and Emma, without whom my life, and the entire world, would be far inferior.

CHAPTER 1

Although Joanna Matthews had few memories of childhood—or rather, few *happy* memories of childhood—she did recall long lazy summer days, so free, such a relief from having to sit in a classroom glued to a chair. She remembered bursts of energy, and spinning, spinning, spinning until she fell on the grass, any thoughts of injuring ankles or breaking hips decades away. Spinning until adrenaline raced, looking up and spinning until she couldn't tell the white clouds from the blue sky and her heart pounded and her throat went dry, finally collapsing on the warm vibrant grass and feeling the earth itself spin and her young body trying to hold on, until the earth and her breathing slowed, but the exhilaration continued, as shapes magically began appearing in the clouds. Childhood, the good and the bad parts, was long gone. She was a settled married woman with a respectable job. The job, and the marriage for that matter, offered no carefree spinning, no delightful falling on the grass. The only adrenaline now produced was of the harmful variety, caused by deadlines and self doubts about meeting those deadlines competently. There was little time for cloud watching, and only limited views between the buildings of Manhattan.

Adult though she was, a recent major decision could be traced back to a childhood incident, a visit to the Red Lion Inn in Massachusetts when she was very little. She was five and her sister ten, and their parents took them to Stockbridge. Older sister Cynthia thought the ancient inn, functioning since the 1700s, was creepy and boring. Joanna loved it, and dragged whomever would come with her to see every floor and public room. Of course she was too little to express more than "I want to stay here forever" to her uninterested sister, or to her parents who were going through their own revelations. The trip was organized by their mother in an effort to remind her straying husband how important family was. It didn't work. But instead of possibly hating the Red Lion Inn because it had split up her parents for good, Joanna loved it even more, for it represented the last place the four of them had been happy together.

Two decades later a boyfriend of Joanna's booked a room at the one-hundred and fifty year old Fox and Gables in northern Connecticut, rented a car, and whisked her away for a few days. Instead of blissful moments between the sheets, Joanna was off exploring the inn any chance she got. Long chats with the young couple who owned the place —people not unlike herself—opened her eyes to the possibility of ownership. When the weekend was over, she knew two things: she didn't want to see the boyfriend again, and she did want to run a bed and breakfast someday. She longed to own a piece of history, history you live in and care for and pass on to the next generation. The need to earn a living led to various jobs in a decidedly nonlinear career path, from bookstore manager to secretary to copy writer and now medical editor, and the B&B dream faded.

Until about eight months ago.

Joanna was being treated to a belated fifty-ninth birthday dinner. Her friend raised a glass of a complex Barolo and said, "To the second half of your life." (Ha-ha. More likely the final twenty years, but still.) "May you be happy." It made Joanna think. *"Happy"*? She left the restaurant, still thinking. That night she couldn't sleep. Her marriage was fine, if not filled with unending joy. Work rarely made her happy, but lots of people didn't like their job. On the plus side she had her sister, and a few good friends, and enjoyable hobbies, but was it enough? No. In bed, next to her sleeps-like-a-dead-rock husband, she felt suffocated by the condensed molecules in the dark room. Positive, happy thoughts do not come to people in the dark in the middle of the night. Joanna was no exception. Recent events jumped before her eyes like newspaper headlines in a 1930's movie. The deaths of two people she went to high school with (thanks for the news, Facebook). One from cancer, the other a heart attack. The clichés she'd been hearing and reading, in letters, emails, and in person echoed in her head: "No one lives forever" and "You can't take it with you" seemed to be the most popular. The latter was uttered most recently by the doorman of her apartment building, in reference to the now empty spot on the bench in their lobby. He added, "God came for her, but didn't take the dog." It would take some getting used to, not seeing ancient Marion and her tottering tiny dog, Pola, sitting there every morning and night.

She sat up in bed and pushed the negative thoughts away, using newly learned techniques enforced upon her and her coworkers by management hoping for an increase in productivity. She resented it, but had to admit the techniques did help, and she looked on the more positive side. Not "I'm going to die soon so why bother" but "I'm going to make the rest of my life a thing of beauty and a joy forever." She took a moment to visualize herself getting up, happily, in the morning, and getting happily dressed, and happily doing _____. At first nothing came to her. She breathed deeply a few times, and tried again. "Me, happily doing _____" and she suddenly saw, actually saw herself back at the Red Lion Inn, a little girl overflowing and dizzy with exhilaration. The little girl transformed into Joanna, now, in an inn. Her inn.

The vision had spurred her into action, almost immediately. She had to stop herself from waking Brian up. The next morning she had sat her husband down on the couch and essentially told him, "I need a change. A very big change." A nice guy who genuinely wanted her to be happy —or who hoped if she were less miserable it would also improve his life—he wished her well on her quest.

It began with three-day weekends or vacation days visiting towns hundreds of miles away from her New York City base. Sometimes Brian or her sister Cynthia accompanied her, sometimes not. So far those exploring trips, to towns and houses in Connecticut, Vermont, and other areas in the northeast, had proved fruitless, but she wasn't giving up. Just thinking about house-hunting, and moving, and painting rooms started more positive adrenaline flows.

***

About to embark on another weekend exploring trip, first she was having breakfast with Brian before working at her office for a few hours. She sat at a little table at which she'd sat with him almost every day for two decades.

Now, instead of feeling the usual malaise, the upcoming weekend filled her with anticipation. The trifold brochure in her hand interested her so much, she couldn't help but read aloud to her husband, "'*Cape May has the second-largest collection of Victorian houses in America, right after San Francisco.*' Sounds promising. I love Victorians. Painted Ladies." She took a sip of coffee.

"Isn't that like being the Miss America runner-up? *Second* largest."

"I'll settle for second best. I'm a lifetime East Coaster. San Francisco would be too much of a change." She skimmed the brochure. "'*The entire New Jersey seashore town is a National Historic Landmark.*' A landmark. I like that. I can't wait to see it in person." A quarter of a toasted everything bagel with light cream cheese remained on her plate.

"Great," Brian said, shoving the rest of the bagel in his mouth. "We'll live in a landmark."

Joanna turned away from her husband's sarcasm (and chewing) and gazed out the living room window. The immediate view from their eleventh floor tiny two-bedroom apartment on West Eighty-Sixth was nothing special; however, if she stuck her head out the window and looked left, she could see the tops of a few trees in Central Park. Friends told her she was crazy to even think about moving from this apartment and neighborhood.

Brian walked the six feet to the kitchen for more coffee. He emptied the pot into his Yankees mug, flipped off the coffee maker, and said, "Oh, did you want?"

She shook her head. "Cape May can't be as nice as it seems, can it? I mean, *everyone* would move there."

"Well, honey, you'll know soon enough."

"I suppose. I just want the perfect house in the perfect location at the perfect price. How unrealistic is that?"

"Very. Very unrealistic but also very endearing, and optimistic, considering that you didn't find anything in Connecticut..."

"Too expensive."

"Or Vermont."

"Too rural."

"Massachusetts."

"Oh, I loved that house. I put a binder on it, remember?"

"And then we wasted a lot of money finding out it was in horrible shape."

"Brian, I'm learning. I've been doing my homework. Don't worry."

"Yeah, great, whatever."

"Your confidence in me is palpable."

"Jo, darlin', I told you I'd move, if you so desperately want to move. It's your money. But I don't have to also be your cheerleader." OUCH, BRIAN.

"Okay. You're right. But I really feel there's a perfect house out there for us."

"For *you*, Jo. If it were up to me, I'd live here until they carry me out in a pine box. As for 'perfect,' in your almost sixty years on earth, haven't you learned that perfect doesn't exist?"

"In myself, yes."

She brought her plate to the sink in their tiny kitchen. If they moved, they might have a real kitchen, maybe with an island. Heck, she'd be happy with a 1950's Formica table, like her family had in their Queens apartment when she was a child. If the kitchen is the heart of a home, her and Brian's apartment was dangerously low in cardiac function.

He said, "This'll be, what, your fifth trip hunting for a house? Maybe you need to lower your expectations. Or stop looking."

"I can't rush this, Brian. It's not just finding a house and a town. It's finding, well, a new lifestyle. It could take years." She added a grim afterthought: "Although I may not live long enough for this change if my job ends up killing me."

"You could quit that job anytime now that you got that inheritance."

"That's for the house. Whenever I find the house."

"We have a good life here, you know."

"I know. Look at it this way: at the very least, we'll get a weekend away."

***

Joanna and Brian met when they were in their early thirties. After a slow start, they became good friends. Movies, museums, Scrabble, and companionable meals where they talked about who they were dating and how it was—and usually wasn't—going. One December 31st, after a long dating dry spell for Joanna and a bad breakup for Brian, they sat on his worn couch watching TV, waiting for the ball to drop, and drinking too much. They later christened that night "New Self-Pity Eve."

"I'm sick of dating and getting my heart broken!" slurred Brian.

"At least you date," Joanna said, pouring herself another glass of wine, determined to match him in drunkenness.

"I haven't met anyone. And at my new job, there's no one even egglyable."

"Eligible?"

"Yeah. You meet girls everywhere and you date."

"Great. Lucky me! I date and get hurt. At least you don't get hurt."

"I'm hurting right now, Brian. I'm lonely, and I'm feeling like it's all my fault, that there's something about me guys just don't like."

"You've dated some nice guys, Joanna. You're too picky."

"Just because you like them, to play basketball with or watch boy movies with, doesn't mean they make good boyfriends."

"You push the good ones—even guys I don't want to hang out with—you push 'em away. I've seen you do it."

"What about Simon? I liked him, but he didn't like me. Lots of 'em don't like me." Somewhere inside she was relieved to be complaining, letting it out, and mixing whining with the wine. Normally, she tried to be positive, and didn't admit to herself how lonely she frequently was.

"Well I like you, a lot. We always have fun together."

"I don't mean fun. I mean sex. Love. A future."

"I love you like a friend. And I'd have sex with you like a friend." With that, he kissed her. Fueled by a long period of celibacy plus the alcohol, she returned the kiss. The fact that he was tipsy made it easier for her, too. In his state he probably wouldn't notice how inexperienced she was, and insecure in bed. Even though she wanted to get to it before the wine wore off, she wouldn't head to the bedroom until he located a condom. Some mistakes are so big you only make them once.

When Joanna woke up, alone in Brian's bed, she had a hangover, and the suspicion that she'd done something stupid. She shook her head, which made it hurt more. "Ouch."

Brian came in with a cup of coffee. "If you feel like I do you'll need these," he said, taking a bottle of aspirin out of his pocket and throwing it next to her on the bed. He sat. She inched to an upright position, covering herself with the sheets, and reached for the medicine. He pointed to her breasts, and smiled. "I saw 'em last night, and I liked 'em."

She laughed, and smacked his arm, spilling some coffee. He said, "Oh, now I'll have to wash the sheets. I was going to frame them."

"Oh, Brian, we didn't, did we?"

"How much do you remember?"

"It's coming back to me hazily, slowly."

"What about my incredibly huge…"

"No, please, laughing makes my head hurt more."

That was the start of their occasional "sextogethers," a word they made up because they hated "fuckbuddies." After a breakup, or when things got desperate, they'd meet, split a bottle of wine or two, and have sex. Sometimes it was okay for her, but more often she was just there for him, trying to be a good friend. She figured use it or lose it. It was better having meaningless sex with Brian than not having sex at all.

love this (handwritten marginalia)

***

"You sure you want to take the bus to Cape May?" Brian said, cleaning sesame seeds from his bagel off the table. "Can't you wait until tomorrow and drive down with me?" He pulled hard on a stuck cabinet door and reached for the jar of vitamins. He downed a few with a cup of water.

"No," she said. "This is the best time workwise to get away. And I know you: you'll speed the whole way and make me feel like there's something wrong with me if I have to go to the bathroom. Also, this way I'll have some time alone to walk around, to form my own opinions. Yours are very loud, even when you don't say them out loud."

"Whatever."

"I also want the full tourist experience of going to Cape May. Like for research. I want to know exactly what it's like on the bus, and how guests will feel when they arrive at our door, how we can help them relax after a long trip."

"You sound pretty gung-ho."

"I am. Well, let's say gung-ho with reservations. How's gung-so-so?" She sat on the couch.

He plopped beside her. "I'm sure most people drive there anyway."

"No! I read...about four thousand people live in Cape May, right? During the summer, forty thousand people visit! They can't all be driving. There'd be no room for all those cars."

"Sounds like nine or ten months of the year Cape May is boring and empty, and the other times it's jammed with annoying tourists."

She gave him a look.

"Or, I could think of it as peaceful and quiet and then exciting and bubbly." He put his hand on her shoulder. "You know, I am trying to warm up to the idea of moving. Spending our declining years in a picturesque seaside town." His hand cupped her breast. "And maybe we can, you know, resume..."

She took his hand off her breast and rubbed it against her face. "Uh-huh."

"You would be one of those annoying, weird women who get better looking as they get older."

"Thanks?"

"It was meant to be a seductive compliment. I want you to know I'm interested," he said, then closed in on her for a kiss, and she responded. She touched his smooth face. No matter how early he got up, five minutes later his face was shaved smooth as a baby's bottom. A decade ago, when he started freelancing from home, he felt it was important to maintain a level of professionalism. He had stopped wearing a tie in the house after a few months, but shaving made him feel work-ready, he told her. The only times she saw him scruffy were when he was sick and couldn't lift a razor, and she had to admit he did look pretty awful. He continued, "Well, it's time for me to hit the spreadsheets." He got up to leave, then turned around to say, "I hope things go well for you in Cape May. Really."

"Thanks for being the agreeable spouse."

"I'm doing my best 'cause you have your heart set on moving."

"I do. Manhattan is wearing me down. I'm exhausted. All the time. And here's a news flash: I hate my job."

"You always hate your jobs. A few days away from it all will do you good."

She made the bed, then finished packing her weekender bag. She entered their tiny second bedroom, which was Brian's office. A line of file cabinets in that awful putty color lined one wall, with his fat CCH Master Tax Guides among the books on top of them. He sat behind his desk, with a laptop and a desktop computer, folders, papers, and open books splayed before him. Other than his thinning and graying hair, he looked much the same as when she met him. Tall and skinny. He had reminded her, when she first saw him, of comic-book Archie's best friend, Jughead.

She said, "I'd think you'd want to move just to get more work space."

"I'm used to it after all these years. I can reach everything without getting up. You leaving?"

"Yes. I have to get to work. See if I can retrieve a PowerPoint presentation I somehow misplaced."

"Jo, you stink on the computer."

"Thanks for reminding me."

"You're smart in many other ways."

"Oh shut up."

"What time is your bus?"

"At 2:30. I'll stay a few hours then walk to the Port Authority."

"I'm glad you're leaving. I need quiet. I have a new client I have to impress." As he walked her to the front door he said, "Phone?" She nodded. "Phone charger?" She nodded. "Cash?" She nodded. "Credit cards?" She nodded. "Good girl." He opened the door for her, and Archie, their orange tabby of uncertain age, ran into the hall.

Joanna said, "Come back, little Archie." She scooped him up and scratched under his chin. "Where do you think you're escaping to?" Handing the purring bundle to Brian, she said, "Maybe he wants fresh air and grass."

"Yes, Archie, obviously, has always wanted to live the

life of a B&B cat." He let the cat jump out of his arms. "Oh, I forgot to tell you: my sister called. She's found three assisted living places for my Mom to check out next week."

"Awww."

"No, Mom's okay about it. All her friends have moved or died. At least this way she'll have people to play cards with."

"She has a better attitude than I will, I bet."

"You have many good years left in you, old girl." He put his hand on her shoulder and kissed her. As always, even though she didn't mean to, she pulled away before he did. "Well, I'd better get to work," he said. "Meeting you in Cape May tomorrow, and looking at places with my Mom next Wednesday, I'm losing too many work days. There will be some late nights for me coming up, that's for sure."

"Good, I'll be able to watch a romantic movie or two without you complaining through the whole thing." She took a MetroCard out of her wallet. "Are you still going out to dinner with Frank?"

"I have to. I canceled on him last time."

"Where are you going?"

"I'll let Frank pick. It'll be four star, I'm sure. He's such a foodie."

"Good. We'll need his advice for breakfasts at our inn."

***

After Joanna pecked Brian goodbye, she reluctantly headed to work. Through a friend, she had gotten a job as an associate managing editor at a medical education company. The work wasn't easy, and lately she'd made a lot more mistakes. It paid well, but the hours were long, the work detailed and multifaceted, and her heart wasn't in it. Her boss wasn't thrilled having her for an employee but didn't have enough reason to fire her, yet. Her office was small and unimpressive but at least had a window. The second she walked through the door, she got a text message from her sister: "Find a great house." Cynthia's voice in her head read it as a command, not a good luck wish. Joanna turned on her computer and began hunting for the missing PowerPoint presentation.

Susan, Joanna's recently hired editorial assistant, bounced in. Although certain Susan could've found the presentation in minutes, Joanna was too embarrassed to ask. Twenty-three and newly graduated from college with a 4.0 in her double English/Communications major, Susan earned a not-so-whopping $34,500 a year. Joanna wished she had the clout to get the girl a raise. Susan was full of hopeful, helpful energy and enthusiasm and peppermint breath, wore a bright yellow V-neck shirt that was cut too low, a floral-print skirt that was too short, and unintentionally made Joanna feel old and sexless.

"Are you excited about your romantic weekend?" Susan glanced from the Cape May brochure on Joanna's desk to a picture of Brian thumbtacked to a bulletin board in back of Joanna's head. "Your husband is hot."

Hot? "I guess he is cute," Joanna said, throwing the brochure into a drawer, tired of looking at the couple on the cover: young, impossibly good-looking and fit, walking hand in hand on the beach. How many couples, of any age, felt inadequate when looking at these Photoshopped models? The sand and the ocean behind the irritating pair invited, but she and Brian wouldn't be strolling wearing tiny bathing suits. In reality, she and Brian had never frolicked on a beach in their entire marriage.

Her phone rang. It was her sister. "I'm faxing you something. It's a list of questions I found in *Real Estate Magazine*: 'What to ask a realtor.' Get all these questions answered. Make sure you understand what you're getting into."

"I'll do my best, Cynthia."

"Are you sure you don't need me to come with you? I can get my assistant to run the shop."

"No. I want to do it alone this time." Actually, she would've loved assistance, but not from her overbearing sister, who tended to commandeer events, small or large, or her husband, who wasn't enthusiastic about the project. Joanna had found it impossible on previous house-hunting trips to hear her own thoughts about a town or a house when either of those two joined her.

Joanna found the presentation in the bowels of her computer and spent the rest of the morning painstakingly going over facts and figures, trying to ignore the truth that she didn't care about any of it. She entered the latest statistics into a simple chart, using her limited PowerPoint skills. What took her an hour took the other editors, or her assistant, ten minutes. She wasn't keeping up with the younger people in the office, and they were all younger, much younger, and seemed to learn things instantly, through their pores. A friend had suggested she take a course. She looked into it, and then realized she didn't want to learn because she had to. Not any more. She wanted to learn because she wanted to. And she wanted a bed and breakfast.

***

Due to a last-minute meeting with her boss that she couldn't miss, Joanna ended up leaving work later than she had planned. Adrenaline, the kind that felt damaging, the kind filled with spikes, was speeding through her as she raced out of her office and headed west.

Recently researched statistics floated in her head. Population density of Cape May, New Jersey: approximately thirteen-hundred people per square mile. The corresponding number in New York City, almost twenty-eight thousand. On this fine June day, on the corner of Forty-Second Street and Sixth Avenue, Joanna felt like she was right in the middle of all twenty-eight thousand of them. She stood on the curb, her overnight bag starting to cut into her left shoulder. Her eyes darted from the red light hanging above the street to the red "Don't Walk" hand on the other side of the lanes of traffic. Her goal, the Port Authority bus terminal —what she jokingly called her Gateway to a Dream—was just a few blocks away. There, the bus to Cape May would be leaving in about half an hour. In New Jersey, the first words of a new chapter of her life might be written.

But first she'd have to cross this street.

Yes, New York was one of the greatest cities in the world, undeniably, but right now, Joanna didn't care about its restaurants, theaters, and museums. She just wanted the light to change.

At last, the red light turned green, and the red hand switched to a white figure walking. The northern flow of cars, buses, cabs, pedicabs, bikers, and roller bladers halted, and Joanna cautiously stepped off the curb and continued westward with the other pedestrians.

As she zigged and zagged to avoid the people heading east, her brain spat at her—Why didn't I take slightly less crowded Forty-First Street? Why didn't I pack my lighter-weight bag? Why didn't I wait until tomorrow and drive down the Jersey shore with Brian?

Joanna lowered the volume of her internal critic, which was always awakened by that spiky adrenaline. She walked quickly, her peripheral vision slow to take in a homeless woman with a crutch. She U-turned and bumped into a teenager with a patchy beard and huge headphones. She said, "Sorry!" even though it was his fault for tailgating. She neared the woman, who was sitting on a plastic crate, holding out a paper cup. The scribbling on the cardboard sign propped up in front of the woman, detailing a hard life and a request for food or money, was full of errors, and Joanna suppressed the urge to whip out her red pen to correct it. Instead, she dug in her pocket for a dollar, accidentally pulling out a $5 bill. About to shove it back into her pocket, she remembered her new credo, her own version of carpe diem: "Change. Improve. Every day," and pushed the money into the partially crushed cup.

"Bless you," said the old woman, a threadbare shawl barely covering her matted hair.

Joanna tried not to breathe in the rank odor. "You, too. Have a nice day!"

Was that a stupid thing to say to a hungry homeless person? Joanna continued her walk/run to the Port Authority, saying a silent prayer of gratitude. She was healthy and had high hopes for the rest of her life, starting in less than twenty-eight minutes, when she'd board a bus and travel south on the Garden State Parkway. Approximately one-hundred and eighty miles later she'd be in quaint, quiet (she hoped), Victorian Cape May. Tomorrow Brian would drive down, wanting to avoid any bus at any time, and accompany her when she met with the realtor.

It took five minutes to reach Times Square. Billboards, neon, construction, and lots of noise. Joanna once loved this area and the excitement, but she was younger then. Now it was an area to rush through. It was so frenzied crossing Seventh Avenue and then Broadway that she didn't feel her cell phone vibrate the first time. Finding an unoccupied spot against a building, she answered the phone. She knew it was her sister, again.

"Hello, Cynthia," she yelled into the phone.

"I can hardly hear you," Cynthia snapped. "Why is this city so damn loud?"

"Well, I am at the Crossroads of the World. It has a right to be loud."

"Not when I need to ask you something."

"Ask, but yell so I can hear you," Joanna said, checking her watch again.

Cynthia loudly whispered, "I can't. I'm in the shop." She was standing behind the reproduction Louis XV desk in her antiques store on Madison Avenue. "Are you sure about this realtor? Did you check her credentials?" Cynthia's disapproval always added up to more than two cents worth of opinion.

Joanna said, "Yes. Cynthia, I have to go. The bus leaves soon, and I have to get through this wall of tourists."

"Keep in touch. You need your older sister now. I can help. I have business savvy. You don't."

As Joanna continued walking, she tried to make sense of the assaulting theme park that the street had become. Funny that she missed the way it used to be. In the seventies and eighties, Forty-Second Street was slummy, with porno shops and bums, and movie theaters you wouldn't take a kid into. Now it was an outdoor strip mall of chain restaurants and attractions, from Applebee's and McDonald's to Rite-Aid and Duane Reade to Madame Tussauds and Ripley's Believe It or Not. *"Give me a head shop over this anytime,"* Joanna thought, laughing to herself, she who had smoked marijuana a grand total of three times.

By the time she got to the front of the Port Authority building, Joanna was exhausted. Hundreds of people entered the travel hub or exited with luggage and confused looks on their faces. Some people browsed counterfeit merchandise laid out on tables, others glanced at the statue of Ralph Kramden. Her inner core craved quiet.

Safe inside where it was slightly less crowded, Joanna slowed down and followed signs to her gate. She was winded from walking so fast but she'd made it in time. The huge clock over the archway read 2:17. Nearer her gate, she went into the ladies room, assuming it would be slightly less awful than the one on the bus. She fluffed her hair and checked her general appearance. Her preferably chin-length hair, neater for business and easier to control, was getting a little too long. Time to make an appointment at the salon. It still looked good, though, with waves that, she hoped, softened her aging face. She peered a little closer: yes, maybe that new miracle moisturizer was, indeed, "erasing" some fine lines. Heavens, she hoped so. Although the thought of a face lift made her feel queasy, so did the sags, wrinkles, and other joys of being fifty-nine.

At the Starbucks near her gate, she bought a cup of peppermint tea. Although there were empty seats at tables, she stood, leaning against a column, having just recently read that sitting too many hours a day was fatal. Tomorrow she'd probably read that drinking hot tea was fatal. Or breathing.

She drank slowly, trying to calm down her insides, which were still racing from the hectic sprint to the Port Authority. No need to rush to the bus. Her prepurchased ticket guaranteed her a seat and, after all, how many people would be going to New Jersey midday on a Thursday? She glanced at the other customers around her. Would Cape May offer such extraordinary people watching? No. Joanna had done her research—Cape May was almost ninety percent white; New York was thirty-five percent white, almost twenty-seven percent Hispanic, and about a quarter Black. After growing up in multiracial Queens, and living in Manhattan all these years, that disparity was unnerving. She had hopes of making her own inn—IF she bought one—somehow more welcoming to all. The thought of being surrounded by white, middle-aged people for the rest of her life didn't thrill her. She gulped. That was *her*, wasn't it? When and how did that happen? And what came between middle-aged and elderly? Older aged? Ugh. She felt young inside, and still looked pretty good on the outside. Her pale skin kept her out of the sun, which cut down on the wrinkles she might've had at her age. A few extra pounds refused to leave her average-sized frame, but she ate carefully and even her older clothes still fit, mostly. Infrequently she went to the gym and more frequently she thanked her slim parents for passing along their DNA.

A couple, in their late teens or early twenties, sat kissing at a small corner table. Unable to stop herself, she stared at them. When was the last time she and Brian had really kissed? Not just a peck hello or goodbye. A few days, and nights, together away from work, commitments, and routine would do them good.

Downing the remaining bit of soothing peppermint tea, Joanna listened to a Port Authority loudspeaker announcement in a lyrical Spanish accent: "The 2:30 bus to Atlantic City, with connections to Wildwood and Cape May, is now boarding at gate three nineteen."

Over the rim of her paper cup, Joanna risked one last glance at the kissing couple. After peeking (they were still kissing), she gathered her things, tossed the empty cup, and walked to the gate. She was surprised to see a line and, as she climbed aboard the bus, was again surprised to see it almost packed. Apparently one of the Atlantic City hotels was having a special mid-week offer, luring people south to the casinos, hence the crowd. Close to the front of the bus, where she preferred to sit, was an empty aisle seat next to a teenage boy with spiky black hair. The seat was comfortable and she managed to settle in, despite a strange cleaning-fluid smell.

A raspy smoker's voice over the bus speakers announced, too loudly, and with an awful accent, "Dis is da tooo-thurdy bus to Alanic Ciddee, wid transfuhs ta Wildwood an' Cape May." Her seatmate put in neon green ear buds, which emitted a steady thump thump thump. The engine also made a lot of noise. So much for a few relaxing traveling hours. Joanna pulled out her new notebook. Even if she didn't move to Cape May, she was keeping a journal about this midlife change, or attempt at change. She loved to write but was usually too tired after work and always too self-critical. She was learning already: her first "Note to Self" was *Visitors may crave quiet after a not-so-relaxing bus ride.*

Joanna looked out the window, but the kid with the headphones made a face, as if she was intruding on his space. So instead, she gazed at the rainbow pattern on the back of the headrest on the seat in front.

She concentrated, and jotted down: "*After twenty years of marriage, a woman and her accountant husband contemplate moving from Manhattan to buy and run a B&B, far away from the noise and crowds of the city.*"

Wow. Individual days might be long and draining, but years really did fly by. Twenty years of marriage.

Her seatmate turned up his volume and through the thumping she could hear the screaming of the singer. The bus driver was loudly conversing with a passenger, too. She needed to move away from the noise. She craned her neck and saw, all the way in the back, a few empty seats. Grabbing her overnight bag, she stood up, and carefully inched her way to the back of the bus, hurrying to find a seat. She wanted to sit alone and spread out but there weren't two empty seats together. The bus made a turn and she almost fell in someone's lap.

"Please siddown, ma'am," came the voice over the speakers. Joanna assumed the driver's concern for her well-being was rooted in the bus company's reluctance to be sued.

There were three empty seats: her prospective trip mates were a sleeping woman, a very large man, and a man who was reading. She decided on the woman, who suddenly snored, so she sat down next to the reader. He didn't look up or budge an inch.

She settled in: bag at her feet, notebook on her lap, pencil in her hand…and nothing in her mind. One sentence completed, she was already losing concentration. Was that age? Postmenopause? Disinterest? Or did she just desperately need to relax.

Too often lately she'd been feeling that, about to turn sixty, "It's all downhill from here." Sixty now wasn't what sixty was for her mother but, most likely, the best of life was over. Maybe her need to move, to start a business, to change everything, was simply a stab at slowing the inevitable decline. Maybe she wanted to shake things up with Brian. Things had gotten dull, and she was at least fifty-one percent to blame.

It was odd, really. She and Brian had started radically. All their friends thought they were crazy for marrying the way they did.

One night over twenty-five years ago, she went to Brian's apartment, lonely and desperately needing someone to just hold her. She wasn't in the mood for anything more, but quid pro quo. An hour later, over scrambled eggs and bagels, Brian had said, "You know, I have more fun with you than anyone else. If we don't meet anyone…"

"Oh, please, not one of those *we'll be married soul mates* kinda thing," Joanna said.

"Why not? I'm not saying we should get married to-morrow. But if we hit, let's say, forty, and neither of us is married, we could live our lives together. I'll watch your boring black and white movies, and you can go to baseball games with me. That's the one with the small round hard ball, and the bases."

"Got it."

"And you could help me to get home after I've had a colonoscopy."

"How romantic." She giggled, "You know, it doesn't sound bad, really."

"You know I love you, Joanna. Like my best friend ever."

"You, too, Brian," said Joanna, knowing full well she had years to meet someone and truly fall in love. But despite an assortment of boyfriends and a range of relationship lengths, she never did.

***

She jotted down in her notebook, "*Change, selfish? Poor Brian the New Yorker.*" Avoiding veering off into negative self-hate territory, she gazed out the windows past the man sitting next to her. The rocking of the bus, and scenery shushing by, began weaving a hypnotic spell. Her shoulders relaxed. She breathed slower, more deeply.

The man next to the window continued to read, with the brim of his denim baseball cap shading his eyes from the sun streaming through the window. She wished she had his ability to tune everything else out. Maybe it was the book? She stole a look at the title, and chuckled. What a coincidence. She tried to make eye contact but his eyes never left the page.

One of the many books she was always reading about how to run a B&B said "*The importance of warm, open personal interactions with guests cannot be overstated.*" That was definitely something she'd have to practice. Talking to strangers wasn't her thing, but no time like the present. She took the plunge, and quietly said to the man sitting next to her, "You enjoying the book?" The man didn't answer. A little louder: "Do you know there's a sequel?" No answer. So much for her attempt at being outgoing. "Never mind!" She resettled into her chair, semi-accidentally elbowing the man.

He reached up to his ear, pulled out an earplug, and said, "Am I in your way?"

"Earplugs. Great idea."

The man nodded. "I don't like being disturbed…"

Joanna threw up her hands. "Great."

"No, I didn't mean you."

"First I sit next to a sullen teenager and now a grumpy old man."

"Hey lady, I'm not grumpy. I'm not old. And I'm not *that* rude. I don't like to be disturbed by all the bus noises. I didn't mean you personally."

"Oh." She settled back in her seat, more than a little embarrassed. She smiled a little shy smile. "Then I'm sorry for what I said."

The man huffed, then slowly turned away, pushed his earplug back in, and returned to his book. Joanna opened her notebook.

CHAPTER 2

Hours earlier that morning, on West Seventy-Third, Michael Leighton had exited his apartment building and made a right onto Amsterdam Avenue. He pulled his denim baseball cap a little lower on his head. The brim, plus his sunglasses, made it easier for him to people-watch. The humans of Manhattan were well worth staring at. Invariably he saw someone or something that made its way into his writing.

He swung on his backpack. It didn't weigh much. Long ago he learned to pack only necessities for these long weekends away—the usual extra pair of pants, underwear, socks, and toiletries. He didn't need trunks; he didn't go to Cape May to swim. The beat-up leather briefcase in his left hand contained the important things, the tools of his trade: writing materials, including two notebooks from that new, hip Japanese store, along with a variety of pens and pencils and a folder full of research. There was something about putting a writing tool—be it a #2 pencil or a mechanical one or a fountain, felt-tip, or ball-point pen—to paper that made him feel connected to Hemingway, Fitzgerald, and other authors he admired and to whom, unfortunately, he compared himself unfavorably. Once he had enough pages filled up, he sat at his tiny desk at home, or brought his new laptop to a coffee shop and typed, editing and revising as he went.

This trip he was going to be disciplined and work on the new book. All he needed was resolve and another long bus trip. Maybe he should've rented a car? No, he wanted those extra hours on the bus to read and think, to decompress from Manhattan and be ready to immerse himself in Cape May.

The weather was perfect for his walk to the Port Authority. In Manhattan, forty blocks flew by—once he was warmed up so he wouldn't get shin splints...ain't aging grand?—and he liked the exercise for both body and mind. He headed east in the upper sixties to walk through Lincoln Center, a place he treasured, and which always offered great visuals. The face-lifted patrons walking side-by-side with teens in artfully ripped jeans, and the ballet students with hair in buns and toes pointed outward. During one walk through the plaza he saw magician David Blaine in a water sphere. Another time he encountered actor Michael Caine arriving to receive a lifetime achievement award from the Film Society. Never a dull moment.

Warmed up, he walked, faster now, past the fountain where eons ago he shared a rare, tender kiss with his wife Donna. Memories flowed, and not just the good ones. To his left, in front of Avery Fisher Hall, his wife told him, years after that rare, tender kiss, that she wanted a divorce because she didn't love him any more. That was almost eight years ago and no longer stung when he thought about it. He hadn't been a great husband, and they had never been the kind of madly in love that some couples are, but still it hurt and derailed him. Fortunately, their son was in college when they split, and wasn't traumatized or even surprised by the event. When Donna signed the divorce papers, she said she "didn't want to waste another day" of her life. She proved it just days after the divorce was finalized by marrying the guy she had been having an affair with. Husband number two was wealthy, serious, and successful, everything Michael wasn't. On the positive side, he never had to pay alimony. Another benefit was having more time to work. He had a steady income from a freelance job writing speeches for executives at a Fortune 500 company. Under a pseudonym, he had written mysteries for middle schoolers, but that was years ago. A lover of Cape May since his boyhood vacations, he was working on a novel about the nation's oldest seaside resort. His expenses were low, his apartment close to being paid for. If he could finish the Cape May book he was working on, he'd be content.

***

The bus rolled along south on New Jersey's Garden State Parkway. Michael took his out earplugs. He said to the woman sitting next to him, "Excuse me." She looked up at him. "I need to use the bathroom."

Joanna gathered the things on her lap and stood, allowing him to pass. Michael walked to the back of the bus and Joanna stretched. The seats were comfortable, but it was hard sitting in such a little space for a long time.

When he returned he slid past her into his seat, saying, "Good thing we're both slim," and put the earplugs in, and went back to reading.

Settled in again, Joanna tried to concentrate, but a woman two rows away was on the phone, talking so loudly she didn't need a phone. And every fifth word was a curse. Joanna tapped Michael on the arm, gently. He took out the earplug. "You wouldn't have an extra set of those, would you? I brought work with me," she said, holding up her notebook, "and it's so noisy."

"Sorry, no. These are my last pair..." and he dropped the one he was holding. It didn't just drop down, it sort of leaped out of his fingers, and began to roll out of view. They both bent over to try to stop its progress and bumped heads. "Ow!" said Michael.

"Ouch!" Her hand went to her head.

"I'm sorry!"

"No, I'm sorry. Was that really your last one?"

"Yes, and judging by how much it rolled, it may be in Atlantic City already." Rubbing his head, "Ow, that hurt!" and he started to laugh. "No good deed, huh?"

She joined in, laughing. "Should I ask the bus driver to take us to the nearest hospital?"

"Or the nearest earplug store?" he said, and removed the other earplug. "No. I've heard misery expands the character."

"Listening to that woman's phone conversation for the next three hours may make us explode."

"I'm trying to tune her out. I'll tune you in. What did you say to me when I was rudely ignoring you?"

"Oh, nothing important. I saw your book, *Time and Again*. It's one of my favorites. I think it's the best time travel book ever. I've read it about five times."

"This is my third. It's perfect for a bus trip."

"Or a horse-drawn carriage ride."

He wondered where she was from, as her appealing voice was so unlike the woman still on the phone, still loudly demonstrating her grating Noo Yawk accent. He said, "I've never seen the bus this crowded."

"I was surprised, too. I figured a Thursday wouldn't be." Joanna wished she were better at small talk. "Maybe a Friday. You know, people getting a jump start on the weekend."

"Gambling away their life savings. You, too?"

"Hmm?"

"Atlantic City."

"I'm not going to Atlantic City. I'm going to Cape May."

"Oh, me too."

"I've never been. You?"

"I go pretty often. I lived there awhile, and I have friends there."

"You live in Manhattan now?"

He nodded.

Joanna shivered, "It's chilly back here. The a/c must be on high." She searched around her, and under the seat. "Oh! I left my sweater over there," she said, pointing towards the front of the bus.

"You want my jacket?"

"No, thanks."

"It's fresh from the dry cleaner." He pulled it out from behind him. "I don't know why I brought it. I never get cold."

"You don't mind? I'm afraid I'll wrinkle it."

"I don't mind."

"Thanks. I couldn't face negotiating that aisle again." She blanketed his jacket around her. "I'm sorry about your earplugs."

"They made you think I was rude," he shifted in his seat to face her, partly to save wear and tear on his neck, and partly because he was intrigued. She had a gleam in her eyes that he found curious. "They deserve to die on the dirty bus floor."

"I thought you were rude or had an amazing power of concentration." She smiled and continued, "You reminded me of me. I used to get so involved in a book I'd sometimes miss my subway stop."

"You a New Yorker?"

"Yes. I live on the Upper West Side. Twenty years now. Before that, the Lower East Side, and before that Queens. I still take the train but I read all day at work so I don't read as much for pleasure as I used to. My eyes are too tired. Easier to be a couch potato."

They were quiet. He reopened his book, and she picked up her pen. A few minutes later the bus jarred and Joanna's notebook fell on the floor. He made a movement to reach down for it and stopped. "I don't want to risk concussion."

"I'll get it," she said and retrieved the notebook.

"You managing to get some work done?"

"Oh, not work, really," she said, self-consciously hiding the words with her hand.

"Hmmm, a book of your own?"

She smiled. "A book? An article in *More* magazine? More likely just a diary. I'm thinking of starting a business in Cape May. No big deal. *She said, gasping for air.*"

He was nodding. "I understand the anxiety. It's a big lifestyle change."

"A big scary change. Moving my husband and cat two-hundred miles away from home. Leaving behind the known for the unknown. I make it sound like we'll be traveling in a covered wagon. Sometimes it seems that drastic. To my husband anyway."

"He's retired?"

"No, he's an accountant. He'll never retire. Works out of our second bedroom."

"Rough commute. No wonder he doesn't want to move."

"As long as he has a computer he can work anywhere. He has a highly organized mind. He'll probably die with a calculator in his hand."

They were quiet again, writing and reading. It was comfortable on the bus, and the loud-talking-on-the-phone woman was asleep. Then Michael turned and said, "I know a lot about Cape May. Wait, that sounded braggy. I mean if you have any questions or anything. My ex-wife and I lived there for about a year, I mean before she was my ex. I've been a tour guide, worked in a shop, and slept in many an overly decorated, creepy room."

"I sat next to the right person."

"Just wait. It's a long trip, and you never know what'll come out of my mouth due to boredom and leg cramps." He turned his head to look out the window. Then he said, "Where are you staying?"

"The Manor Rose," she said.

"You'll love it," he nodded.

"And we may tour the Captain's Bed."

"Uh huh."

"Or the Hat Pin."

"Nice variety."

"I want to get a real feel for the town."

"First a four-star inn, then a mid-level, and then an

economy inn, if you can call $195 a night a bargain. You've done your research."

Shaking her head she said, "Not nearly enough. I browsed county websites, thumbed through some travel books. But I don't know good or bad streets, what the walk to the ocean is like, the quality of the sand, you know. All that stuff you need to see and feel in person."

"The quality of the sand? That's thorough."

"I want to know everything."

Joanna returned to her notebook and Michael to his book. About ten minutes later he noticed she wasn't writing any more. "I don't suppose you're dying to play Scrabble."

"That came out of nowhere!"

"Is that a 'no'?"

"No! Yes, I <u>love</u> Scrabble," she said.

"If you can scoot out for a minute, and I can get to my backpack," he said, pointing upward to the luggage rack.

Joanna put her notebook in her bag, and stood up, holding onto the railing on the overhead rack. There wasn't much room. Michael stood and stepped out into the tiny aisle. The bus jerked along, and even though Joanna held tightly to the handrail, she nearly fell, but Michael grabbed her arm. "You don't have your bus legs yet." When she was steady again, he reached up and into his backpack.

The bus driver's voice chastised them: "Please ruhmain seeded when da bus is in mowshun."

Joanna giggled, "You'd better hurry or we'll be thrown off the bus."

"It would be quieter by the side of the road." He pulled out the game and a dictionary and sat down. Joanna plopped in beside him and they both laughed. He said, "I hope you have a strong bladder because I don't think the driver will allow you to walk to the bathroom!"

Michael opened the Scrabble board and handed her a tile rack.

She said, "Are you prepared to be beaten?"

He flexed his bicep. "By you and whose dictionary?"

"I know all the two-letter words allowed by the Scrabble Gods," she warned him. "Even the newer, seemingly made-up ones."

They balanced the playing board on their thighs. It was slightly uncomfortable, and they were sitting at odd angles, with their knees clashing, but somehow it didn't seem to bother either of them. He held the bag of tiles for her. "Ladies first."

She reached into the faux velvet bag and picked a letter. "P." He did the same. "P." He said, "What are the odds? Remind me to buy a Lotto ticket." They tried again. He picked a D, and she an M.

Joanna said, "You go first." As he picked his seven letters, she asked, "So, what do you do?"

"I'm a writer." He rearranged his tiles a few times, then put down each of the seven tiles, one with each syllable, as he said, "Or. Should. I. Say. I. Am. An. *OUTLIER*."

"It's a good thing we aren't playing for money."

"We aren't?" He reached for his pen. "I'll keep score."

"It's your game and your dictionary. And unfortunately your seven-letter word."

He looked up at her and furrowed his brow. "I know this is personal, but I'll have to write your name on the top of this little column. What is it?"

"Joanna. Matthews," and she held out her hand.

He shook it. "Michael Leighton." He picked up his pen. "*Joanna*," he wrote on the sheet of paper. "Well, Joanna, that's eight points, doubled for the first move is sixteen, plus fifty for the seven-letter word equals sixty-six."

Joanna narrowed her eyes at him. "Now I recognize you! From Fox TV's *America's Most Wanted Scrabble Sharks*. Preying on innocent women riding in crowded, horribly loud buses to Cape May."

Joanna put two tiles down on the board and realized she was having fun. Brian was right that she needed to get away. "*XI*, a Greek letter, and *XU*, Vietnamese money. It's only thirty-six points, but I'll catch up. Shark."

Farther along in the game, while Joanna shuffled her tiles and sighed and said things to them like, "If you were a different letter I'd have a seven-letter word," Michael's thoughts drifted to his novel. His in-the-works book centered on an attempted assassination of a politician vacationing in late 1800's Cape May. He was weaving historical figures in with the fictional ones, and in this one scene Harry Houdini visits the town to investigate a medium claiming to have information vital to the case. There would be some romance, too, between the inexperienced detective assigned to the case and the young medium, who may or may not be a fake. Well, that certainly was enough plot for at least one book. If it turned out well, perhaps he'd write another with these characters. He was becoming fond of them, and hoped readers would, too. He'd have to work it carefully, revealing small details, make the reader want more and more. It was an emotionally and sexually repressed time, the late 1800s, and Michael wanted to explore all aspects of love and sex, history and society in Cape May.

Michael knew the basics of Cape May's history by heart, starting in 1620—the same year the Pilgrims landed at Plymouth, Massachusetts—when Cornelius Jacobsen Mey, a Dutch sea captain, discovered a peninsula while exploring the Delaware River. He named it after himself.

Its foray into life as a resort town began in the early 1800s when rich Philadelphians, needing to get away from the summer heat, were more than willing to pay "townies" for the use of their homes by the shore for the ocean breezes. The money the townies made during the summer months supported them for the rest of the year. The wealthy from other major cities in the northeast began traveling south, often staying in Cape May's public houses or taverns. The first hotel, which had started life as a tavern, was called the Atlantic Hall. Cape May became a summer resort destination.

In 1847, the Great Compromiser Henry Clay visited Cape May. In 1855, President Franklin Pierce. In 1858, President James Buchanan. And approximately a hundred years later, future author Michael Leighton visited with his tired parents. When they were napping, he snuck out to explore the streets of Cape May, fascinated by the large, ornate houses. Now in his early sixties, he still loved the town, and wanted to incorporate that love into his novel.

CHAPTER 3

Two decades ago, Joanna and Brian played Scrabble on the deluxe set he received from his Aunt Flo for his Bar Mitzvah. It miraculously still had all one-hundred tiles even though it was over twenty-five years old and had moved apartments with him at least four times. Joanna and Brian still had sextogethers, but more frequently hung out and drank wine. Midway through the game, with Joanna ahead by fifty-two points, Brian said, "You know we both turn forty this year?"

Joanna was glad to talk about anything that wouldn't lead to sex. She was far more interested in Scrabble. "We should have a party, huh?"

"We should have a wedding." He stopped shuffling his tiles and got really serious. "Remember our pact? If we weren't involved with anyone when we hit forty we'd get married? To each other?"

"It wasn't a *pact*."

He put his tiles face down on the table. Even about to propose he still upheld the sanctity of the game. He kneeled next to her. "Joanna. Let's get married."

"Really?"

"Yeah, let's just do it. You can move in here."

"But my apartment is rent controlled."

"And falling apart. And this one is twice as big."

She paused, trying to think of other objections. "It seems…unromantic?"

He kneeled closer to her. "It's just right for us. Come on, Jo. When's the last time you went on a date." She didn't answer. She had no answer. "We spend most Friday and Saturday nights together. We have sex…infrequently, like a real couple. We go to movies together. Dinner, shopping. What's the last thing you bought for over $10 without me going with you?"

"I bought that dress by myself. The brown and red one?"

"And then we returned it together."

"Oh, yeah."

"I admit this isn't conventional, but I think we're our best option. We can make a life together. And when half of our friends are divorcing—they say one out of two marriages end in divorce anyway—we'll still be best friends playing Scrabble."

She thought a moment. "What about kids?"

"Jo, you're almost forty."

"Ursula Andress was in her mid-forties when she had her first kid."

"And you've never been a Bond girl either."

"But I want children."

He said, "Child*ren*?"

"Well, could we do one?"

He sighed. "I guess I could stand it."

She said, "Maybe we both need to think about this."

"All right. I will. But I think I could live with a little Jo running around."

"Or a little baby accountant."

"Yes, and I'm positive this would be good for us," and he kissed her. It was a nice kiss. She could do this. It would be nice to have someone to depend on and to brush your teeth for. She'd think about it.

***

The bus rolled along and Joanna and Michael continued playing Scrabble. Her cell phone vibrated. "Excuse me," she said to Michael. "Hi, Cynthia."

"I was looking on the internet at houses for sale in Cape May. Some are fully or partially furnished. If they have any good pieces, we could work out a trade."

"I don't know if the houses I'm looking at are being sold furnished or not."

"What are their names. I'll look them up."

"No. Cynthia, thank you, but I want to do this alone this time."

"Take pictures."

"I'm not going to buy a house based on its furniture anyway."

"But why waste good antiques on guests?"

Cynthia was always on the lookout for worthy pieces. She began her career at the antiques store as a saleswoman. Then she married the owner, whose family had started the business in the 1940s. With her impeccable taste, Cynthia was a natural at running the shop. She came to know the clientele, some of whom were third-generation patrons, by name and preferences, and she was well liked. When she divorced her husband, Cynthia could've been handed millions in the settlement. But she knew the best way to hurt her ex was to wrestle the shop away from him. His family liked her more anyway. Plus, now she was set for life, as the shop had loyal, wealthy customers with money to spare, no matter what the economic climate.

Joanna said, "But Cyn, the antiques…you just don't get B&Bs, do you."

Michael looked up at her, barely suppressing a smile, his eyes twinkling.

"Oh I *get* it," Cynthia continued. "I know you don't know antique from IKEA. Just take pictures of everything. Damn. I knew I should've come with you."

Furniture was the last thing on Joanna's mind, but she wasn't about to admit it to her sophisticated sister. Their once edgy relationship had evolved into a tentative friendship. With age, they were getting closer and Joanna didn't want to impede the progress. They'd come a long way since childhood. They were separated by five years and radically different personalities. When their mother divorced their father because he was having an affair, Joanna was heartbroken while Cynthia was mostly relieved not to have to live with the hostility any more. Joanna knew her parents didn't get along. The whole neighborhood did. But Joanna's little girl heart, shaped by fairy tales and TV shows, still hoped love would win in the end. It didn't.

Dad didn't take care of himself after he "lost" his wife. That was how he talked about her. Strangers thought he was a widower. He never forgave himself or his wife. Or his daughters, because he blamed them for somehow coming between him and their mother.

From an early age, Cynthia was the practical, no-nonsense one, and Joanna was the "happy idiot," trying to accommodate others and worrying about everyone's feelings. When their dad came to pick them up for dinner or the weekend, he'd wait in the car and honk, as if exposure to his ex-wife would be fatal. Cynthia would storm out of the house but Joanna would first spend minutes reassuring her mom that she was loved and still the favorite parent.

As they got older, Cynthia never hesitated to point out that her baby sister's decisions were usually bad, or at least impractical. Cynthia had spent hours and hours trying to talk Joanna out of marrying Brian. Still, at the ceremony in front of a judge at City Hall, Cynthia provided flowers and support as Joanna's matron of honor. Now, Joanna's yearning to buy a bed and breakfast threw her sister into overprotective mode. Both had inherited money from an uncle. Cynthia's grew steadily thanks to her own money smarts combined with advice from customers in the financial field. She disapproved of Joanna's aspiration to blow it all on a potential money pit.

"I'm a grown up," Joanna said. "Please stop worrying about me. Live your own life."

"I'm sorry. I'm nervous. I've got a blind date tonight. My ex-sister-in-law set me up. I'm meeting him at the Russian Tea Room. His choice. I hope he isn't eighty years old."

"You'll sleep with him anyway," said Joanna, and her hand flew to her mouth as her eyes flew to Michael's.

Michael only smiled and raised an eyebrow. He was finding the whole conversation amusing.

Cynthia continued, "Maybe. Probably. Why not? Life is short."

"Have fun, at *dinner* that is. Call me tomorrow?"

"You're rushing me off."

"I'm playing Scrabble with the man in the seat next to me. Being on the phone is probably breaking a Scrabble-playing-on-a-bus rule."

Cynthia was about to reply when a customer, Mrs. Delaney, walked in, for the second time that day. Cynthia deduced from the woman's body language, slight smile, and level of excitement she had decided on a purchase that would bring Cynthia thousands in commission. Not a bad day's work. She rushed off with a "Customer. Gotta go."

Joanna put her phone away and turned her attention back to Scrabble. "Sorry."

"No, don't be." It was Michael's turn, and he was losing to Joanna by only fifteen points. "That conversation is sure to end up in my novel."

They played for another half hour. Joanna was feeling relaxed and sleepy. As Michael concentrated on his tiles, she openly stared at him. He was probably her age, but looked younger. Damn men. He was flipping pages of the dictionary, tilting it and his head, to read the tiny print. The sun caught his long blonde eyelashes.

She said to him, "It's not a word."

"Hmm?"

"Whatever you're looking up. Don't bother; it's not a word."

He smiled. He had a nice smile. "Is this your Scrabble psychological warfare strategy?"

"Mm-hmm."

"Well, you're right, unfortunately. It isn't a word." He put the dictionary down and returned to his tiles.

She said, "Do you mind if we talk a little. I'm getting sleepy."

He looked up from his rack. "Do you want to stop playing?"

"No—I'm winning."

He held the small plastic rack in one hand, and moved the half inch tiles with the other. "You talk to me, then, and use words with lots of vowels in them. I need hints."

"That was my sister who called."

"Older, right?"

"Oh, yes. Apparently she thinks she gave birth to me. She also thinks I can't do anything by myself."

"But it sounds like she loves you, and you her. You're lucky. I'm an only."

She nodded. "Can I ask you a question?"

"Sure."

"Do you always travel with a Travel Scrabble set and a Scrabble dictionary?"

"To Cape May, yes. I have a lady friend there, Madeleine."

"Ooh, a lady friend. How gentlemanly of you."

"That's what she is. Anyway, her house is tiny and she won't buy a Scrabble set just for the few times a year I visit her. She's a tour guide at a private estate. Actually she's the Executive Director, and gives tours as a volunteer. If you'd like, I'll try and get you in. It's hard to find a slot unless you book in advance."

"Thanks, I'd love it. But I do have an appointment with the realtor, so it'll depend on the timing."

They continued playing. She said, "What type of writing do you do?"

"My writing…well, you can get my first novel, the only one written under my real name, from Amazon for one cent plus shipping."

"Do you get to keep the whole penny?"

"Yes. I'm a nickelaire now."

"I'm impressed."

"I write speeches for executives who make more in a week than I make in a year but don't know how to write. I used to write mysteries, like *Goosebumps*, but better and therefore not as profitable, to get kids into reading."

"Ooh, tell me."

"My pseudonym is 'Chester Worthington.' I know. I didn't pick it. The books are better than the name. I haven't written those in years, but I still get checks. And, of course, I'm working on a novel."

"Wow. I envy you. I used to write, in my twenties. But I also used to read a lot." She yawned, covering her mouth. "What I wrote wasn't nearly as good as what I read."

"Maybe you were reading only the really good stuff?"

"That's a nice way to think about it. Yeah, I like that theory. I don't think it's true, but it's nice. Now I'm attempting to write just for fun. And to get the editor half of my brain to mind its own business...or something. You know what I mean." She yawned again. "I'm sorry. I've been working late so I could take days off for this trip."

"Are you a napper?"

"Oh God yes."

"Take a nap."

"How would it look? Our first Scrabble game, and I quit."

"I promise I won't inform the National Scrabble Association."

"Well, okay then. I am exhausted." They put the tiles in the bag, and closed the board. Joanna pushed the recline button on the arm of her seat, but nothing happened. "Well, I guess I'll have to nap sitting up. I hope I don't drool on your jacket."

Michael leaned across her. "It's probably just stuck."

Joanna flattened herself back into her seat. Michael was intent on fixing the release button and didn't realize he was practically on top of her. He was so close, she could smell the too-long hair curling on the back of his neck. It smelled good. She cleared her throat.

Michael banged on the arm a few times then looked up. "Oh, personal space invasion." He moved and said, "It was jammed. I think I fixed it."

Her seat reclined easily. "Thanks." She settled in, closed her eyes, and fell asleep.

***

"Ladies and gennelmen!"

Both Joanna and Michael jerked awake at the loud announcement. "We will be arrivin' in Alanic Cidee in ten minutes."

"Oh, that's too loud," said Joanna, pulling Michael's jacket over her head.

Michael shielded his ears. "And I was having such a peaceful dream."

More noise from the speakers: "There'sa infamation desk, fuh drekshins, transfuhs, brochas."

Joanna ran her tongue over her teeth. "I hope there's someplace for me to buy mints."

"I have some," said Michael, reaching into his shirt pocket. "Here. I never travel without them."

She pulled a mirror out of her handbag. "I hope I look better than I feel."

Michael turned to survey her. He squinted and nodded. "I think you look fine. However, you may want to pat down that little hill of hair."

She reached up. "In the back? I've had that since I was a kid. Hard-to-manage hair spot."

He was about to reply but instead stuck his fingers in his ears when the bus driver made another announcement. Joanna did the same.

"Here we are, folks: the Alanic Cidee bus terminal. When da bus comes to a complete stop, please gadda ya belongins. Check unda ya seat..."

Joanna interjected, "for runaway earplugs."

"...and in da overhead racks. For thosaya makin a knecshin to da bus fuh Wildwood and Cape May, there'ill be infamation posted on da boards. If ya need asitans ax someone in a monagram jackit. Thank ya fuh traveling wid us."

The announcement over, Joanna released her ears, and saw that Michael was doing the same. She said, "Is it because we're older, and our ears are worn out and overly sensitive?"

"No, I think all these kids have damaged their ears and are partly deaf. They need everything loud."

Michael stood up, knees bent so his head wouldn't smash into the overhead rack. Joanna maneuvered herself into the aisle to give him room. She said, "You'd better come out of there. You look like Quasimodo."

There was very little space between them. She looked up at him. "You're tall!"

He put his hand flat on his head. "Six-one and a half, ma'am," he said in his best John Wayne voice. "You're five-six?" he asked, moving his hand down from his head to the top of hers.

"Almost. Five-five and a half inches of soon-to-be screaming woman if I don't get off this bus <u>now</u>. My claustrophobia is kicking in. I thought I should warn you as your ear is so close to my mouth."

When there was room for them to move, he got his backpack down from the rack, and she grabbed her overnight bag. They walked down the aisle to the front, where she grabbed the sweater still on her original seat.

They stepped down off the bus and both took big deep breaths of 'fresh' air. When they saw each other, they burst out laughing. Other passengers, standing by the side of the bus and waiting for the bus driver to pull out luggage, turned to look at the source of the sudden noise.

"Yeah, that's just what we need," Michael said. "Nice, fresh exhaust fumes in our lungs."

"Please tell me Cape May smells better than this."

"I promise it does," he said, holding up three fingers in a Boy Scout salute. "Did you bring a suitcase?"

"No. My husband is bringing it tomorrow with the car."

They walked towards the terminal. He said, "It feels good to stretch. I think my aging knees are telling me it's time to start renting a car for this trip." Once inside the waiting room, Michael said, "I'll see if the bus is on time."

Joanna grabbed some Cape May brochures (the few she didn't already have) from a rack. Michael came back and said, "Right on time. It'll be leaving in about half an hour."

"Good." There was an awkward moment as they stood there. She said, "I think I'll sit and read these. Make the time go faster."

They each found seats next to other waiting passengers. Michael jotted down notes for upcoming chapters of his novel. Joanna read the brochures and continued listing things to do, ask, and research while in Cape May. Some information was available on the internet, such as average monthly temperatures, taxes, crime rates. What research and all the brochures in the world couldn't tell her was how she'd feel away from a big city, with a depleted nest egg, and none of her friends nearby. She wasn't the first in her group to be leaving expensive New York, though. In the past few years, three had relocated to warmer climates and two had moved to be closer to grandchildren, which, unfortunately, wasn't a move Joanna would ever get to make. Yet another friend, her best friend in Queens when she was growing up, had made that much farther move into the great beyond, from which no traveler returns.

Joanna lived in Queens for the first seventeen years of her life. From the time she was nine, she and her mother or sister traveled into Manhattan half a dozen times a year, to see theater (when they could afford it) and museums, go to the Central Park Zoo, shop, or just walk around. She still loved it, but Manhattan was more overrun with tourists every year, and becoming less nonmillionaire friendly. Joanna loved the brownstone apartments on the quiet tree-lined streets—who didn't?—but they were affordable only to the very rich. Not that she should complain: she and Brian were comfortable, and whether they stayed in

New York or moved to Cape May, they'd always have a roof over their heads.

New York was exhausting her. Work, too, and commuting on the subway. When there was time she preferred to walk at least part of the way. In the summer the descent into New York's underbelly was accompanied by the increasingly powerful smell of urine and sweat, and overflowing garbage cans. It wasn't New York's fault. Unlike transportation systems in other major cities, which closed a few hours every night for maintenance, New York's ran 24/7. The tunnels and trains were actually relatively clean, but she was less tolerant. One upside to commuting was people watching, which was always entertaining. On crowded platforms waiting for the train there was a fascinating variety of humans. The people, even just at her subway stop, represented every ethnicity, age, height, weight, style, and economic status, including no status at all. That diversity was the best thing about Manhattan. Well, that and theater. And museums. And restaurants. And—"*STOP it, Joanna,*" she mentally yelled at herself, "*or you'll never leave New York.*"

She took out her cell phone and called Brian.

He answered after a few rings. "You on the bus?" with his mouth obviously full of food. How did he manage to stay slim while she had to watch every bite?

"No, the Atlantic City bus terminal. The Cape May bus should be here in half an hour. You meeting Frank soon?"

"Nah, I had to cancel. This client is very demanding, and work's going slow. I've been waiting for an e-fax from California for two hours."

"Oh, I know you were looking forward to dinner."

"It's more important that I keep this client happy. If you insist on moving me to God-forsaken Cape May, I'll need my work to keep me sane."

***

Michael only sat for a moment, electing instead to walk around the transportation center. In Manhattan whenever he got stuck writing, he'd go for a walk, any hour of the day or night. It helped him think. He was thinking now that the working title of his book wasn't working. *Assassination: Cape May* was too contemporary. He wanted his readers immediately immersed, starting with the title. Immersed in the time period, the people, the town. He wanted to convey his own fascination with Cape May. As a kid, he'd fallen in love with the town, the gingerbread houses, proximity to the beach, the climate, everything.

His knew his memories of Cape May were prejudiced by the fact that his parents, when the three of them vacationed there, were happy and relaxed. Those were adjectives rarely attached to his mother or father. They saved all year for a week at the shore away from the small grocery store they owned. The other fifty-one weeks his parents worked long hours, and money was tight. Michael was often left alone to fend for himself. That helped fuel his incredible imagination. From an early age he loved to write. Though he was a C student in math and history in his earlier years, it was always A all the way in his English classes. By the time he was ready for college, history had equaled writing in the subjects about which he was passionate, and his overall grades were good enough to get him into almost any school. His parents wanted him to be a doctor. Feeling he owed them something (especially because they were paying), he tried it, wasting two years studying science and medicine before transferring to a "regular" college. After graduating, he earned a living at various nonwriting jobs, but wrote before work, at lunchtime, and after work, until he completed his first book. It was about two unhappy shop owners and their disappointing misfit son. They say write what you know. Miraculously, it was published. He didn't make much money from it, but the prestige of a published book got him a teaching position at a small community college. There, he met his future wife, who was working as the Dean's assistant. They got married, had a son, and his creativity moved to the back burner. Living with Donna wasn't easy. Attempting to keep her content took a lot of his energy, but he was determined to have a happier married life than his parents. When their son was thirteen, Donna went back to school to get her masters in psychology. She was a dedicated student and her few moments of free time were devoted to their teenager. The time apart didn't help an already strained marriage. She didn't miss Michael and he didn't miss her. Donna met another man, fell in love, and asked Michael for a divorce. He had no real reason to contest it.

A free man once again, Michael threw himself into writing. He wrote, and sold, mysteries for the adolescent set. He also moved into a friend's house in Cape May. Various part-time jobs later, supplementing his frequently fickle income, he returned to his small Manhattan apartment and started corporate writing. It cut time for his own writing but made bill paying easy. To salve his soul, he visited Cape May twice a year.

Now he was working on his fiction again. Writing about Cape May again. This trip was about research and getting color for the book. Trying to see the town a little differently.

CHAPTER 4

"The 5:47 bus to Wildwood and Cape May is ready for boarding." The announcement broke through the music playing over the speakers.

Joanna quickly put away her things and stood up, looking around for Michael. He was no longer sitting on the bench. What if he missed the bus? Something jumped in her chest.

She slowly walked outside to the waiting bus, its door open and engine running, and scanned the area for him. One foot on the first step, she told the driver, "Someone else is coming. He should be here in a minute."

The bus driver eyed her a moment. "Anything for you, pretty lady."

The gambling crowd was gone and only five other people were scattered throughout the bus, including the young man with the green earbuds still in his ears. She sat down by the window in the second row, looking out towards the terminal entrance. There he was, rushing towards the door. She was relieved. In one leap he was in the bus, eyes searching for then landing on hers. He smiled back at her, as he said hello to the driver.

He sat down in an aisle seat across from her. "I had to take a call. Possible freelance work. Couldn't get the guy off the phone."

"I bet it's a long walk to Cape May," she said.

"I'da made it in a week or two."

The driver shut the doors and headed back to the Garden State Parkway. "Ladies and gentlemen, we are on our way further south in New Jersey. First stop Wildwood, then Cape May. If I drove any further, you'd need a wet suit." A few giggles from the passengers. "Settle back and enjoy the ride." This bus driver seemed friendly, his laid-back vibe permeating the bus.

Joanna relaxed, sinking back into the comfortably padded bus seat. Michael opened his book.

The bus driver looked at Joanna in his mirror and said to her, "You're the Queen of the Bus."

"As I'm the only woman on the bus, that's not saying much."

She opened her notebook again, but her eyes kept drifting to the window. The Garden State Parkway was lined with fully blossomed trees, in more shades of green than even an Impressionist could capture. Despite being in the confines of the bus, Joanna could sense the fresh air outside. It was a picture perfect day. When she and Brian took walks in Central Park, she tried to breathe in extra hard, to fill her lungs with new, fresh air, to replace the exhalations of the millions of people on the streets and in the subways. Again her thoughts seesawed between her longing to move someplace with sweeter air, a little slower pace, a lot less crowded, and more aging-friendly, or stay in a city that never slept, where every moment seemed alive and important and youthful. Did everyone have such a love/hate relationship with Manhattan?

The bus drove on and on, and eventually the trees and grass of the parkway gave way to *Wildwood* signs. After a brief stop to let two multipierced teenagers disembark for the boardwalk and rides of Wildwood, the bus was back on the parkway. Soon Joanna saw "End of Parkway" and "Cape May Courthouse" signs, renewing her excitement about visiting the place where she might spend the rest of her life. She had not been this hopeful about any other inn hunting expedition.

Michael saw her gathering her things. "We still have awhile, Joanna."

"I'm so ready to get off this bus," she said, smiling.

"It'll be worth it, I promise." He slid his longs legs into the aisle, for comfort and to face her, making it easier to talk. "You'll see to the right the Court House entrance. There's a liquor store, too, that's very popular. Most of the restaurants here are bring-your-own-booze. When I drive down I usually stop in. Nice selection of local wines."

Michael pointed to the left, "There's the Lobster Hideaway. You can eat inside, or out by the boats, on huge wooden reels turned on their sides. Self-service, plastic utensils. Sometimes it's crowded, but the food's pretty good and not too expensive. Though there's always the possibility that a sea gull might drop a gift on your plate."

The bus slowed, driving on the one lane south and close to the cars on the one lane north. He said, "This is Lafayette Street."

Joanna flashed forward to Monday, when she'd be sitting in the passenger seat with Brian driving home on that north lane. Would their decision be made? Would they know they wanted to move to Cape May, start a whole new life, with new work, climate, scenery, or would they realize that New York City was still the place for them? It was such a monumental decision, it seemed impossible that in a few days she might know. Was moving a foolish thing to do at this stage of her life? Too daring? Her first and pretty much last daring act, marrying Brian, all too quickly became normal and rote. Maybe everything that begins unconventionally, adventurously even, somehow rapidly becomes routine. Maybe transporting their life to Cape May was just what they needed.

As the bus headed deeper into Cape May, glimpses of the occasional Victorian house, intermingled with regular houses, snapped Joanna out of her thoughts. The gingerbread and multicolors made them stand out next to aluminum-sided or stucco or brick houses. Many of the Victorians even on the outskirts of Cape May were bed and breakfasts, and inviting, despite the further distance to the coveted beach. These inns would be competition for Joanna and Brian's possible future inn. The bus passed an especially enticing house, like the witch's in Hansel and Gretel, but without the danger, and she *ooh*ed and *aah*ed.

Michael said, "You ain't seen nothin' yet."

The bus driver abandoned his microphone to shout out the simple announcement to the few people left on the bus: "Lady and gentlemen, in a moment, our final destination: the Cape May Transportation Center." Michael glanced at Joanna, who was almost jumping out of her seat. Her excitement was infectious. The bus turned right into a small driveway and stopped in front of what looked like a 1950's train station. The driver continued, "You can get a cab, information, use the restrooms, grab a map or whatever you need. Thank you for traveling with us. Have a wonderful time here in Cape May. Looks like we've conjured up a fine-looking evening for you."

Joanna stood and made her way out of the bus. She said to the driver, "Have a nice evening."

"You, too," he said, and winked at her.

Finally on solid, Cape May ground, Joanna put her overnight bag down and did a standing forward bend.

Michael was standing over to the side. He said, "You do that like a professional."

"Yoga classes. I haven't gone in years, but I've kept up with this one stretch. All I do at work is sit. I refuse to become one of those hunched over old women who look like they're hunting for quarters."

"That explains your excellent posture."

"Not too soldierly, I hope."

"Not at all."

She pulled a map out of her bag and unfolded it. "Guess I better get my bearings." She looked back up at him. "Um, I guess this is goodbye, too?" She stuck out her hand. "Well, thank you for making the ride so much more pleasant. That Scrabble game saved what's left of my sanity." Their eyes stayed on each other's a moment.

He took her hand but didn't shake it. "Listen, Joanna, do you know where you're going? I can walk you to your B&B. The Manor Rose is that way," he said, pointing.

Joanna felt a little jolt. "I couldn't…"

"Oh, I see. You think I'm a Scrabble shark *and* an ax murderer."

"They so often go hand-in-hand, don't they."

"I practically have to pass your street to get to mine. Oh, wait. I'm an idiot! Maybe you want to be alone."

"No, I like your company," she said. "I have to call my husband first, to tell him the bus didn't crash or anything." She took out her cell phone and hit redial. Brian picked up. She said, "Hi. I'm in Cape May."

"Great. You like it?"

"I'm still at the bus terminal, about to walk into town with this nice man I met on the bus."

"Picking up strangers again? I thought I broke you of that habit."

Joanna looked at Michael and shook her head. Into the phone she said, "This one is not that strange." Michael produced a comical sinister look, which made her laugh. "Well, he's pretty strange, but also a self-proclaimed Cape May expert and could provide us with a wealth of information."

Brian said, "Good."

Joanna said, "How's work?"

"Don't ask. See you tomorrow around noon, okay?"

"Bye, Brian. Good luck."

Michael said, "Ready?"

"You know, before I see Cape May and it sees me, I would be happier if I could wash off some of the bus grime."

"You look pretty grime-free to me, but the bathroom's in there. Meet you by that bench in a few minutes."

In the ladies room, Joanna brushed her teeth and fluffed her hair. She was pleased with how it looked. Never one for make-up and beautifying, her one vanity was having her gray roots touched up every eight weeks. The gray had made her feel like her own grandmother. She'd spent many hours and even more dollars at a salon restoring the original brown and, in the past year at the suggestion of her stylist, adding red highlights. It wasn't up there with other midlife crisis Band-Aids, like buying a sports car, but it did make mirror gazing less painful. And right now, despite the bathroom's harsh lighting, even with the wrinkles she'd never get used to, she thought she looked happy, and pretty. Subtracting the stress of Manhattan and work and adding a minivacation was apparently equaling relaxation. Her eyes were sparkling. She smiled at herself, put the brushes away and left the room.

Michael was already waiting outside. He, too, had cleaned himself up a bit and washed his face. Some wet hair clung to his forehead. She reached up to brush the locks aside.

"Oh, I'm sorry," she said, pulling her hand away.

He paused before saying, "I don't mind."

She'd once read a book in which the hero's eyes were described as hooded. She'd never been quite sure how that looked until she saw Michael's hooded eyes.

"Let's go," she said.

He pointed and said, "This way." As they walked, he dug his baseball hat out of his backpack and pulled it on.

They left the Visitor Center parking lot and walked across the two lanes of Lafayette Street. Joanna said, "The weather couldn't be more accommodating."

"Yes, it's perfect."

"And the air is…soft and tranquil?"

"It's that lazy southern air. We're as far south as parts of Virginia and Kentucky." They continued walking, past a strip mall and parking lot. "Over there on your left is a grocery store. There's also an Asian restaurant with good dumplings. Light. There's a pizza place, deli, and lots of tourist shops. One sells painted hermit crabs. The perfect Manhattan studio pet. Of course they'll be dead in a few days."

"That's very sad."

"That's true. Many a child's heart has been broken by the death of little Harry or Harriet Hermit Crab."

They walked through the parking lot to Ocean Avenue. On the corner was an old stone church, cast in a traditional Medieval revival style. "That's quite a church."

Michael put on his best tour guide voice: "That's the Star of the Sea, built in 1911. There's a stained glass window of Mary ascending to heaven. It's worth seeing." He dropped the voice. "Although honestly I haven't been in there in five years."

"Not a *regular* church goer, are you?"

"No! I'd rather have root canal. Oh, are you a… religious type person?" he asked.

"No, I'm not. I was born to nonreligious parents. Never went to church. I do consider myself to be, for lack of a better word, spiritual. I believe in…something?" She looked up to see him smiling at her. "I know, I sound ridiculously indecisive for a middle-aged person."

"No, I'm smiling because I feel exactly the same way. Except I would never admit to being middle-aged."

"Ugh. Age. I shouldn't have mentioned it. Please let's talk about anything else. Tell me more about Cape May."

He pointed to the right. "This is a pedestrian-only shopping mall, closed to cars in 1971. Full of restaurants and shops where you can buy anything from post cards to diamonds, fudge to books, T-shirts to, well, you get the idea."

They continued walking slowly in the evening summer sun. Joanna sighed.

"What?" said Michael.

"If I walked like this on Forty-Second Street I'd be arrested, or trampled. It's kind of nice, just strolling. I'm feeling, I think the word is relaked? Relassed? I read it somewhere."

"Sounds like you've been working too hard."

"Yes, but I really have to stop complaining about it. In this economy, at my age, I'm glad to be employed."

"I hear you. I'm grateful for every boring job that pays the bills so I can write."

"See, you're doing something you love."

"Most of the time."

"I want to do something I love. I'm determined to follow my dream."

"Dream?"

"I'm looking for a house down here, to buy and run as a bed and breakfast. That's why I came. I'm meeting with a realtor tomorrow. Even though I know I'll end up working more hours than I do now, at least it'll be for me. Us. I'll be the boss. Meet new people and live someplace calmer."

"Sounds like you know what you want, too."

They continued walking quietly until Joanna said, "Oh, that house is adorable!"

"Captain Mey's Inn, built around 1890."

"Do you know every house in Cape May?"

"No, not all. A lot though."

Joanna said, "And what's that one, over there? The small one."

"Is this a test? That is M'lady's Glove and Bonnet. Silly name, I think, but the house is very sweet. It is small. Two guest bedrooms. What size B&B are you interested in?"

"Depends. On the house, the price, the location, how we feel about it." They were both quiet a few moments. She changed the topic: "So, what are the things I have to see and do here?"

"Judging from your pale..." his eyes swept her face "wow, flawless skin..."

"Someone needs glasses."

"...you're not a sun worshipper." Joanna shook her head. "How about your husband? Is he a sun lover?"

"Brian hasn't set foot on a beach in years, since one of his west coast clients insisted on having a lunchtime meeting on Pacific Beach. He almost had sun poisoning."

"Ouch. He has clients that far away? Must be pretty smart."

"He's had some clients for decades. Wherever they move, they still want him doing their accounts, via fax, email, Skype, smoke signals, whatever."

"Blisters aside, while you're here, if you have the time, you should go to the beach, sit under an umbrella. There are kiosks where you can rent them, and chairs. Talk about relaxing. You might even see dolphins."

"I'd love that. What else?" She crossed the street to look in a shop window. He followed.

"The boardwalk. Sunsets. The stars. The Washington Street Mall back there is worth exploring, if you like to shop." They peered in the store window and among the sweaters, pants, jewelry, and scarves were greeting cards of nude six-packed men with actual long thin balloons hanging out of the card where each penis would be. They glanced disbelievingly at each other. He said, "Classy." They switched to another window. A small candle of a ghost sat on a display. "Oh, there's a haunted Cape May walking tour that's very popular."

"Have you been on it?"

"Wouldn't be caught dead on it."

She chuckled. "Okay, no church, no ghosts…"

"I'm an open-minded doubter," he said. "Just because I've never seen a ghost, and don't really believe in ghosts, doesn't necessarily mean there aren't ghosts."

"Who would you want to see, if you did believe in ghosts?"

"Is this a trap? If I say Einstein, you'll think I'm pretentious. If I say Marilyn Monroe, you'll think I'm shallow."

"Would either of them be true?"

"No. I think I'd want to meet Michelangelo, but I don't speak Italian, so, maybe Lincoln. Although in death maybe we all speak one language. What about you?"

She thought a moment. "Abigail Adams. I've read all the biographies. I feel like I already know her. She was an admirable woman. Smart, loyal, funny, ahead of her time, a great mother and businesswoman, and wife. I'd ask how she managed all that."

"She didn't spend time on Facebook."

"Ah, how very very true."

"So you *do* believe in ghosts."

"I'm not sure." She paused. "It's hard to believe that we are all there is, that this is all there is."

"People say that about life on other planets, too."

"I wish I were more sure of what I believe."

"I find it refreshing that you're not. So many people are positive what they believe is right and they're willing to kill those who don't."

She was shaking her head, "Every day in the news. Very upsetting. Stop. I'm on vacation. Go back to the ghosts."

"Well then, I'll admit that I've heard ghost stories— from people I consider sane and reliable—about some of these houses that made me doubt my doubting."

"Really? Tell me. No, don't tell me or I'll be scared alone in my room tonight. Tell me tomorrow when Brian can protect me if a ghost shows up." She stopped in her tracks. "Oh, wait, oh my gosh, *that* is the most amazing house I've ever seen." Joanna was looking across Ocean Street...

And there was the Queen Victoria.

As described in many a tourist brochure, the 1880's house sat with fitting regal splendor on the corner of Ocean and Columbia Avenues. A favorite tourist destination, the glorious example of Victorian architecture also showed influences both Italian, in the twin turret windows, and French, in the mansard roof.

"That is the Queen Victoria, and a Queen she is. I know the owners. If you want I could introduce you. That's the main house, and they also own the Queen's Cottage," he said, pointing to the house behind them, "and this one, called the House of Royals," pointing to the building on the corner, "and the Prince Albert Hall around the corner. It's a bit of a monopoly."

"They must have a lot of non-Monopoly money."

"Apparently."

"Well, I've been here less than an hour and I'm dazzled."

"It's magical here, and romantic, and you get the feeling that, well, you almost feel if you're not careful, you'll accidentally time travel right back to 1880. I was slightly drunk one night and, oh, never mind. That's a story for another time."

"No wonder you're reading *Time and Again*!"

"Ha, yes."

"I can't believe these houses. Look at that one on the corner. Oh, look at the one next to it! This is too much."

Michael smiled. "Maybe you should just mention the ones you *don't* like!"

"It's more...everything...than I expected. Even after visiting all the websites and reading so many books."

"But you'll wear yourself out. You know, Cape May has the second..."

Joanna chimed in: "...largest collection of Victorian houses in the world." They both laughed.

He said, "I guess you read that brochure, too, huh?"

"I should have been a historian. I find research fascinating. If we decide to move here, I'll read every book ever written about Cape May."

"I hope mine is on the list, if I ever finish it. It takes place in Cape May."

"I'll be the first in line to buy a copy. What's it about?"

"It takes place in Cape May."

"Ohhhkaaayyyy."

"I shouldn't have mentioned it, since I don't want to talk about it. It's still young."

"I understand."

"Your inn is just around that corner. It took us half an hour to walk a few blocks!"

"It's my fault," Joanna said.

"No, I've enjoyed every minute. Your enthusiasm is catching. I'm so familiar with all of this I've become a little complacent." They turned the corner and there stood the Manor Rose. "There it is. Your bed and breakfast, your home for the next few nights. I don't think you'll be disappointed."

The Manor Rose was almost as impressive as the Queen Victoria. While the Queen Victoria was majestic and awe-inspiring, the Manor Rose was welcoming and warm, suggesting a house full of love and family dinners and hugs. Everything her own childhood home wasn't. The Queen Victoria was deep dark shades of green; the Manor Rose was painted a burnt umber, with pink, salmon, and apricot accents. It was bright and cheerful, but not overly storybook. In the front of the house, the bottom of the windows were level with the wraparound porch, allowing easy access. Looking in from the street, Joanna imagined the mother of the house, a hundred years ago, baking cookies with her daughters on cook's day off. Too many feelings rushed over her. She needed a minute.

After delighting in all her *oohs* and *aahs*, the sudden thick quiet surprised Michael. He thought maybe Joanna didn't like the house. He turned to her, and saw her eyes were filled with wonder, and some tears. She turned away from him. He dug a tissue packet out of his pocket and handed it over her shoulder.

She wiped her eyes and blew her nose. "I don't know why…I mean I'm…it's just so moving. Such an example of time passing. That house is still there but all the people who fit with it, *in* it, cleaned and ate and loved in it, even the people who walked past it every day, they're all gone. Oh, God, I must sound…" she shook her head.

"No, I understand. Being moved by this."

More composed, she turned to him to reply and was surprised and silenced by the warmth and understanding in his eyes.

He continued, "When my son was born I was apparently implanted with a 'sappy' chip and I've gotten sappier as I've gotten older. It hurts but I actually like it. I'm willing to feel more now. Aging does bring with it some unexpected pluses, I guess. I'm certainly a better writer now."

"You have a son?"

"Yes. Robbie. *Rob*, he likes to be called now. He's in his late twenties and lives in California."

"Do you get to see him much?"

"No. Our relationship is complicated."

There was a pause. "Well," she said, "I should check in."

He opened the gate for her and they walked up the front path. "I bet you're tired."

"Yes, tired and very hungry."

He hesitated. "I was just on my way to dinner. On the boardwalk. A place called Henry's. You're welcome to…"

"I should…" she gestured to the door.

"Yes, of course," said Michael. He backed down the path. "Enjoy your evening."

"Thanks for everything, Michael."

"You're welcome. I'd better get going. I am hungry." He walked further down to the gate and shut it behind him. He looked back at her, now standing on the steps of the house. "I enjoyed getting to know you, Joanna."

"You too."

He walked to Ocean Street and made a right, heading towards the boardwalk.

Joanna stood a moment, contemplating joining him. She took one step back down the stairs when the front door opened and she heard a tinkling bell. A short plump woman called to her through the screen door.

"Oh, hello! Are you checking in?"

Joanna turned around. "Yes. Hi. I'm Joanna Matthews," and went inside.

"I'm Marie. Welcome to the Manor Rose," she said, while looking on her iPad. "Oh, yes, you're visiting from Manhattan, I see."

Joanna nodded, eyes taking in the surroundings. She and Marie stood in the entranceway of the house, a grand immaculate example of Victorian architecture and décor. Straight ahead was the staircase with a runner carpet of royal blue background with a multishaded blue floral design, held in place with shiny brass rods. The banister's dark wood gleamed, the railings intricately carved. The doorway to the left of the entrance hall led to a sitting room. Joanna peeked in, feeling the intruder, and saw a burnt orange satin love seat, a small table with a chess board and pieces set up ready for play, a sideboard with sherry and eight Old Galway glasses on a polished silver tray. On the round, main table in the room, local newspapers lay side-by-side with *Architect Digest*, *Travel in Luxury*, and *ARTNews* magazines. Adding to these anachronistic touches was a shelf of DVDs to borrow.

It suddenly occurred to Joanna that, if she wanted to, she had no way of contacting Michael. She didn't know where he was staying, she didn't have a phone number. He obviously knew where she was staying, but would she ever hear from him?

Marie was saying, "...and a full breakfast served from..."

"Marie, I'm sorry, I just remembered something. Can I leave my bag here and come back later?"

"Of course. I'll put it in your room. Here's the key. If you're back after eleven, please use the side door. It's quieter."

Joanna bolted out of the house, and missed hearing the tail end of, "...but you can always..."

She rushed back into the house. "Where is Henry's?"

CHAPTER 5

After dropping Joanna off at the Manor Rose, Michael walked leisurely towards Henry's. Maybe he shouldn't have asked her to have dinner with him, but he enjoyed talking to her. How come he hadn't met women like her when he'd attempted dating. Dating. A ridiculous word and thing to attempt over the age of, oh, thirty. After his divorce and mourning period, he tried dating, but didn't have much hope or patience. Everyone had baggage and was set in their ways. He knew he was guilty himself on both counts. Although he'd gotten involved with a few women, nothing ever became serious. He'd hurt feelings, and had his hurt, too. Some of the friends who'd set him up lost patience, but what could he do? He tried, but wasn't interested enough. Now he seemed destined to stay single and was okay about it. If he examined himself too closely, he'd have to admit he was occasionally lonely. Lonely, but too lazy to do anything about it. No, it wasn't really laziness. It was fear of being hurt again. Fear of being rejected. Trepidation about letting someone get too close.

Back in his married days, when counseling lonely single friends, he'd recommend museum tours, or singles' cruises, or a theatre-going group. Now that he was single, he did none of those get-to-meet-people things. Writing was a solitary endeavor. He certainly wasn't going to meet coworkers, not working alone in his 750 square foot apartment. In a different universe, he might try being a docent, or feeding adorable baby animals at the zoo, where perhaps he'd just happen to meet a woman he wouldn't lose interest in after two dates. He'd let his Match.com account lapse. There were far more women looking for men than men looking for women, which should've worked in his favor, but somehow didn't.

On Beach Avenue he made a left. How could he miss her company already? Well, usually he took the bus alone. He'd never struck up a conversation with a fellow traveler before. But he liked her. (Maybe he'd like her sister?) It must be her enthusiasm, which was nice to be around. His few friends in Manhattan were very insular and apt to stay put, not understanding his love for Cape May. For them, heading south meant visiting the South Street Seaport. He played poker once a month with a bunch of people, all of whom claimed to be looking for prospects for him. Over the years, some set him up—with sisters, neighbors, friends, coworkers—occasionally inviting him to dinner where another guest, a woman, would unexpectedly be there. After dating a few of candidates, he began to wonder if his friends really knew him at all. Some women were physically attractive, but empty. He was (he'd admit if forced to) still good looking, with all his hair, graying at the temples in a distinguished, rather than just old, manner (he hoped). Thanks to walking around the city he was in good shape and health. He read a lot of books, saw a lot of plays and movies, and basically enjoyed his life. Loneliness never killed anyone. He'd rather be alone than with someone like Donna. His ex-wife had a way of making him feel wrong and awkward. The fact that he chose and married Donna, and stayed with her far too long, made him doubt his self-matchmaking abilities.

He walked into Henry's Restaurant. A young waitress in a white blouse and short black skirt came over to him. "Michael! How are you?"

Michael hugged her. "Sophie! I wondered if you still worked here. How are you?"

"I'm good. Rob still in California?"

"Yes. You heading back to school?"

"Finishing my masters starting September. I'm here for the sun and beach and some spending money before devoting my life to five year olds. I want to enjoy myself now. Outside."

"You're smart. You'll have enough time inside a class-room, as a student or a teacher. You'll be a great teacher."

She sat him at a table outside under the canvas roof, which was everybody's favorite spot. He took out *Time and Again*, and started reading. Funny Joanna liked the book so much, too. He'd heard that the time travel romance had a loyal following, but the only people he knew who'd read it were the people for whom he'd bought copies. His ex-wife thought it was "sentimental," and she wasn't sentimental about anything, was she?

***

The houses on the way to the boardwalk all deserved more of her attention, but Joanna rushed past them, want-ing to get to Henry's. She liked Michael and wanted to talk with him more. When was the last time she met someone with whom she clicked. She was sure that Brian would like Michael, too. The three of them could get together back in Manhattan, if they meshed here.

She walked to Beach Avenue and made a left, as directed by Marie. Beach was parallel to the boardwalk and more heavily trafficked. Joanna crossed Beach and climbed the few cement steps to the boardwalk. The weather was pleasantly warm, and she was perspiring from walking so fast. The building up ahead on the right seemed to be the right one, as described by Marie. She put her hand above her eyes to shield them from the still bright sky. Large letters spelled out "Henry's" above an awning. An American flag waved on a high pole, its rope clanging against the metal. The place looked lived in and, especially now, welcoming. She opened the screen door, and entered. Inside, it was a basic and warm diner. Her eyes scanned the tables, but he wasn't there. A waitress walking past with trays of enticing food impossibly balanced up her arm said, "You can sit anywhere. There's tables in the back, too, if you want to eat outside."

Joanna said, "Thanks," and walked into the back area of the restaurant, and saw Michael sitting at a table, reading. He looked up from his book, saw her, and smiled. She was still breathless from her sprint, and squeaked out a "Hi!"

He walked over to her. "I'm glad you came."

"I suddenly realized how hungry I was."

He guided her over to the table, with his warm hand light on her upper arm. She sat across from him and looked around, taking it all in, and giving herself time to catch her breath. The space had a canvas roof with awnings, which made flapping noises in the breeze. In cooler weather, the clear plastic walls, currently rolled up and out of the way, would be down. In the winter, the room would be closed off. Now, it was just warm enough to be pleasant in the shade, and the table afforded a panoramic view of the beach and the ocean. The scent of sunscreen lightly wafted in and mixed with the fried-food smell of the restaurant. The combination tugged Joanna right back to her childhood summers. She breathed in deeply. "Oh, this is just what the doctor ordered."

Michael called Sophie over. He gestured across the table. "Sophie, this is Joanna, and it's her first time in Henry's."

Sophie said, "Welcome. You want to start with our lemonade? It's the best in town."

Joanna nodded. "Sounds great."

"I'll bring two right away. Here's some menus, although you don't need one, Michael," Sophie said, and went to get the lemonades.

Michael said to Joanna, "My son was friends with her. I think we both had crushes on her."

"Eww."

"It's not like I pursued it. I saw, and learned from, *American Beauty*."

"Good. There's nothing worse than a man dating a girl his granddaughter's age. Unless it's a woman dating a man three years younger than she is. Or perhaps I read too many tabloid headlines at the supermarket."

"Actually it was her mother I was…" he was interrupted by Sophie bringing the lemonades. Michael said to her, "I forgot to ask, how's your mother?"

"She's fine. Happy she moved to Atlanta. Still wishes you had moved down there, too, when she did."

"Oh, that was a long time ago. But I'm flattered," Michael said. "Tell her I said hello."

Joanna listened to their conversation as she took the inch of paper cover off the top of her straw and sipped. "Oh, yummy."

"Good! I'll be back in a minute for your order."

Michael turned to look out at the beach, lost in thought. Joanna was comfortable just being quiet, and watching him. She wondered if he used to eat here with his wife and son. He'd mentioned that he'd been coming to Cape May for years. He was somewhere else right now, miles away. She realized his eyes were an intriguing shade of blue, which made her also realize he was staring back. She snapped out of her own little trance and said, "Sorry. Daydreaming," and turned to people watch.

There were a lot of people on the beach, many strolling fully clothed except for bare feet. The young, skinny girls paraded in their tiny bikinis. "Oh, I see why you like it here."

"Can you imagine: in the 1870s, women wore bathing dresses made of flannel, about ten yards worth," Michael said.

Sophie returned and said, "Are you ready to order?" as she put down a basket of rolls and butter. Michael shook his head, and the waitress left them alone again. Joanna broke off a bite-sized piece of roll and popped it into her mouth.

He sipped his lemonade. "Did you like your B&B?"

"The little I saw, yes. Just inside the door. It seemed perfect. I'll be honored to sleep there tonight. I hope I'm worthy."

"It does seem bizarre to be in an elegant, formal house in jeans and a wrinkled shirt, or even worse, shorts and a T-shirt."

"Sacrilege! Some houses should have real Victorian clothes for houseguests to wear."

"You could do that at your B&B," he smiled. "But don't make it mandatory or people might not come back."

"It would certainly change our romantic views of that time period, if we had to wear corsets and suits in August." She picked up the menu.

He said, "I could make a suggestion, as I've eaten here about a thousand times. Left column, about midway down. Henry's Specialty."

She scanned the menu following his directions: "*Big Ass Clam Platter*! Can they say that?"

"Yes. And it's delicious. With cole slaw and french fries."

"Why not? It sounds like fat and cholesterol heaven, and I am officially on vacation."

"One greasy meal can't hurt, huh? Oh, there's Sophie. Sophie! We're starving."

Sophie came over. "Gee, Michael, let me guess what you're having. Did you talk her into it?"

"Yes," said Joanna. "That's me, falling prey to peer pressure again just like in high school."

Sophie left to place the order.

Michael said, "She's about to fulfill her dream of becoming a kindergarten teacher, and it seems like yesterday I was helping her with algebra."

"Time really does fly, doesn't it?"

He paused. "Most of the time I don't mind so much, you know? Then something will happen and I'll think, shit, what's happened to my life."

"I don't even like to admit I'm middle-aged, and then I think, how many 120 year old women do I know?"

"You're not sixty, are you?" Michael asked, shaking his head.

Joanna's palms flew up to her face. "Not quite yet, please! I'm still in my fifties, for a few more months. I always forget I'm not supposed to tell people my age."

"You shouldn't because they'd never guess it."

"Thank you. Well they do say that sixty is the new twelve, or something."

"I'm over sixty on the outside, with an internal maturity of about seventeen."

"Uh oh, are your hormones raging?" she said, embarrassed the moment the words came out. Her own hormones were making her blush again. At almost sixty. Would that ever stop?

"Yes, they still get me into trouble, but at a slower pace. No raging any more. Now it's more like a swift current."

Wanting to change the subject, she asked, "Are you working on any projects other than the Cape May book you won't even give me a hint about?"

"Next week, back in the city, I have a speech to write, then nothing lined up. I have to start hunting for work. Hell, can anyone retire any more?"

"It's too bad you don't have a science background. My medical education company always needs freelance writers."

He squared his shoulders. "And who says I don't have a science background?"

"Do you?"

"My parents didn't believe I could make money as a writer, so they forced me into medical school. I made it through two long, awful, painful years."

"Loved it, did you?"

"It was my parents' dream. Certainly not mine. But I did learn a lot. I learned how to work like hell and attempt to be satisfied with so-so grades. It really was humiliating. However, having seen an autopsy in person gave me some good copy for my mysteries."

She reached into her purse. "We do seminars, slide presentations, that sort of thing. If you're interested in some freelance work…wait, let me impress you," and dug out a business card. "Here. My company gave me 100 of these, and I think this is the fifth I've actually given anyone."

"*Joanna Matthews, Associate Managing Editor.* Well, I am impressed."

"Yeah, big deal, huh? Email me your CV when you get back to New York. I'll give it to the editorial director. You never know. It's hard work, but it pays well. You're sure to do it better than me. And my cheap company would love the fact that you'd be freelance and they wouldn't have to cover your health insurance."

"If anyone saw what I'm about to eat, the health insurance I currently have would be revoked."

Sophie put huge plates down in front of them. Joanna said, "Wow, that's a lot of food."

"Here's some extra napkins." Sophie asked, "You need anything else? Water?" They both nodded and she was off.

Michael said, "Looks greasy and good" as he handed Joanna the ketchup bottle. She took it just as she bit into a big ass clam. It was hot and some juices dribbled down her chin. He grabbed a napkin to give her but her hands were full, so he wiped her face and she started laughing.

She managed to say, "Oh, I'm glad this isn't a first date. What would you be thinking?" as she continued laughing and dripping.

He laughed, too, and said, "I'd be hoping for a second one." Their laughter slowed.

Sophie arrived with two glasses of water. "If you need anything else, just let me know."

They gazed out at the beach and the pink sky while they ate.

***

They finished eating, quietly and comfortably, watching people on the beach. Joanna consumed her last fry then wiped her hands and face on a wet-nap. After vehemently turning down dessert, she settled back and sighed.

"It's hard to believe we're on the same planet as Manhattan, let alone the same coast, just miles apart."

"You're renewing my love for Cape May. Thank you."

"No, thank you for inviting me here. I probably would've just gone to bed too early."

"Doesn't sound bad."

"I'll be dead asleep by eleven anyway." She looked at her watch. "I should get back to my B&B. Prepare for tomorrow. Let's get the check," she said, looking around the restaurant for Sophie.

Standing and stretching, he said, "It's all taken care of."

Confused for a second, she then said, shaking her head, "You can't treat me."

"I *did* treat you. It's your first meal at Henry's. Your first meal in Cape May."

"Then I accept graciously. Can I leave the tip?"

"I tipped more than the meal cost. For Sophie's textbooks," he smiled.

They exited and Michael lightly put his hand under Joanna's elbow to escort her out of the restaurant. It struck her as a gentlemanly, old-fashioned thing to do, fitting right in with the Victorian structures they were about to see.

It was dark when they exited Henry's and the street lamps and shop windows were ablaze. She gasped. "It's so, I don't know, World's Fair, or Disneyworld, but real."

"You see what I meant about time traveling? It doesn't look all that different than it did a hundred years ago." A man wearing only tiny tight yellow shorts roller bladed past them. "Well, that ruined my point."

The street was full of pedestrians, bikers, skateboarders, and cars, surreys, and scooters. The air hummed with activity.

Joanna said, "Oh, I smell warm, fried dough covered with powdered sugar."

"You smell powdered sugar?"

"Why do unhealthy things smell so good?"

They started walking, and Joanna headed back to Ocean Street. Michael said, "Let's take Gurney Street so you can see some different houses."

Joanna yawned. "I can't believe how tired I am. I guess it's a combo of the bus trip and too much food."

"And the fresh sea air." He sniffed.

She sniffed. "I can't smell it, can you?"

"No, as a matter of fact." He sniffed again and shook his head. "Maybe it's seeping in through our pores." They walked quietly for a few moments. Then he said, "I'm falling down on my tour guide duties. More about Cape May: Do you want to hear about the seventeenth century, and the Kechemeche Indians of the Lenni-Lenape tribe?"

"Keep it simple. I'm really tired," she said.

"Well, for me, things started hopping in the early nineteenth century. In the 1830s, the elite of the major cities—New York, Washington, Philadelphia—came and stayed in the boarding houses. There were only a few then, but within the next ten years, the New Atlantic was built. It was huge. Would accommodate three-hundred guests."

As they walked, Joanna gaped at the row of sister Painted Ladies on Gurney Street. "Oh my, I'm dazzled just looking at the outsides of these houses. What am I going to do tomorrow when I'm inside some of them? My heart may not be able to stand it. I'm meeting with a realtor also, to get an idea of prices and what's available. I'm supposed to be a sensible businesswoman, not a rabid fan."

"Look, I've stayed in over twenty B&Bs. I have friends who own Victorians. I could probably be of help."

"That's nice of you to offer, Michael."

"It's no big deal. I love it here. Been visiting since I was a kid, lived here, would move here again in a heart beat. I know a lot. There I go bragging again."

"No, that's not bragging." She thought a moment. "My husband is coming tomorrow. Let me see how he feels about a third person joining us. Although I think you two would get along really well. That is, if he's not in one of his 'I already know enough people' moods."

"I do that, too. I'll give you my phone number. If you guys want me to come with you, if Brian's feeling social, I'd be happy to join you. My time here is flexible."

"Thanks." She pointed to the houses on the left. "Are all those bed and breakfasts?"

"Only the ones with the inn signs. The others are private homes. Some people fly south in the winter. Florida, the Carolinas. The wealthier go to Bermuda or the South of France. But many people live here all year long."

"It must be cold and lonely in the winter."

"Cold, yes. Lonely? Of course you can be lonely anywhere, any time. But Cape May is busy at Christmastime: tree lightings, caroling, theater, there's a parade, too. You see how pretty it is at night? In the winter it gets dark earlier."

"Yes I've noticed that in Manhattan, too," she said.

He narrowed his eyes at her. "I meant, more time to enjoy all the lights. The town is all lit up and festiv…"

"WAIT." Joanna stopped and stared across the street. "Wow. Is that the Abbey?"

"Yes."

"I read about it. But the website doesn't do it justice."

"Gothic revival villa. It's one of the most popular bed and breakfasts in Cape May."

"I can see why."

"All of the bedrooms are named after cities, like the rooms in your inn are named after roses."

They walked, turning left onto Columbia. In back of the Abbey was a creepy, glum black and red house. Joanna said, "That *has* to be on the Haunted Cape May tour."

Michael said, "If you're interested, the book store on the Washington Mall sells a series of books about Cape May's ghosts. I've read a few. They're fun."

"Shouldn't they be terrifying?" She glanced around. "Oh, I see where we are: my inn is right over there. Everything is so close."

"It's a small town."

She lowered her voice: "I love being able to see into the houses, with all their lights on."

"Cape May brings out the voyeur in all of us."

"Maybe those alleged hauntings weren't ghosts, just Peeping Toms," and she yawned. "Excuse me. I'm so sleepy."

They were now right in front of the Manor Rose. "Good timing. You can be asleep in minutes."

They stood for a few seconds, Joanna scanning the architecture of the block, soaking in the ambience, and reluctant to say goodbye. "Where's your bed and breakfast?"

"About five blocks from here," he pointed, "that way." He smiled slightly. "I hate to say goodbye."

"Me, too. It's been really..."

"It's been nice showing you around, someone who appreciates it, you know? The year we lived here, my wife and son spent all their time wishing they could move back to a big city."

"I understand."

"Remember, if you need any help, let me know. I don't have business cards with me, but you could record my phone number the old-fashioned way and write it down."

"You can have some of mine, just cross out my name," she said while fishing paper out of her bag.

"Or I could change my name to Joe Matthews."

"Everybody calls me 'Jo.'"

"Oh, I'm sorry. Should I?"

"No, I like being called 'Joanna.'" She found a pen. He rattled off his cell number. They stood for a moment. "Well, maybe see you tomorrow then," he said.

"Yes. Thanks." Their eyes locked for a moment before he turned and walked away. This time Joanna didn't watch him go, she just went through the gate and up the front steps of her bed and breakfast.

CHAPTER 6

Joanna entered the Manor Rose and closed the screen and the side door carefully, so they wouldn't slam. She turned left into the parlor and saw a bell on the mantelpiece over the fireplace next to a sign: "If you need *anything*, just *ring*." Joanna decided then and there that if she had a B&B nothing cutesy would be allowed. She had to admit that the sign was beautifully calligraphied and the bell appropriately period. The wooden handle and brass bell were heavy and expertly crafted. She moved her hand and the clapper hit the bell's curve, making a startlingly loud noise. Joanna silenced it, not wanting to disturb the rest of the house, even though it wasn't late. In an instant, Marie came through a door that presumably led to the kitchen.

"Ms. Matthews! Did you enjoy Henry's?"

For a moment Joanna was puzzled that Marie knew she went to Henry's but then remembered. "Yes, it was delicious, unhealthful food. I loved it."

"Great! I've put your bag in your room on the second floor. Are you ready to go up?"

"Please. I'm exhausted."

"Oh, before we go," Marie said, "I should tell you that breakfast is served from seven to ten in the dining room right through there. There's a pantry on each floor with complimentary coffee, tea, and hot chocolate. There's also a small refrigerator in your room, stocked with water and juice. If you need anything else, call one of the phone numbers on these sheets." She handed Joanna a few typed pages.

"One or two of us is always nearby, either here or in the house next door. Only a call or intercom away."

Marie led the way up the stairs, narrating as she went about the history of the house. Joanna took one quick look around the ground floor, anticipating exploring it tomorrow, when she was less tired. Her foot landed on the stair's plush carpeting, sinking in luxuriously. The banister's wood was shiny and cool and Joanna loved the smooth feel of it under her hand. Marie kept talking but Joanna's tired brain wasn't taking any of it in.

"This is your room," Marie said. "The key also opens the front door, but don't worry. It doesn't mean every guest has access to your room. I don't understand how it knows, but our locksmith says it all has to do with math."

"Never my strong subject."

"No, me neither."

The door swung open and Joanna gasped. She stepped into the room, a living museum full of antiques, or excellent reproductions. Opposite a gas fireplace stood a bed, occupying a huge amount of space. One look at the dark wood four-poster, with elegant sheets and too many pillows, filled her head with romantic visions, and caused a tightening between her legs. She walked over to the mantel, which held framed pictures of Victorian families. One little girl in a photo was so adorable, in her hat and braids with ribbons, that tears came to Joanna's eyes. When she was overly tired she also became overly sensitive. A vase with red roses sat on the marble-topped dresser next to the already turned down bed, complete with an inviting gold packet of chocolate on the pillow. Joanna could get used to being pampered like this.

"There are terry cloth robes hanging in the bathroom, and extra soaps and shampoos." Marie put brochures, *What to Do in Cape May* suggestions, and the list of phone numbers and emergency procedures on the table. Joanna liked Marie, and appreciated both her knowledge and dedication, but was relieved when the woman said goodnight and left. The sudden peace and tranquility of the room was jarring for a moment, but Joanna happily adjusted.

She peeled off her clothes, so happy to slip into her cool, cotton rose print pajamas. Brian, Archie, and work seemed many days ago. She entered the bathroom, and whispered, "Wow!" The bathroom was pristine, and so different from her New York City apartment built in the 1960s. A claw-foot tub sat invitingly under a small sea blue and green stained-glass window. She ran her finger along the faucets, which were gleaming white porcelain and shiny brass. The wallpaper was off-white, with lavender sprigs and little red rosebuds on it. Everything was delicate and—odd for a bathroom?—sensual.

After a lackluster teeth brushing, she crawled in between the crisp, sage-colored sheets, stretching her legs and toes all the way down the bed. These sheets, eighteen-thousand plus thread-count, were much more expensive and softer than any she and Brian ever bought. She curled up, closed her eyes, and the first thing she saw was Michael's face. An intake of breath accompanied the instant opening of her eyes. She closed them again. This time she let her mind go blank, and fell sound asleep.

***

That night, staying in a room at his friend's small, moderately-priced bed and breakfast, Michael wrote down ideas for his book. He wrote rapidly, wanting to get them on paper before his internal editor criticized him.

He wasn't sure how to work it into his book, but a piece of Cape May history that fascinated him was its unfortunate involvement with fire. In 1856, the partially constructed Mount Vernon hotel—advertised as the biggest in the world with a twenty-one hundred guest capacity—burned to the ground in an hour and a half. Cause unknown. Six deaths. The following year, the Mansion Hotel burned to the ground. In 1862, a mysterious fire in the United States Hotel was extinguished before too much damage was caused.

In 1869, the "breath of the dread Fire-King," as it was referred to by reporters, began in an Oriental goods shop, and was thought to be deliberately set. The United States Hotel didn't make it this time; neither did the New Atlantic, the American Hotel, numerous cottages and boarding houses, and two blocks of the oldest section in Cape May.

In 1878, the work of arsonists destroyed seven hotels, more than thirty cottages and boarding houses, and two-thousand bathhouses. Thirty-five acres wiped out. The fire smoldered for days. Amazingly, no lives were lost.

In 1889, the New Columbia, thought to be fireproof due to its brick construction, burned to the ground. In 1918, a Naval base, for coastal defense training, was destroyed in a suspicious fire. In 1979, the Windsor Hotel burned to the ground.

Michael planned to weave historical details into his novel; the closer to the truth, the better. The devastation caused to Cape May could be played up and made to seem suspiciously excessive. Maybe there was more behind the headlines: corrupt officials, building code violations, arsonists covering up other crimes. His fictional detective, nosing around looking for information about the assassination plot, would surely stir up trouble in the small town, involving delicious (for a writer) unsavory characters and doings.

***

Joanna woke up early, still on work time, thirsty and not quite sure where she was. The morning sun cast moody shadows on the busy wallpaper. The window treatments were appropriately Victorian and heavy and would block out much of the natural light if not tied back. Being warm and snug and half asleep, she was overtaken by a usually repressed memory. So many years ago, in her second year of college, in her small writing class...

Being the perpetual early bird even then, she was the first person in the classroom on that first day. As the other students entered the room, she peeked at them from under her bangs. Some walked in with head held high, some slinked in. Then he walked in. She looked at him, he looked at her, and she felt like someone punched her in the chest. For a moment, she actually lost her breath. It wasn't that he was so handsome, but his essence, his presence attracted her. All she knew was her heart was beating faster, and when the teacher came into the room and introduced herself and the course outline and goals, Joanna missed most of what she said.

From her earliest days, Joanna heard her parents, mostly her mother, commenting on "slutty" girls and the evils of premarital sex and cohabitation. Although her teenage years coincided with the swinging sixties, the "swinging" part had been reviled by her Catholic mother. Her sister Cynthia's rather busy love life put more pressure on Joanna. Their mother was determined not to let her younger daughter tread the same path. Joanna was brought up to be, God help her, a good girl, to overcompensate for Cynthia's failings. As a young college sophomore, more interested in reading and writing and other solitary pursuits, Joanna was a loner. It was okay with her that she was boyfriendless, although she did feel pangs when she saw couples kissing on the school lawn.

By the second class, Greg (she heard him tell another student his name, that much she paid attention to) had moved closer to her, and she even managed to smile. A week later, he asked her to go out for coffee with him. They talked for hours, and he walked her back to the dorm she shared with three other students. Even all these years later, she'd never forgotten their first kiss.

Greg cared about her and wanted her, and attempted to bed her from their first date. Her grades were falling. She couldn't concentrate. It was hard to hear the teacher over her pulse pounding in her ears. After being in a perpetual state of arousal for months, one night she couldn't resist him any longer.

Two things kept her memories of Greg on a tight leash. One: it all ended so painfully. Two: her cognizance of the fact that she'd never felt that way about Brian.

The birds chirped and she stayed in bed to listen. The air coming in through the open window smelled sweet and clean. In August, she imagined, the scent of flowers would be intoxicating. This would be a delightful town to move to. Of course, if this were her bed and breakfast, she'd be in the kitchen already, overseeing breakfast. Her day would start very early, and be long, spent greeting guests, suggesting restaurants, giving directions, answering questions, ordering supplies, and general upkeeping of the house. Not an unpleasant day at all, she thought. If she could stop herself from missing New York bagels.

New York. Just yesterday she was there, in her tiny apartment, then tiny office in a tall building on a busy, crowded street. It seemed so many days ago. Now she was just a block and a half away from the beach and boardwalk and Henry's. That was a really fun dinner. Michael was a nice, interesting man. He was lonely, too, she sensed, and sad underneath his smile. What had happened between him and his son? There was a lot more to that story, of that she was sure. But it was none of her business.

She sat up, slowly slid off the high bed, and her feet landed on the Asian rug. "Ooh," she said out loud as the stiff fibers massaged her feet. She tiptoed, why she wasn't sure, to the window and pulled back the heavy outer curtains and the lace inner curtains, to peer down to the street. What she saw wasn't the horse-drawn carriages and women with parasols she wished she could see, but the view nevertheless made her smile: early morning Cape May. The street was almost empty, with just a few joggers and a woman walking her dog. Did some B&Bs allow pets or was this woman a Cape May resident? Would the Brian and Joanna B&B allow animals? Dog fur on antique sofas? Cat claws digging into one-hundred year old material? But Joanna felt animals made a home. That was going to be a hard decision to make as an owner.

Thirsty, Joanna went to the mini-fridge for a bottle of water, and drank it down in a few gulps. The french fries at Henry's were salty. There was Michael's face again, as clear as when he was sitting across from her at the restaurant—his blue eyes and crinkly wrinkles that somehow made him look charming where they just made her look older, his light brown hair, gray at the temples and curling on his neck, his chest hair peeking out from the top of his shirt.

Time to call Brian. She got her cell from the bedside table and punched his number. It was early but he'd be up. Even though self-employed, he kept himself on a strict schedule. Sleeping late meant staying in bed until eight. Besides, he'd be getting ready to leave, to drive down to meet her.

Brian answered after a few rings and his clipped, too loud, "Joanna," signaled stress.

"Uh, oh. Work not going well?"

"No, it's going well but there's too much of it. I was going to call you later. I thought you might want to sleep late."

"I went to bed pretty early and slept like a log, or a baby, or whatever sleeps really well. You leaving soon?"

"I have to finish this work first and I'll drive down later."

Joanna paused. "But our appointment with the realtor is at eleven. You know she's showing us houses."

"I know, but my client cut my deadline by a week."

"Can they do that?"

"Yes, and I negotiated a few thousand extra for it."

"That part's good. I'm sorry about the deadline, though. When did you find out?"

"Last night. That's why I canceled on Frank. I was up until three. The figures were swimming in the columns."

She sat on the surprisingly comfortable rosewood chair by the window. "I don't like you driving tired. Be careful." One hand held her phone, and the other traced carved rosebuds on the arms with the tips of her fingers.

"I'll be okay. What about you?"

"I'm feeling stressed, but I'll do what I can."

"Maybe there's a business development office and you could hire someone to go with you."

"I can handle it. I don't really want a stranger with me. I'll go alone."

"What about that guy from the bus? Didn't you say he offered to help?"

Joanna swallowed to get rid of the sudden lump in her throat. "He did but..."

"He wouldn't've offered if he didn't mean it. Didn't you like him?"

"Yeah, he's nice."

"Great. Call him."

She could hear him walking around the apartment. He spent so much time in front of the computer that when he was on the phone he paced for exercise. She knew he was probably standing in front of the living room window right now, probably pulling dead leaves off the African violet. She said, "I don't want...I mean..." Archie meowed in the background. She hoped Brian remembered to feed him, but this wasn't a good time to ask.

"Oh, call him. You didn't want Cynthia's help either. You don't know everything. Ask for help, Joanna. Get over yourself."

"Why are you snapping at me," she stated. "You're worried about this job, aren't you."

He sighed. "Yes," he said. "This new client. Plus the moving thing. You know I don't do change well."

"I know. And I'm scared, too. But it'll be fine. Get here as soon as you can, okay?"

"I promise. Meanwhile, ask that guy, what's his name?"

"Michael," she said.

"Ask Michael to go with you. I know it's the twenty-first century but it's still a good idea to go with someone, someone who knows the in's and out's of a place."

"Someone with a Y chromosome, you mean?"

"You little geneticist, you. I'll feel better knowing you've got someone—male or female—with you. For advice, for company."

She sighed. "I'll see. I'll do what I can."

"Good," his voice was softer. "Good, Joey."

"You know I'd hit you if you were here. Don't call me that."

"I know. I'm just teasing you. I have to work now, okay?"

"Good luck with work, Bri-Bri. See," she smiled, "two can play that game."

"Yuck. Only my cousin Libby called me that. Luckily she moved to Denver when I was ten." He paused. "Well?"

"Well, what?"

"You can ask now."

She heard Archie meow again. "How's my furry baby?"

"Fine, and very cute, and being fed, so don't worry."

"Brian, thanks. I'll see you later."

"I'll get there as early as I can."

"Keep in touch, okay? Stop at rest stops. Drink coffee. Arrive alive," she said.

"Yes, dear. I love you," he said.

"You too. Bye."

***

In the mystery Michael was writing, a Newark detective is dispatched to Cape May by the New Jersey Commissioner of Police. Newark in 1880 had a population of almost one-hundred and forty-thousand people. A police presence was obviously necessary. During that same time period, only nine-thousand people lived in all of Cape May County; less than seventeen-hundred people lived in Cape May itself. The Cape May police force was accustomed to escorting drunks home or locating lost dogs, not handling major crime. How did the big city detective see the quaint little town?

Spending time with a visitor to Cape May was giving Michael insight for the detective, also an outsider. "Outsider" Joanna may have been a newcomer to Cape May, but she seemed to love it and fit right in. He wondered if her husband would love the town as much. What was her husband like? Maybe he'd get to see for himself, if they called him. He hoped they'd call. He loved Cape May, and sharing his knowledge of it. His ex-wife thought Cape May was a waste of time, except for perfecting her tan. He once took her to the arcade, and she couldn't stand the noise or being surrounded by kids. Whenever their son wanted to go,

Michael took him. It was just the two of them, the men of the family out alone, and they had a great time. Donna, preferring sleek modernity, found no beauty in the carefully preserved homes either. Michael, on the other hand, loved to walk every block, revisiting houses he'd first stared at many decades earlier. He got older, friends died, the world changed at an alarming rate, but some of these houses remained the same. He took every house tour, and became acquainted with not only the architecture, but also the owners. He and Donna lived in Cape May only a year, and it was a great year for him. He would've stayed longer but Donna couldn't stand so small a town. At least she gave it a try, for him. Perhaps he should have been more grateful at the time.

After divorcing Michael, Donna and her new, rich husband moved into a large two-bedroom apartment in Manhattan in a building that was about five minutes old. Doubtless he was being too sensitive, but that move felt like her final "fuck you and your old houses." Michael moved into a friend's Cape May bed and breakfast in what used to be the maid's room in the hot attic. He didn't mind the size of the room or the heat. In contrast to his years of discontent and then a broken marriage, the room was a haven.

It continued to be a haven, even after many visits. Every trip he tried to see something new. In all his visits, he somehow had never been to the famous lighthouse. Sometime this weekend he was going to see it. A few scenes in his novel took place there, and he needed more information than his preliminary research had provided: built in 1859, first lighted on October 31. Full height, one-hundred fifty-seven feet, six inches. Even with the renovations that took place from 1987 through 2002 and cost about $2,000,000, he'd still have to get to the top the old-fashioned way. He hoped his knees would let him walk up the one-hundred ninety-nine steps to see the reportedly spectacular view.

If it worked out, he wanted the fight between the detective and the assassin at the top of the lighthouse. An homage to Hitchcock's *Saboteur*.

CHAPTER 7

At her B&B, Joanna drank another bottle of water before heading into the bathroom for a shower. She undressed, trying to avoid her reflection. Lately, every glimpse seemed to unveil another wrinkle or sag. However, the lighting in the bathroom was low key and forgiving and she glanced at herself, not displeased. When the water temperature was right, she stepped gingerly into the tub, her recently developed fear of falling and breaking bones making her wary. The linen shower curtain hung on polished brass hooks, which matched the faucets, and smoothly slid closed. So unlike the jerky plastic K-Mart curtain and hooks in the bathroom back home. It was time for an upgrade.

As the hot shower woke her up, she perused the complimentary, custom-made shampoos, conditioners, and soaps, all with the Manor Rose label, and also available for purchase in the tiny gift shop near the kitchen. Unlike her usually quick water- and time-conscious showers in the morning before work, she stayed in for twenty luxurious minutes. Oh, this really was a vacation!

The plush white towels were warm off the rack. After she patted herself dry, she moisturized and slipped into the robe, which had the B&B logo on the pocket. Delicious smells floated in from downstairs: coffee, bacon, cinnamon. All this pampering and elegance! No wonder people were willing to pay so much to stay here. She dressed quickly, got her notebook, and left the room, feeling like a new person.

The house was still quiet. She hadn't paid much attention to Marie's little tour the night before and was seeing everything as if for the first time. She was appreciating each well-made item of furniture, decorating touch, and lovingly displayed antique.

At the turn in the landing stood a headless mannequin in a period dress, with a hat resting between the shoulders. Joanna gasped. In the space of nanoseconds she first thought it was a person, then a ghost, then she was in awe of the clothing. The dress was velvet, a deep garnet color. Since no one was looking, she touched the fabric. It felt like...velvet. Joanna smiled. What had she expected? Joanna wished she had a dress like it, although this one was many sizes too small for her. The waist was tiny. Of course, the woman who wore it would have been corseted. No thanks.

Next to the figure was a settee with a large, worn leather photo album on it. Joanna made a mental note to browse through it when she had more time. At the top of the staircase she looked down into the entrance way, and automatically stood more erect, as if whalebone were suddenly supporting her. Imagine being the wife and mother here, walking down the stairs to greet callers or welcome your husband home from work. There probably were many kids running around. Their friends. Servants. Tradesmen coming and going. Her own life was so quiet, the thought of all that activity made her envious. Was the first lady of this house, almost one-hundred and fifty years ago, happy? Maybe she would've envied Joanna's self-focused existence.

The powerful smell of the coffee lured her down the stairs. She could ruminate later.

No one was visible, although Joanna could hear people in the kitchen. It was a strange feeling walking around someone else's house, looking at their pictures on the wall, browsing the books on their shelves. It was possible, if everything fell into place, that paying guests would be walking around her house. The thought filled her with joy and hope for the future.

What she saw when she walked into the dining room made her smile like a little kid at Christmas. The long table was set for twelve with elegant rose-patterned china dishes and real silver cutlery. It was surrounded on three sides by food. One sideboard had homemade breads alongside blueberry muffins and cinnamon scones. Another handsomely displayed a cut-crystal bowl filled with fruit salad alongside small individual boxes of cereal. Glass pitchers filled with milk, and orange, cranberry, and grapefruit juices nested in a tray of ice, the colors vibrant. The third had hot plates, patiently awaiting the main course. She dished out some fruit salad, determined not to gain weight in these few days away from her disciplined eating routine. It was hard passing the scones. Perhaps she'd just have half of one.

As she sat down, a woman came out of the kitchen. "Good morning!"

"Hello. Something smells delicious."

"Yes, it does, and it is. I taste-tested it. One of the perks of working here. The cook's made her signature dishes. Can I get you some coffee? Tea?"

"Coffee, please."

Cream, milk, sugar, homemade jam, and butter, all in fine china containers, sat atop a beige, hand-loomed, hemp linen runner embroidered with pink roses.

When the woman came back with a pot of coffee she said, "I'm Rebecca," and poured a steaming stream into Joanna's china cup. "You checked in last night?"

"Yes, and I'm in love with the town already."

"I've lived here my whole life. It's small but has everything, and I never tire of it."

"I can imagine." Joanna looked at the grandfather clock in the other room. It was 8:15, and she had an appointment to meet the real estate agent at eleven. Plenty of time for a leisurely breakfast and some porch chair rocking.

Rebecca went into the kitchen through the swinging door and was out again a second later. "The hot food will be out in a minute."

"I don't mind waiting," said Joanna, holding the delicate cup in both hands and not missing her chunky mug back home. "I'm enjoying sitting here, looking at everything. I love bed and breakfasts. I've always wanted to run one."

"There are some nice ones for sale here in Cape May, and a couple of lousy ones, too. Owners who didn't take enough care. These houses are old old. They require a lot of love and a lot of work."

Joanna gulped down the bracing coffee.

"Some people are too eager to sell sell sell, no matter what," Rebecca said, topping off Joanna's cup.

Joanna wanted to ask a thousand questions but a couple entered the dining room, saying "Good morning," and Rebecca played hostess to the new arrivals.

Over the next few minutes, more guests came down for breakfast. Joanna chatted with some of them, but mostly took notes. She wanted her potential B&B to be as nice as possible. Even in her wildest dreams, however, she couldn't imagine running an inn of this caliber. This house must've cost a fortune. How many $350-a-night bookings per year did the owners need to cover costs? Joanna felt her heart begin to race. "Stop it, Joanna," she silenced herself. It wasn't just about making a living down here, it was about a change in lifestyle. No more jobs about which she was indifferent. No more immersing herself in the mechanisms of disease. Other than doctors, who really wanted to learn about these awful things? These various ways to get sick and die?

A middle-aged white couple entered the dining room and said a general good morning and sat down. The woman said to Joanna, "Where are you visiting from?"

"Manhattan," said Joanna, grateful to cut off her negative thoughts. "And you?"

"Atlanta," said the woman. "We visited New York once. Too crowded for me."

"Some areas are awful, but it's an incredible city. Did you get to any museums?" Joanna asked.

"No, my husband thinks museums are boring."

"That's not true!" chimed in the husband. "I just don't want to look at paintings all day."

Joanna said, "What about the Museum of Natural History?"

The husband said, "Nah. That's for kids."

"Did you see any theater?"

"I don't like theater much," said the husband.

"Well, in my opinion those are some of the things New York does best. If you don't like those, I understand why you didn't like New York," said Joanna out loud, all the while thinking, *"Oh, you idiot! If you're an example of the clients I might get at my B&B, I'm in trouble. And I'll make a rotten host."* Stop judging. Be nice, Joanna.

She returned to her note-taking as Rebecca brought out hot food.

Rebecca said, "This is our stuffed French toast. There's warmed maple syrup on the table. The omelet is onions, mushrooms, and cheddar. There are sausages as well. Can I bring anyone more coffee or tea?"

After eating far too much food—the French toast was the best she'd ever tasted—Joanna excused herself from the table and waddled upstairs. She still hadn't made up her mind about contacting Michael. He seemed sincere about wanting to help, and it would be helpful to have someone in her corner. And they had fun together. It was nice finding someone with whom conversation came so easily, unlike the people at the breakfast table.

By the time she reached her room, her stomach hurt, and it wasn't the luscious food or two much coffee. She was nervous...about possibly making a huge mistake moving. She was also nervous about calling Michael. Wouldn't she be imposing? No. He made the offer and she was sure he meant it. He seemed to be an honest, straight-forward guy.

She'd call right now, before she lost her nerve. He answered after one ring. "Hello?"

"Michael? This is Joanna Matthews, from yesterday?"

"I remember you from all the way back to yesterday. How are you?"

Joanna said, "Honestly? I'm a little anxious about meeting with the realtor. Was your offer sincere?"

"Absolutely."

"You'd look at houses with me?"

"Yes. I'd enjoy it. Should I meet you and Brian at the Manor Rose?"

"No. Just me. He had to work. He's coming tonight."

"You should have someone with you. Realtors throw a lot of info at prospective buyers and it's easier having two sets of ears to catch as much as possible."

"She's picking me up here at eleven. Could you be here by then?"

"Yes."

She sighed. "Thank you. You're making this so much easier for me. I really appreciate it."

"No problem. I love looking around these houses. I'll be there at 10:50."

***

Joanna paced on the wraparound porch. The rocking chairs were comfortable but she couldn't sit still due to her surplus of adrenaline. She managed to enjoy watching the endless stream of people, mostly heading toward the beach. The morning air was warm and soft. She was still for a moment and closed her eyes and breathed it all in. Somewhere in back of all the chatter and footsteps, and getting louder, Debussy's "Girl with the Flaxen Hair" was being whistled. It was one of her favorite pieces of music. She knew it was him. Peeking from behind her sunglasses, she saw him walking up the street. She couldn't help smiling. He walked briskly, with a youthful lope, and was wearing khakis, a wrinkled white shirt, sneakers, and his blue baseball cap.

He waved. "Good morning!" and leaped up the porch steps.

"Hi," she said. "It's really nice of you to do this, Michael. Brian asked me to thank you. He had to finish some work and couldn't get away."

"It helps me, too: seeing inside another Victorian might give me fodder for my book. I'll be taking notes."

"I keep interrupting your reading and your writing."

"Not at all." He sat in a rocker and she did the same. "How do you want to work this? Do you want me to listen, or be annoying and ask questions?"

"Let's see how it goes." She looked at her papers. "If there's something major I'm not saying or asking, please say or ask it. Her name, the realtor I mean, is Ruth Halemayer."

"I don't know her."

"She's taking me, uh, us, to see a house on Burns Street. It's called the Widow's Shawl."

Michael said nothing, and Joanna saw he was trying really hard to have a poker face.

Joanna said, "What."

He lightly shook his head.

"What?"

"I don't want to be negative first thing."

"You're scaring me."

"No! That's not what I intended."

"Michael, I'll be honest with you," Joanna put down her papers and turned to him. "Brian and I are not rich. But even living in superexpensive Manhattan we've managed to save. You know, two jobs, no kids, my only sister has no kids, Brian has one niece he doesn't like. We live frugally, which you'd know instantly if you saw our apartment. I've traveled a lot, alone or with friends. Brian doesn't like to travel much. And then the impetus for this move: my uncle died and left me some money. But it's all we have, and I have to be careful with it. You know, we could live another forty years, heaven help up. If you know anything, tell me."

"The Widow's Shawl. I've heard things. It has a bad reputation."

"Bad?" she said. He nodded. "How bad?"

"Unless they're selling it for $50,000, and you have half a million to put into it, and don't mind a year's worth of renovations, run the other way."

"Oh. *Bad* bad."

He leaned closer and said, confessing, "Wet basement. Mildew. Like a hopeless drunk: still a mess after drying out. Tons of wood damage. It was a rental for a while. The people who lived in it didn't take care of it. Owners just gave up. It's been on the market for years."

"How do you know all this?"

He paused. "When my marriage collapsed, I lived here for a year. People like to talk. People here still tell me things. I also ran a friend's B&B while he was on vacation."

"I read about that: inn-sitting."

"Yes. It's hard for owners to get away. I liked to help my friends when possible. So I learned a lot living here."

"Well, I'm sorry about your marriage but I'm grateful for your knowledge."

A smartly dressed woman walked up to the house and through the gate. Joanna smiled at her and said, "Ruth?"

The woman thrust her hand at Joanna and said, "I'm

Ruth Halemayer. Nice to meet you, Ms. Matthews."

Something about Ruth's white teeth, starched clothes, and too perfect blonde highlighted hair, coupled with her instantly aggressive personality, made Joanna dislike her. "*I'm doing it again. Instantly being judgmental*," Joanna scolded herself, and then overcompensated, smiling too widely: "Call me Joanna. Thanks for agreeing to meet with me."

Ruth said to Michael, "This must be your husband Brian."

"I'm a friend. Michael."

Ruth adjusted, made some small talk about the trip down from New York and the weather, then got down to business. "I have four or five houses to show you today, depending on your time constraints. The first house we'll see is the Widow's Shawl. Full of history. It's a reasonably priced fixer-upper, at the low end of your price range."

Joanna glanced at Michael and he winked at her. She said, "Ruth, Michael used to live in Cape May. As my old, old friend, he's here to advise me."

Michael smiled. "Yes, Jo and I go back, wow, how many years now?"

"Oh, twenty at least." Joanna said. "No, twenty-five. I met you on my birthday."

"Yes, that party at Proof of the Pudding wasn't it?"

"We closed the place down."

"Drank two bottles of the 1897 Château Lafite-Rothschild, remember?" said Michael.

Ruth said, "How nice. Well, shall we walk to the house?"

Joanna said, "Michael told me about the Widow's Shawl. I don't think I can afford all those repairs."

For a moment Ruth was silenced, but being professional she recovered. Her starchy all-business personality dissolved. "My boss is trying to unload the place. I wasn't trying to scam you. It could be a good house if someone has the money and patience to renovate it. The price is reasonable."

"I understand," said Joanna. "I work in medical education, and I've occasionally pushed the second best medication, or even the third, because its manufacturer was paying my salary. I'm okay with renovations, but nothing terribly extensive. "

Ruth nodded. "I do have nice houses, in various sizes and conditions, to show you." She turned to Michael. "Do you know the Baroness E, the Teal Dream, or the Tea & Scones?"

He said, "I knew the first two were for sale, but not the Tea & Scones."

"It's been closed for a while and a bit neglected. Not like the Widow's Shawl, I promise. The owners couldn't decide what they wanted to do but are now retiring and the house will be on the market officially in a few weeks. But you're here now, so I'd like to show it to you. The owners are still living there, but won't mind stepping out for an hour to give you some privacy to look over the house."

Michael turned to Joanna. "They are all worth seeing. You'll get an idea of what's out there." He turned to Ruth, casually, and said, "I haven't seen the T&S since I stayed there years ago."

"Since then," Ruth continued, looking down and checking her notes, "they've renovated the kitchen…"

Michael motioned to Joanna discretely, first miming drinking tea then giving her the thumbs up and okay signs.

"…replaced the boilers, and did the roof. Minor repairs need to be made—broken windows, steps, nothing too expensive."

"How many guest rooms?" said Joanna.

"Five bedrooms, four bathrooms. Two rooms can be used as a suite with a connecting bathroom. Small apartment upstairs for the owners to live in or it can be rented, too. Six blocks from the beach."

"I'd like to see it," said Joanna. "I'd like to see all three houses."

"Great," said Ruth, as she tapped into her iPhone calendar. "I'll call the Tea & Scones now. No Widow's Shawl, and I'll try to move up one of the later appointments." She left the porch and walked to the sidewalk, for some cell phone privacy.

Joanna turned to Michael. "Am I glad I sat next to you on that bus!"

"I can be useful sometimes."

They were smiling at each other, unable to look away. A small bomb of heat exploded in Joanna's core, as if she had downed a strong brandy. She could feel the heat rising in her face, so she turned and walked away towards Ruth.

Ruth said, "We can go see the Baroness E now. It's only a few blocks from here. If you don't mind, I just got a message I have to respond to. I'll be off by the time we're there."

"Please go ahead," said Joanna, as she and Michael began strolling behind her.

Joanna's level of excitement was high: she was about to see the inside of her first potential Cape May home. She didn't feel like chatting and somehow Michael sensed it. They arrived at the house. Ruth got off the phone and unlocked the door as Joanna and Michael walked around the property then on the porch. Everything was in good condition but too ornate for Joanna. She carefully and systematically walked through the empty house, its halls and bedrooms and bathrooms, kitchen, attic, basement, garage, all of which confirmed that the Baroness E was not for her. She tried to be open minded, but she couldn't picture herself living in the house.

Next on the list and geographically was the Teal Dream. Although architecturally pleasing and immaculate, it felt too creepy. Ruth dutifully pointed out all the positives and seemed to genuinely like it. Joanna used all her powers to imagine less oppressive furnishings, the walls with different paint or wallpaper, but nothing could cover her feeling that there'd been a brutal murder in the house. She felt like the kid in *The Shining* seeing blood and brains splattered on the wall, while no one else noticed the mayhem.

The three of them then walked to the Tea & Scones, chatting about Manhattan—Ruth visited there four times a year to see her sister and nieces—restaurants in both New York City and Cape May, and mortgage rates. They turned a corner and Ruth said, "The Tea & Scones is up ahead on the left. Three houses down."

Joanna gasped when she saw it. It was like the younger, smaller sister of the Queen Victoria or the Manor Rose. Charming, elegant, and, in Joanna's eyes, perfect.

Opening her loose leaf binder, Ruth began reading from various sheets of paper: "One of Cape May's best kept secrets, the Tea & Scones boasts a stunning entryway and front door with stained and beveled glass."

Joanna's eyes took in every detail of the house. That sense was so attentive she suddenly realized another wasn't working at all: she hadn't heard a word of Ruth's narration. Words didn't matter at this point. The house, from the outside anyway, was everything Joanna had ever envisioned owning, despite the chipped and faded pale pink paint, the revolting green trim, a few broken windows, and splintered shutters hanging on for life by rusty nails. On the front path, Joanna looked up: the house had three floors with three porches that decreased in size as they went up. It gave the impression of a tiered wedding cake, with the smallest porch at the top for the bride and groom. Joanna walked up the pathway, flanked by overgrown rose bushes. Seven— lucky number!—steps, some missing a brick here and there, led up to the wraparound porch, which was missing some posts, too, here and there. The stained glass of the front door formed an abstract work of art that instantly brought a smile to Joanna's face. She felt welcomed. She felt she'd come home.

The porch needed stripping and refinishing, but the wood seemed good. When she stepped onto it, and walked the full length of it, she knew she was hooked. Michael saw her eyes shining with tears, and knew she loved the house. Her face was an open book.

Ruth said, "This isn't in as good shape as the other two. It needs work, but nothing horribly expensive," and continued reading over her papers. "Let's see. There's an apartment on the third floor that needs some dry wall and kitchen updates. It has a tiny sundeck with ocean views."

"Oh, an ocean view. Just what I've always wanted! Even Brian would like that. Fantastic!"

Michael said to Joanna, "Come and see this," and pulled Joanna off to the side, away from Ruth, who was having difficulty unlocking the door. About to whisper to her, he was momentary stalled by being so close to her. "Joanna," he said, the three syllables tickling her ear.

She backed away. "I-I can hear you," she said, suddenly interested in looking at the small overgrown side garden.

"Sorry. I don't mean to be a killjoy but I wanted to say that while I'm really enjoying your enthusiasm, you might want to dampen it a bit when dealing with" he pointed his thumb over his shoulder "*her*."

"Of course. You're right. I'm an idiot."

"No. You're not schooled in the art of deception. If you manage to lie a little, and like the house despite all of its many, many deep flaws, you might be able to bargain a bit and get it for less."

She smiled. "Thanks for the tip." She walked back to Ruth, with her shoulders squared and her resolve intact. "What's the average electricity bill?" she said, in a clipped, business-like voice.

Michael had to turn away to hide the grin on his face. He took a minute to subdue himself and, with his own blank face now set, he walked through the front door, which Ruth was holding open for Joanna.

Ruth said, "The owners are willing to negotiate and sell the house furnished, if you're interested."

Walking around in the house, Joanna had to suck in her cheek to stop from beaming and "Wow"-ing at everything she saw. Despite the fact that the house, in true Victorian fashion, seemed to have twice as much furniture as it actually needed—her sister Cynthia's antiques shop could benefit from the excess—the house was roomy and welcoming, with the sun streaming in. Something in Joanna clicked, reacting to the house in a way she had only dreamed of. When Ruth led the way into another room, Joanna caught Michael's eye and mutely screamed with enthusiasm. Something in Michael clicked, too.

They toured the entire house, with Joanna reciting her "Oh, this is okay, but I don't like that" commentary, all the while jumping up and down inside and making faces aside to Michael. It was easy for Joanna to see past the broken windows, worn rugs, cracked walls, and chipped paint. Unlike the subdued nightmarish feel of the Teal Dream, this house filled Joanna with happiness. The very walls—despite some hideous wallpaper—felt infused with love and comfort and peace. When they left the house an hour later, Joanna again muted her enthusiasm and said to Ruth, "It's nice. Do we have time to see another one?"

"Yes. It's just a half block away, this way."

As they strolled, Michael said, "It's a buyer's market isn't it, if so many houses are for sale?"

Ruth said, "Yes and no. We are in a downturn but Cape May is always desirable. These are more than just houses—these are history. It's not just about earning a living running a glorified hotel, it's about stewardship. Maybe that's why I wanted to show you the Widow's Shawl. Someone caring needs to buy it and restore it to its grandeur. I wish I had the money."

The last house was larger and more expensive than Joanna would have been comfortable taking on. They did a perfunctory look-through and left. After they saw everything, Joanna said, "Thank you. I've got a lot to think over."

"I think you should have a good idea now of what you can get in Cape May in your price range."

"Yes, thank you. If my husband wants to see any of these houses, could you show us tomorrow, or at a later time?"

Ruth shook Joanna's hand. "Of course, I'd be happy to. You can't be expected to make a huge decision like this in a day or two. You have my card. Call anytime. And if you'd like, I can email you when anything suitable comes on the market."

Joanna and Michael watched as Ruth drove away, around the corner. Joanna turned to Michael and was so excited, she almost hugged him, but squealed instead, "You were right. I love that house! It's perfect. Even the name: the Tea & Scones. Perfect!"

They started walking, mostly because Joanna couldn't be still.

He said, "The house had a remarkably friendly, light feel to it, as if it were filled with happy memories."

"You felt it, too?"

"Oh, yes. I've walked into a few of these houses and felt...I don't want to be dramatic, but I swear I've felt evil. Like that teal one. You can't paint over that, you know?"

She stopped, and looked at him a moment, unable to comment. "I've lost track of where we are. I'm incredulous. It's a dream come true, Michael. It really is. I've been searching and hoping, and I've found it. The house. Cape May. This is it." Tears came. "I need to sit down. I'm dizzy."

He led her up a path to the steps of a house. "Sit, Joanna. Do you want me to get you some water?"

She checked her watch and laughed. "It's 3:30? I think I'm just starving."

"Me, too," said Michael.

"After that huge breakfast I thought I'd never want to eat again."

"You just found the house of your dreams, so I think you should get to choose where we have lunch, too."

She smiled at him. "I'm thinking big ass clams, but two days in a row would be asking for a stroke. There were other, less lethal items on the menu, weren't there?"

"You want to go to Henry's again?"

"That lemonade took me right back to my grandma's house. Also, if I order a salad, I can try one of those desserts that looked so good."

They started walking towards Henry's, and Joanna's heart fluttered. What if Brian didn't like the house, or changed his mind about moving? She knew he was moving just for her. Or what if someone else was willing to pay more for the Tea & Scones? As she and Michael walked to Henry's she said, "Do you mind if I call Brian?"

"Of course not. Do you want privacy?"

She shook her head as she speed dialed Brian. As soon as he picked up, she said, "I found it!"

"What?"

"Our new home!"

"Oh. Okay."

She stopped walking. "That's it?"

"Jo, I'm in the middle of something."

"You could at least pretend to be excited." She turned her back to Michael, embarrassed. He noticed and walked away, suddenly determined to study a lavish iron fence.

"Maybe it's all getting too real: moving," Brian paused. "I think I assumed you'd be onto the next thing by now."

"What?"

"I'm happy for you. Honest. We can talk when I'm there."

"Okay. See you later. Bye." She waited a few moments before walking over to Michael.

He said, "You okay?"

"I guess I can't expect him to be as happy as I am. He's not really thrilled about moving."

They didn't talk again until seated at a table, looking at the menu. Joanna said, "I'm taking up so much of your time. Aren't you supposed to be writing?"

"I am, in my head. Hanging out with you has given me ideas for my book. It's been good for me."

"For you? You may have saved us tens of thousands of dollars just by telling me to keep my mouth shut."

"I hope I said it a little nicer than that."

"You did."

"The house is a beauty. Special."

"Yes! And I didn't see any foundation problems." She took a small notebook out of her purse and began jotting. "No floor flexes or recesses. No moisture discoloration. There was a crack in two of the walls on the second floor I'll want someone to look at, and the apartment upstairs needs some new walls entirely, but I don't think the house was leaning, or structurally unsound. The mantelpiece on the large fireplace was missing some tiles. I'm sure they're replaceable although I'll probably have to have them made to order."

"I didn't notice most of those things." Michael smiled and shook his head at her. "You know your stuff."

"I've seen so many houses, dragged Brian or my sister Cynthia, or another friend for support. I've had to learn a lot. At work during lunch I read and read and read. I can't think about spending this much money without educating myself about everything. I still have so much to learn, but I can tell that this house won't cost me hundreds of thousands to renovate."

Again they were seated outside. Again the breezes brought smells of summer. Joanna already felt at home here, after barely two days. She gazed out. "Hard to believe New York has the same sky."

"Maybe you can't see it because of the tall buildings."

"Maybe. What about you? Do you live in one of those tall buildings?"

He shook his head. "Second floor of a ten story building. In a tiny one-bedroom apartment on Seventy-Third just off Amsterdam."

"We're practically neighbors."

"I could kick myself now. I had the opportunity to move about four years ago. Same building but a bigger apartment with a nicer view. But I didn't."

"Why?" Joanna said.

"Oh, inertia mostly. Packing? No thanks. But if I wanted to move now, I'd have to wait until someone in the building dies."

"Are you on a waiting list or anything?"

"Yes, but I'm in no rush, to tell you the truth. It's just me there, with two million books."

"Sounds like our apartment."

They sipped their lemonade.

Michael said, "I was surprised you wanted to come back here. I mean, I love it, too, but not everybody does."

"Brian's best friend Frank is a chef and now Brian's into upscale restaurants, so this is different and a lot of fun for me. Tomorrow we'll probably be eating at some expensive restaurant, which I'm sure I'll enjoy, but give me a basket of fried anything, with french fries and onion rings on the side, every once in a while, and I'm happy."

They ate quietly and comfortably, with their notebooks open in front of them. While Joanna wrote down thoughts and questions about the houses she had just seen (pretending that she might be interested in any one other than the Tea & Scones), Michael worked on a scene between the Newark detective and the bodyguards assigned to protect the visiting politician, who didn't appreciate police interference.

"Michael, on the second floor of the Tea & Scones," Joanna asked, her eyes closed, her right hand holding a pen poised over the notebook and her left working its way through the schematic of the house in her head, "when we exited the smallest bedroom was there a window to the right before you get to the staircase?"

"You're kidding, right?"

She opened her eyes and laughed. "I guess you're not as obsessed with the house as I am, huh?" He shook his head. "And I'm interrupting your writing again. I'm an anti-muse."

"I don't mind."

They both returned to writing, until the check came. When it did, Joanna insisted on paying. "To thank you officially," she said.

They left the restaurant and Michael said, "Want to see more of Cape May?"

"Yes but can we stop at the inn first? For a sweater? It's a little breezy. And I want to call my lawyer and ask about putting a binder on the Tea & Scones. If Brian likes it. Oh God he has to like it."

"It's a great house and reasonably priced."

When they approached the Manor Rose, Joanna said, "Do you know the owner?"

"Claire. Yes."

"No, this one's name is Marie. There's also a Rachel, no, Rebecca."

He shook his head. "Neither rings a bell. Maybe they're new? I wonder if they're Claire's relatives. She has a couple of nieces I think. Do you know their last names?"

"I can't remember. I'm sure it's somewhere in my head, but inaccessible right now. Apparently half my brain is closed for vacation."

He laughed. "Do you think you'll recover for work next week?"

"I'd better."

They walked up the few steps to the front door, and Joanna whispered: "Marie's nice, but I wish she were a little less interactive. Maybe it's the New Yorker in me. Sometimes I like to be left alone with my thoughts."

The hallway was peaceful, with some classical music lightly drifting in from the kitchen. Michael sat down in one of the burgundy wingback chairs and said, "Think how great an innkeeper you'll be, armed with all this insider information. Number one: give guests some peace and quiet."

He grabbed a magazine and settled in.

"When you come and stay with me and Brian, contrary to this trip I promise to leave you alone to write. And we'll give you ten percent off."

"That's all?"

Entering the pantry, she said, "And a complimentary cup of coffee or tea, right now."

"Now you're talking. Coffee. Black with one sugar."

Joanna prepared her tea and his coffee. It felt surprisingly comfortable preparing drinks for herself and Michael on the ground floor of this magnificent house. When Brian came, she'd do the same for him, and feel the real mistress of the house. Carrying the cups out to the parlor, Joanna spotted Michael gazing out the window. He looked pensive.

She didn't mean to pry, but said, "You okay?"

He took the cup of coffee. "Oh, I know sometimes I'm miles away. I didn't mean to be aloof."

"Not aloof. It's just, you seem sad sometimes."

"I thought I hid it well. Being in Cape May brings up memories of my failed marriage."

"Oh," she said, "Do you want to talk about it?"

"God no," he said, with a laugh. "I don't like to fail, or talk about my failing."

She smiled at him. "I understand. You're a man. If you were a woman I'd already know every detail. Would've in the first hour on the bus."

"I'm actually a good talker, for a guy. Haven't you noticed? I think it's because I'm a writer. I have to explore things, and stir up memories and feelings. But now I'm having a good time, and I don't want to actively depress myself."

She put her tea on a table. "I'll go get my sweater." She trotted upstairs. When she entered her room the cell phone rang. "Brian, where are you?"

"Still in Manhattan. I'll be able to leave in a few hours."

"I hope you have an easy drive."

"I doubt it. I'll hit traffic somewhere. You still with what's-his-name?"

"Yes, we just had some lunch. I think you'll like him. Oh, he got us in a tour of a private estate tomorrow. They limit attendance because they don't want thousands of people traipsing through each year. And then you have to see the Tea & Scones."

"Whatever."

"It's perfect. I love it."

"Okay. I'll see it this weekend. Probably tomorrow."

"I don't want to pressure you but I don't want this house to get away."

"Jeez, Jo, I get it."

"I'm sorry. I'm just thrilled with the house. I'll stop now."

"Good."

"You sound tired. Wait until you get here. You'll love it. I feel great. Relaxed. Like I've been on vacation a week."

"Sounds good. I better get off now. The sooner I finish the sooner I'll be there. See you later, Joanna. I miss you."

"You, too."

Joanna put her phone away, grabbed her sweater, and walked downstairs, to find Michael sleeping soundly exactly where she left him, with a magazine open on his lap. He looked so comfortable, she didn't have the heart to wake him. The leather photo album she'd spotted that morning popped into her mind. She quietly walked over to it then carried it gently to a comfortable chair across from Michael's and began looking through the pictures, as she sipped her tea.

According to the hand-written labels, which were starting to peel off the worn pages, the photos were from the 1880s. Everyone looked old, even the children, and no one looked happy. As she judged the women in the photos, she wondered what people one-hundred years from now would think of her own photos. If she and Brian did buy an inn— her mind instantly visualized the Tea & Scones—would they take pictures, put them in a leather photo album? Would it stay in the house for years after they died? The photos would be of just her and Brian, with no children. She felt the stab she always felt at that thought. Would guests speculate on Joanna's level of happiness, of love. Joanna had everything, didn't she? Devoted husband, excellent prospects for the future. She tried to ignore the suddenly empty feeling in the pit of her stomach.

***

The antique grandfather clock in the parlor chimed. Joanna opened her eyes after counting four, and was shocked to hear three more. She sat up and looked around, trying to focus. Michael was watching her from his chair, a book open on his lap, and a cup of tea on the table beside him. He really had a very likeable face.

He said, "Hi," quietly, looking at her from under his hooded lids.

"How long have I been asleep?"

"I'm not sure. I've been up for half an hour. Made myself some tea and I've been reading. I didn't want to wake you. Marie brought me some cookies."

"Ooh, homemade! Leave one for me." She stretched. "I think I needed that nap."

"What is this narcoleptic effect we have on each other. First the bus, then here." Michael closed the book and put it on the table.

"Maybe we're boring," she said.

"I think it's more of a trust thing. I don't fall asleep with people I can't trust."

"Have you checked your wallet? Maybe I fleeced you while you were sleeping."

He shook his head. "I doubt it. I'm ticklish."

Their eyes unlocked when Marie's loud, cheerful voice said: "Well, I see you're up now, too, Ms. Matthews. Would you like a cup of tea?"

"No, thank you," Joanna stood up, and stretched again.

Marie said, "It's the sea air, you know. Makes people sleepy when they're not used to it."

"Thanks for the tea, Marie," said Michael. "And the nap."

"You're lucky it's Friday night. Everyone's out, so it's quiet." She picked up his empty teacup and left the room.

Michael walked over to Joanna. "Do you want to call it a night?"

"No!" she replied. "I'm wide awake now, and I need some fresh air."

"Let's walk."

"Tell me more about Cape May," Joanna said to Michael, as they strolled away from the Manor Rose.

After their naps and his tea, they were both refreshed.

"Well, let's see. Basic stuff. Cape May is named after a Dutch captain called Cornelius Jacobsen Mey, spelled M-e-y. It was the first American resort by the sea."

"We passed a B&B called the Captain Mey. On Ocean right?"

"You must've been a straight-A student with a memory like that."

"I was a straight-A student, if you don't count math or science."

"Or gym?"

"How did you guess?" she laughed. "Wow, that was yesterday when we saw the Captain Mey? It seems like a week ago."

"Every hour with me seems like a day. It's my lack of charm that does it."

They walked east on Columbia, past the Abbey, past the Mainstay. Michael said, "That gorgeous house, the Mainstay, was a gambling establishment. I like to imagine wealthy men in top hats, smoking cigars, sitting around a large elegant table and losing their band-collared shirts."

On Stockton Place they made a right.

Joanna said, closing her eyes, lifting her head, and breathing in deeply, "I still can't smell the ocean. Can you?" He shook his head. She continued, "Do you mind me not making eye contact? While we talk, I mean? I want to see as much of these houses as I can."

"Sure, then I can make faces at you."

She looked at him. "You certainly aren't very mature."

"You make it sound okay. My wife, uh, ex-wife, accused

me of being immature, frequently. She did not make it sound okay."

"Were you immature?"

"I worked, paid bills, did half the parenting, took out the garbage, loaded and unloaded the dishwasher, and more."

"Sounds pretty mature to me."

"You're lucky, Joanna. It's rare to be in a good marriage."

"Yeah," Joanna said, "well, he's my best friend."

"Maybe that was the problem with me and Donna. I don't think she ever really liked me."

"That had to hurt."

"Yes, but maybe I wasn't all that likeable, who knows. It suddenly all seems a long time ago." After a minute passed, Michael continued, "Funny, looking back, the hardest part was the awkwardness of going from being married, part of a couple with a capital C, to not being married. Everything changed. Took awhile to readjust. Now I like being single."

"Would you ever marry again?"

He laughed, "Who'd want me?" Joanna opened her mouth to say something but he interrupted. "I wasn't fishing for compliments or anything. I mean I'm not getting any younger, I'm set in my ways. I do exactly what I want when I want. You know, stuff like that."

"You ever lonely?"

"Yes. But I was frequently lonely when I was married, too," he said.

"Marriage isn't a cure-all, is it."

"You lonely too, sometimes?"

"Sometimes." They walked silently for a few moments. She said, "Now I'm depressed."

He laughed, "Some tour guide, huh? Robbie, I mean Rob, my son, says a conversation with me is more like being interviewed."

"I haven't minded. You haven't pried."

"Good. Now I probably will."

"Uh-oh," Joanna said.

"You don't have kids?"

"Nope."

"You seem like the kind of woman who would've wanted children. I mean, you're warm and motherly."

She grimaced. "Ugh. Just what a woman wants to hear."

"Sexy, I meant very, very *sexy* woman!" They both laughed. "I meant motherly only in the most favorable way, honestly."

"I...let's just say it was never the right time."

"Oh, foot in mouth again, Mike. Sorry, Joanna."

"No, it's all a long time ago. But you're right, I am the mother type. I would've loved kids. It's a long story."

Michael and Joanna walked quietly, which unfortunately gave her brain the opportunity to remember those few awful months. What felt like both a hundred years ago and yesterday.

How ridiculous to get pregnant the first time you have sex. There ought to be a law protecting stupid virgins. Way back in college when she lost control and fell into bed with handsome, sexy Greg, she wasn't thinking about contraception. She wasn't thinking. Desire had taken over, sucking all power away from her brain. It was all over in minutes, it hurt, and certainly wasn't the stuff romance novels are written about. She convinced herself she was in love, though, probably because nice girls didn't have sex with boys they weren't in love with. (Thanks, Mom.) Greg kept after her, and the sex got a little better with practice and as much patience as a twenty year old boy could muster. She was finally starting to enjoy it and lose some of her inhibitions when she realized she was pregnant. They would be in college at least two more years, many states away from their parents, with no support, no money, and no wish on Greg's part to get married. An abortion seemed the best choice. The arrangements were made and he took her for the procedure, and stayed with her afterward while she cried until she couldn't cry any more. She cared about Greg, but chased him away because he reminded her of the day she did the unthinkable.

It took her a long time to sleep with anyone again. Part of her sexual reluctance had to do with not wanting to be like Cynthia. Her older sister slept with anything that moved and had a penis. That was how it seemed to Joanna, five years younger and much more shy than her elegant and sexy sister. Boys and men loved Cynthia, and she saw no reason not to love them back. When they were younger, as two daughters of a single mom, they were rivals for their mother's attention. Joanna, as the younger and less social, won. When Cynthia was out on dates, Joanna listened to her mother worrying about Cynthia's morals. Joanna knew she couldn't compete with her sister's popularity with the opposite sex, but she could be their mother's favorite child, if she behaved. It cost her a lot to be her mother's favorite.

Michael's "I'm really sorry, Joanna" brought her back to the present. "It's none of my business…"

"No, it's fine." The abortion was a part of her history that she didn't share with anyone. "I got married older, and didn't get pregnant, and that's it really." Her sudden sadness told him it was more involved than that.

"Did you ever want to adopt?"

Joanna looked away from his questioning eyes, with an audibly sharp intake of breath. "I…"

"I should glue my mouth shut."

"No. We're talking. It's a legitimate question. I wanted to, but Brian didn't." She paused, and he was about to attempt to say something, but she continued, "No…it's just, I wish he…you see, he barely even wanted a kid of his own. He was clear about that when we got married. I should've listened, I guess."

"We hear what we want to hear. Or don't." There was a long pause. He said, "We sure are wallowing in depressing topics."

"As Jung said, even a happy life has darkness in it. Or something."

"Well, as tour guide I need to cheer us up and I have just the place."

"Place?"

"The arcade."

"The arcade?" she said and smiled.

"Yes. It's right over there. Just a few stores down. You can't be sad in the arcade. It's impossible."

"Impossible, huh?"

"Unhappiness dissolves when you…" he stopped walking, and stood completely straight, head held high, "play skee ball," he said.

"Skee ball?"

"Joanna, you sound like a parrot." She smiled. "You've never played?" She shook her head. "Then come on!"

CHAPTER 8

One of the reasons Joanna agreed to marry Brian all those years back was that she desperately wanted to have children. She'd felt shut down in her twenties and confused in her thirties. It took getting older and knowing herself better to feel she might be a decent mother. After they were married, she went to her doctor for a full examination. He gave her the go-ahead—she was healthy and everything was working as it should—but she never became pregnant. Factors included not only her age, but their infrequent love-making, both of which, in her mind, were her fault. It was stupid, she knew, but she couldn't help feeling that she was being punished for the abortion. Joanna knew she should've been smarter. At the time she was a well-educated, privileged, grown-up virgin who was so carried away that birth control was the last thing on her mind. With that one event, all those years earlier, she betrayed the oft-repeated tenets of her depressed and controlling mother, chased Greg away, and put her own selfish needs before the life of her baby. After that she kept her emotions firmly in check, and she never let herself get carried away again. Greg wanted to continue to see her, but she wouldn't return his calls. He eventually gave up, not wanting to fight any more. She dated, mostly to have a reply when her friends and family asked if she was dating anyone, but she wasn't really interested. It wasn't just that no one felt like the mythical Mr. Right, no one even felt like they came from the same planet that she did. One by one her friends married, and she managed not to feel jealous. She stayed friends with some of them, although she did lose a few to the sometimes exclusive couples club.

When she met Brian, something clicked, two people who felt damaged, recognizing something in each other. As a child he'd been a poster boy for nerdiness: a skinny loner with really bad acne, glasses, and braces, who preferred numbers to people. The night they met, Joanna had been dragged to a party by a coworker at her new job. The coworker talked to her boyfriend all night, and Joanna sat on a couch attempting to talk to an older, dull man. Brian was sitting across from her, not talking to anyone. As the older, dull man monologued about the rotten state of the world, Brian made eye contact with Joanna, closed his eyes and pretended to fall asleep. She couldn't help but smile. He held up his glass of wine and silently asked if she'd like one. Tilting his head toward the bar, he stood up and walked, and she followed him.

In the "social" department, they were both in the "anti" column, but they managed to talk to each other. In one of the bedrooms, they found a Scrabble set and began playing. That was the building block of their friendship. When people asked how they met, they said they were set up on a blind date by Alfred Mosher Butts. The fact that no one got the joke about the inventor of the game was part of their fun.

***

Joanna and Michael walked into the Cape May arcade. It had an open front, with coin-operated mechanical rides—a horse and an elephant, both with bejeweled saddles—sticking out onto the wooden slats of the boardwalk. Joanna hadn't been in a place like it since she was little. The arcade was filled with kids and, to her surprise, some adults, who were sitting on high stools in front of blackjack and poker machines.

"Don't they have PacMan any more?" Joanna asked, not recognizing any of the games.

"No, only incredibly violent games. Where you blow up dinosaurs, kill zombies or drug lords, Nazis, cheerful stuff like that."

It was loud, with soundtracks thumping, guns firing, dinosaurs roaring, and people screaming. Michael yelled, leading her to the rear of the place. "Skee ball is like mini-bowling, sort of."

When they reached the back wall where it was a little quieter, Michael waved his hand with a flourish. "Look." There, in all their glory, was a row of a dozen skee ball alleys. "Just look at them, Joanna. They are made of wood. Not plastic. They don't kill anything, they require no bullets or batteries. See, the alleys are much smaller than in bowling, and you don't knock pins down. Here, watch him."

A teen, whose underwear stuck out three inches above the waistband of his pants, put a token in the machine's slot. Nine balls released into the holding area. The kid picked up one and rolled it up over the bump in the wooden alley. The ball jumped and landed in the hole marked forty points. Underneath the token slot, a ticket popped out.

Joanna turned to Michael. "These aren't Victorian, are they?"

"They were invented around 1910."

"Corseted women couldn't've bent over to play."

"They should've been home cooking anyway."

The kid continued rolling the balls, getting them in the holes, and tickets kept popping out. Joanna pointed to them. "What's that?" The kid turned around suspiciously. "Oh, sorry," Joanna whispered, as she walked away with Michael.

He said, "We have to get tokens."

"I have some quarters in my purse, I think."

"No, we need tokens. Lots of tokens." He put a $10 bill into a change machine and tokens landed noisily in the cup.

Joanna eyed the pile of tokens. "Uh, how long are we going to be here?"

"You play a few games of skee ball, and then if you want to leave we'll leave, okay?"

"Fair enough."

They walked to the end of the row where there were empty alleys side by side. Michael put a token in one machine, and the balls dropped. "I love that sound." Taking one ball out, he held it up to her face. "Isn't this wonderful? It's wood. Not plastic or synthetic. Feel it."

Their hands grazed.

"It-it's wood all right," she said.

"It's possible that a president held this ball. Some visited here, you know. Do you want me to show you how to play?"

"It looks basic enough."

She put her token in and watched the balls drop. She rolled one up the alley, and it rolled back down. Rolling it again, it jumped a little when it hit the bump, but didn't go over the bump.

"Don't be shy," Michael said.

She rolled the ball harder. It flew over the bump and landed in the ten points target. The machine registered the points and Joanna picked up another ball. All the balls she rolled landed in that same ring. When she was finished, a couple of tickets poked out under the token slot. "What are these for?"

"This isn't all just simple, mindless fun, Joanna. I have saved the best piece of news for last. Look over there. See those shelves full of valuable prizes? See the numbers on them? Like that scary looking bear?"

Joanna turned around to see display cases forming a square in the center of the arcade. A bored young man stood in the middle behind the counters, which were filled with cheap plastic toys, jewelry, decks of cards, model ships, and just about anything else you could think of. Hanging over his head were hundreds of stuffed animals of every color, shape, and size. She saw the scary bear, with a sign around its neck. "It says *fifteen-hundred*. Fifteen-hundred what?"

"Points. Each ticket is worth three points. You get one ticket for every forty points you score in skee ball. Then you redeem the tickets for a valuable prize."

Joanna did some calculations. "Math, math, math. Do you mean I'd have to get five-hundred tickets to win that bear thing?"

"Yep!"

"Wouldn't I have to spend...a ridiculous amount of money on skee ball to get those tickets?"

"Yes."

"Wouldn't it make more financial sense to just buy the bear?"

"Yes! But it's about the enjoyment, dare I say adventure, of the game. Also, there are smaller, still valuable prizes. Years ago, I won a whole paper bag's worth of tiny plastic World War II soldiers."

She couldn't help laughing. "And I bet you still have them."

He stood up straight, head held high, broadening his already broad shoulders. "You haven't really gotten into the spirit of the game yet, Joanna. I'm sure you, too, in time, will come to love it, and behave like a ten year old."

"Great," she said, still smiling, "just what I need." She rolled a few more balls, all scoring ten points. He was bursting at the seams. "You want to show me how to do it, don't you."

He nodded. "I want you to love skee ball."

"Okay, show me."

"Now, take the ball and stand here." She did as she was told, and he stood in back of her, putting his hands on her waist. He dropped his hands, faced her and said, "Uh, is it okay if I…" he motioned with his hands towards her waist.

"I must learn. Do what you have to."

He put his hands lightly on her waist and positioned her in front of the alley. "Good, now over to the left about an inch. Yes." Skee ball lesson or not, Joanna noted his delicate touch. He truly was a gentle man. She did a quick inventory of her single friends, trying to think of someone to set him up with. No one seemed suitable.

Michael moved his right hand from her waist, and cupped her hand. He swung it back, then forth. "Let go!"

The ball rolled perfectly down the center of the alley, jumped over the bump, and fell in the ten point hole. Joanna took a step away so she could turn to him, smiled coyly, and said, "I did *that* without your help."

Michael was determined. "No, really, there's an infallible method. I've studied this more than you'd want to know, or I should admit, on many a long post-divorce, whiskey-fueled night." His eyes on the alley, his right hand again went under hers. "Let's try again." This time his left arm went around her, and his body spooned hers. "Aim down the center, keep your elbow bent a little, and let go when your arm is passing your body. I want you to experience the fifty point thrill."

His head was over her right shoulder, facing forward, concentrating on the alley in front of them. Her eyes slid toward him, surveying his close profile—the straight strong nose, the soft skin, the gray-speckled days' growth of beard, and the attractive crow's feet around his blue eyes. In the seconds they were in this position, the arcade warmed, and she felt faint. She faced the alley and allowed him to mechanically bring her arm back, then forward. As he turned toward her to impart some instruction, she turned towards him, and their faces were just inches apart. The ball fell to the floor with a thud. They quickly stepped apart.

He bent down to retrieve it. "Y-you get the idea," he said, handing it to her. She nodded, still feeling woozy. He moved to his own alley, feeling a little woozy himself. A few minutes later he said, "How's it going?"

"I think I'm getting the hang of it."

"Good."

Exerting her full concentration powers on skee ball, she aimed and rolled the ball right into the fifty point hole. "Yes! Fifty points! You're a good teacher."

"No, some people just got it! Look at that line of tickets."

"Should I take them now?"

"If you want, or leave them until you're finished."

Joanna picked up another ball and scored forty points. "Yes! Yes!"

"Well, Ms. Matthews, do you want to leave? Or are you a convert."

"You couldn't drag me out now, Leighton." She mock spit on her hands, rubbed them together, and grabbed another ball. Michael just smiled. She said, "I know: you told me so."

They played for a full hour—and used another cupful of tokens—occasionally watching each other and getting excited if one of them scored high points. When their tokens were gone, Michael said, "Enough?"

"Let's stop while we're ahead." She rubbed her shoulder. "My arm is starting to ache."

"Okay, then. Time to count our tickets." She followed Michael to the prize counter. The young man in the red and white striped cheesy jacket and Styrofoam straw hat watched them approach. How did they appear to this twenty year old boy. Old? Silly? Together?

The kid said, "Yeah?"

Michael said, "Hi," and handed in his tickets. The kid, "Brad" according to his name tag, put them on a scale. Michael said to Joanna, "In the old days, we actually had to count the tickets ourselves, and then multiply by three."

"Thank goodness for modern technology," Joanna said, holding onto to her long strip of pink tickets, and finding the whole process entertaining.

Brad noticed Joanna's stash. "Sh'I weigh 'um together, or separate?" he asked, sounding as if he couldn't possibly care less.

Joanna looked at Michael who said, "We could we pool our resources..."

Both Joanna and Brad said, at exactly the same time, "by joining forces from now on?" The three of them laughed.

Brad lit up. "I love *Gypsy*! I played Tulsa in my high school production."

Joanna said, "*Gypsy*? In high school?"

"It was highlights from Broadway shows. So, no stripping. But I loved the music and got the CD."

Michael propped his elbows on the display cases. "Brad, I'm Michael. This is Joanna. It's her first skee ball experience, so if you want to add her tickets to the scale, and uh, lean on it a little bit with the old thumb..."

"Say no more," said Brad. "Any friend of Gypsy's is a friend of mine."

Thanks to Brad, they ended up with many more points than they'd earned. Hunched over the display cases for many minutes, they found it hard to decide on just the right prizes. There were no tiny toy soldiers this time, but Joanna did find a plastic flashlight key chain shaped like a lighthouse that she thought was cute. Michael got one, too.

"Bye, Brad. Thanks for your help," said Joanna, leaving the arcade. Michael waved goodbye.

Outside again they breathed deeply. "I didn't realize how stuffy it was in there. The fresh air feels so good," she said. "I still can't smell the ocean, though."

"You want to smell salt? I'll take you someplace to smell salt. Morrow's Nut House, just over there."

"And we're going there because…"

"They sell fudge, nuts, and just about everything else. When your guests ask *'Where can I buy salt water taffy to take home to my Aunt Minerva?'* you'll be able to answer with authority Morrow's Nut House."

"You're determined to make me the most knowledgeable innkeeper in Cape May, aren't you?"

"For purely selfish reasons. I'll be dropping in on you and Brian, drinking all the complimentary sherry on the sideboard, expecting kingly treatment."

"Oh, now I see."

The moment they entered Morrow's, Joanna said, "My goodness, I see what you mean about the salt. You could get high blood pressure just breathing in here."

Michael said, "You wanted salt."

"I wanted ocean salty, not nuts-drowned-in-salt salty."

"Want to leave?"

"No! I love stores like this."

Morrow's had long counters in the front of the shop, filled with nuts and candies sold by the pound. The store also had shorts, T-shirts, and all sorts of kitschy beachside souvenirs with *Cape May* printed on them.

It was crowded and they had to squeeze past people to get to the back of the shop. There, they leisurely browsed the shelves filled with knickknacks, books, sandals, candles, stuffed animals, and post cards. Joanna wanted a little gift for her assistant Susan, in thanks for all her help. While she hunted for a present, Michael wandered the aisles.

After a few minutes of solo browsing, Joanna wanted Michael's opinion about something she'd picked out for Susan: a business card holder. It was a three inch long tree slice with the bark left on, all shellacked and shiny, with *Cape May* painted on it and a tiny pail and shovel glued on the side. Susan was destined to move up the corporate ladder, once she learned how to dress more appropriately. She'd have business cards of her own then, and this silly little tableau seemed a perfect gift. It was that or the bright red lobster-shaped oven mitts! Joanna looked around the crowded store for Michael. She found him waiting in another aisle for her, with an odd look on his face.

She guardedly approached him. "What? What are you up to?"

He was pointing to a display of shell-encrusted objects of all sizes: red velvet ring boxes covered with tiny shells, picture frames covered with tiny shells, tissue box holders covered with shells of varying sizes. Joanna started to giggle. She picked up a three inch high sculpture of a well with a bucket, all covered with tiny shells, for holding toothpicks. It made her laugh even more.

Michael said, "Wait! The pièce de résistance," and brought out from behind his back an eight inch high statue of an owl covered in shells of various sizes, with glued-on googly eyes.

"No. That's too absurd. I don't believe it!"

He was tickled at her reaction and together they laughed a long time. "I ask you, why is this exhibit not at the Museum of Modern Art?"

She said, "It's a travesty." After recovering from the shell sculpture aisle, they discussed Susan's possible gift.

"What do you think of this? It's silly, obviously. Although it's positively staid compared to the owl."

"For business cards?"

"Yes. She doesn't have any yet, because she's 'only' an assistant, but I hope this will show her I believe in her. She's very young. And a lot better at the job than I am. I don't think I'd still be there if it weren't for her help."

"I think that's nice. I'm sure she'll appreciate it."

"You getting anything?"

"Mints. You ready to go?"

They paid for their items and left.

There was an air of excitement and enjoyment outside, with the sun down and the lights on and people roaming the boardwalk. A kid walked by eating an ice cream cone.

"I wish I was hungry. That looks good," Joanna said.

"There's always tomorrow," he said, offering her a mint. Joanna headed toward the street but Michael said, "You haven't seen the beach yet. Let's go for a walk."

She shook her head. "Won't it be cold?"

"Nah, and you have your sweater. Come on. Get the fake salt out of your nostrils and replace it with the smell of the ocean." He walked towards the sand, beckoning her with a wave of his hand. "When's the last time you were on a beach at night, you city dweller?"

"A very, very long time ago."

"Don't you think it's time to do it again?"

"Maybe. All I remember is how black everything looked."

"Scared you?"

"I could practically see huge sea monsters coming out of the water to eat me." Then she smiled.

"What?"

"Nothing," she said.

"What? Tell me."

"I just remembered a Dennis the Menace cartoon I saw once. Dennis saying to his mom, '*It's not the dark I'm afraid of. It's the things in it I can't see.*'"

He put his hand on her arm and said in a superhero voice: "I'll protect you!" She looked into his eager face thinking how boyish he seemed. He tugged at her arm. "Come on! Five minutes. More research. Another arrow in your Cape May quiver."

CHAPTER 9

They walked, not talking, down the wooden planks between two buildings perpendicular to the beach. She stopped at the edge of the wooden steps and looked out onto the vastness of the beach. People dotted the landscape, black shapes distant and two-dimensional. The ocean looked so far away. She took a deep breath. Michael said nothing and just watched her.

They stepped down into the sand and walked toward the water. As Joanna walked away from civilization and toward nature, the hair on her arms stood up, her skin tingling. The noises of the boardwalk and street behind them faded—people talking and laughing, music playing, cars driving by—and the splashing of the ocean on the shore took its place. It took a moment to adjust to the change in sound. She expected to see more people on the beach, but it was prime dinner time, or bar hopping time, on a Friday night.

For the first time since arriving in Cape May, Joanna could actually smell the ocean. The wait was worth it.

An extremely bright light on the roof of one of the buildings on the boardwalk cast strange shadows over everything. She wondered if she and Michael were allowed to walk on the beach, but there had been nothing forbidding their entrance. Was the light there to keep teenagers from loitering? Where was it coming from? A police station perhaps? She turned back toward the boardwalk, curious. Michael's outline was dark against the light, and she couldn't make out his features.

"Don't look into the light," his disembodied voice said, "or you'll see spots." He seemed so far away and too close at the same time.

They walked away from the light and toward the wet sand. Michael stopped to take off his shoes, balancing himself by holding onto her shoulder. His touch was firm, his hand large. She breathed in loudly.

He took his hand away. "Did I hurt your skee ball arm?"

Her voice was unsteady. "What are you doing?"

"Gotta make contact with the water." He tied the laces together and threw the shoes over his shoulder, then rolled up his pant legs. "What about you?" She shook her head. Michael ran to meet the lapping water. "Ah! That feels wonderful!"

They continued walking parallel to the shore but many feet apart, Joanna adjusting her path to avoid the tide, Michael enjoying the water, not noticing or caring as the bottom of his rolled up pants got wet. As their eyes fully adjusted to the moonlight, the landscape coming out of the darkness was almost otherworldly.

He ran over and tugged on her arm. "Take your shoes off, Joanna!"

Catching his enthusiasm, she kicked off her sandals. He knelt down and rolled up the legs of her pants, his hands warm against her bare skin. "Let's leave them here and get 'em on the way back." They dropped their shoes on a pile of dry seaweed, along with her bag from Morrow's, and he skipped back to the water, beckoning to her. "Come on in."

She followed him and gave a little scream. "It's freezing! Oh, *now* I remember. On the bus you said you never get cold."

He took her hands and danced a little jig, making her laugh. "Sorry! But don't you love it?" He saw her shiver, and said, "You'll get used to it in a minute. I hope."

"What do I do meanwhile?"

"Meanwhile, you see the incredible view. It's even better closer. Here. I want to show you something."

She was cold, but curious. He stood close behind her, but not touching her body with his. He lightly put his hands on her shoulders and faced her toward the water. Then he cupped his hands at her temples, shielding her eyes from the lights of the boardwalk.

"You can see more without the light pollution. It's one of my favorite memories of my dad. He showed me the sky like this, here in Cape May, when I was a kid. His hands were bigger than my head. I could feel calluses from his working twenty hours a day. I thought he was the manliest man ever."

She could feel his breath, still heavy from his little dance, on her hair. Her own breathing was becoming more difficult. She concentrated on the view: the dark horizon and the moon's reflection on the water. It was like something out of a movie. She felt very small and insignificant taking in the vastness of the ocean and sky in front of her. It was disconcerting standing there, with only the sound of the water and her pounding heart in her ears. His soft voice broke through both. "Now, look up," he said, and she did, with his hands still shielding her eyes from the lights. He said, "I've never seen more stars anywhere. Or maybe I just see things more clearly here."

The cloudless sky was dazzlingly full of stars, infinite and eternal. For a moment she felt dizzy, as if the sky were still, and they were spinning. She stepped away from his hands, wanting to ground herself again. Before turning to face him, she folded her arms across her chest to cover the hard nipples pushing against her bra. "It's awesome." Her voice sounded distorted to her ears.

There was enough moonlight for Michael to see her hair tussling in the breeze. As he stepped closer, and she didn't step away, he gazed into her questioning brown eyes. Unable to resist, he kissed her on the mouth, lightly and quickly.

They stood silently looking at each other. Joanna's lips were parted and she was breathing hard. Her mouth moved as she tried to form words of resistance, but she couldn't. In slow motion his hand came toward her and brushed a strand of hair off her face, his fingers shaking, but warm. Her whole body shivered, teeth chattering.

"Oh, you really are cold," he said, taking her hand and pulling her out of the icy water lapping at her ankles. "I shouldn't have dragged you in." He rubbed her goose-fleshed arms, "I'm sorry." She shivered again and he wrapped his arms around her, now rubbing and warming her back. A little voice inside her, reason perhaps, or conscience, told her to make a break for it, to turn and run, but he was so warm. She leaned into him.

Michael's hands slowed, and he held her closer. "Joanna," he whispered, his lips skimming her ear, that one word coming from deep in his throat, needy, sexy. It sent a different kind of shiver down her spine, ending in throbbing between her legs. He backed away a little, his eyes not leaving hers, his hands sliding up her arms to softly cup her face. He moved in slowly and kissed her cheek, then brushed her upper lip, his nose rubbing hers. His eyes were open, seeking permission before going further. Her lips responded, kissing his lower lip, shyly and delicately.

Their kiss was tentative and gentle yet immediately filled them with heat. Her hands were on his chest, fingertips tingling from the cotton shirt and his chest hairs underneath it. Her fingers slowly slid upward, seeking the soft, warm skin of his neck, then tangling in the curls that had attracted her since they met. He stopped kissing her for a moment, to search her eyes, and they could only stand it apart for a few seconds. She stood on her tip toes to better reach him, gently pulling his head toward her, and kissed him. The kiss deepened, growing more passionate as the tip of his tongue touched her lips. She moaned with pleasure, never wanting this feeling of aliveness to stop, and held onto him, tight, feeling she'd spin off the planet if he let go of her. She kissed him hungrily, needing him more than she'd ever needed anything. He matched her fervor, obviously feeling the same. When they parted again just for a moment, just for air, he gave her a little smile that made her heart ache. Their lips met again, so tenderly, and the exploration began anew. She caressed his face as they kissed. The stubble on his chin was rough against her fingertips and face, and she liked it, sensual and manly, so different from Brian's always clean-shaven face.

Brian!

She pushed herself away from Michael. "Oh, God!" she said. "What am I doing?" She covered her lips with the tips of her fingers, shaking her head.

Breathless, she turned and almost fell, woozy, but he caught her hand. She pulled away and walked. Anywhere.

Now she was grateful for the bright light on the boardwalk, guiding her back to reality and sanity and the safety of a crowded street. The walk seemed to take forever, the sand grabbing at her feet. Her foot hit the first step of the boardwalk and she realized she'd forgotten her shoes. She turned to see him approaching. His face was troubled as he looked up, handing over her shoes and bag.

"Thank you," she said, the words coming out heavily. The moment their eyes met, she had to look away, and continued up the steps. He followed, but gave her space. What the hell was happening? There was a wooden bench against a building, carved with names and hearts and a few curse words. Joanna sat down to brush the sand off her feet. He did the same, rushing to tie his sneakers, knowing she'd run as soon as her sandals were on.

Shaky legs got her to Beach Avenue. The pounding between her thighs was a guilt-knell. She actually saw spots and felt faint. Waiting for the light to change, she peeked over her shoulder, to see if Michael was still following. She hadn't realized he was right behind her. Their eyes met and she felt little electric shocks in her fingertips. She turned and bolted, and Michael had to lunge and pull her back, away from a speeding bicycle.

"Watch out, lady!" the biker yelled as he passed by.

"Joanna, careful," Michael said, kneading her shoulder.

She looked at him and nodded, but couldn't say anything. The light changed and Michael led her across the street, his hand lightly on the small of her back.

"Let's sit a minute?" he said as they passed a bench. She kept walking, so he followed, worried she might get lost in the dark. Cape May's Victorian gaslight look made for great atmosphere, but was bad for actually seeing anything.

They arrived at the Manor Rose. She opened the gate and headed towards the steps without saying a word, desperately needing to pull away from this magnetic attraction to a stranger. She longed for the safety and solitude of her room.

"Joanna," he said. She stopped on the front path but didn't turn around. "I just want you to know, I didn't know...I mean I wasn't trying to...I had no ulterior motive..." He paused and heard someone approaching from around the corner. "...when I asked you to walk on the beach with me."

She answered quietly, "I know," and met his gaze.

"I was enjoying your company. I wanted to share the view with you. The memory. That's all."

A lantern on the path threw odd patterns of light on his sad face. She had to fight the urge to run to him. "I know."

He took a step toward her. "We have to..."

"Joanna?" they heard from halfway down the block. It was Brian, with his backpack on and wheeling a suitcase behind him. "I just parked in the lot down the street. How did you know what time I'd be here? You Michael?"

Michael tried to regain his composure. "Hi," he said.

Joanna was grateful to be in the shadows. Her hands were icy and her face hot, and she couldn't think straight. All that internal conflict surely must be registering on her face. She turned toward Brian, her mouth finding it difficult to form the words "How was the drive?" She knew he'd be on hyperspeed now, after sitting in the car all those hours, probably downing gallons of coffee.

"Fine. Long. Boring. We touring tomorrow?"

Joanna couldn't make eye contact with either man for longer than a second.

Brian continued, "We still on?"

"Yes, of course," said Michael. He noticed the tears in Joanna's eyes, and handed her a tissue. "Is your eye any better?" Lying to Brian, "It was windy on the boardwalk and some sand got in her eye. I walked her home. *Here*, I mean."

Brian said, "Must've hurt, huh?"

She nodded and took the tissue and the opportunity to pull herself together, but couldn't say anything yet.

Michael stepped in. "We just came from the arcade. I'm afraid we dropped a few bucks playing skee ball."

"I haven't played that since I was a kid." Brian stood next to Joanna.

Michael continued, "Joanna has all the makings of a skee shark. She won a very valuable prize."

"Oh, really." He turned to his wife. Joanna held out the key chain she and Michael had spent so much time picking out. Showing it to Brian made it shrink somehow, made it look even more pathetic than it was. "Time well spent," he said.

Michael took the twin key chain out of his pocket, and held it up for Brian to see.

"Oh, so Jo's is not a one-of-a-kind antique then?"

"No, it's not," Michael said. Joanna heard an edge to his voice.

"I need to relax," Brian said. "What time should we meet tomorrow?"

Michael said, "The tour starts at ten."

"How long is it?"

"About an hour and a half."

"I may have to leave a little early. Jo, I made some calls from one of the rest stops. I've got some plans in the works, for our move, if you make me move. You can finish the tour with Michael and then we can all go to lunch maybe."

Joanna said, too loudly, "No!"

Both men stared at her. Brian said, "What's the matter, honey?" His hand was on her arm and it made her want to scream. And she didn't want Brian to call her honey in front of Michael. She wanted to run into the house and be alone.

She managed to say "I have a headache and really need some aspirin. And a good night's sleep."

"Oh, okay," Brian said as she walked away.

"Goodnight, Joanna," said Michael.

She stopped on the step. "Goodnight," she said, not turning around, and went inside the house.

Michael said to Brian, "Why don't I pick you up around 9:40. The Woodline House is a fifteen-minute walk from here."

Brian said, "Great," but obviously was troubled by Joanna's outburst. He stared at the other man a few moments. "Well, it's been a very long day. I need to get to bed."

Michael nodded, instantly jealous about where Brian would be sleeping.

Brian said, "'Night," as he dragged the suitcase up the front steps.

Michael stood there alone for a moment, then turned and walked slowly towards his own bed and breakfast.

***

Joanna was already upstairs when Brian entered the Manor Rose. She left the door to their room ajar, and when he stepped into the room she was closing the bathroom door. He put his things down and said through the door. "Jo? You okay?"

"I'm brushing my teeth."

Inside the bathroom, Joanna splashed cold water on her face. What was happening? She didn't even know Michael…but that wasn't true. She felt she knew him well— his kindness, his humor, his intelligence, his gentleness.

But what did it matter.

This was ridiculous, having these feelings for someone she'd known less than two days. Was this yet another post-menopausal surprise? She thought the physical changes were over, but apparently not. Whatever was going on in her suddenly excited body, it probably had nothing to do with Michael. Being on this adventure near the majesty of the ocean, and dealing with the life decisions she and Brian were contemplating, all could explain her raging emotions.

She breathed deeply and felt a little better.

She exited the bathroom and walked to Brian. "I've an awful headache."

"How's your eye?"

"Hmm?"

"The sand?"

"Oh, it's fine now. Got it out with water." She turned away from him, not ready to meet his gaze. She went to the mini-fridge and got out two bottles of water. "Amazing how much one grain of sand can hurt, huh?"

"That's how a pearl is made, they say." He embraced her from behind.

She turned, handing him a bottle of water. "I'm so tired. I'm not used to being in the sun all day."

"My turn," he said, going into the bathroom.

She grabbed her pajamas, quickly put them on, and climbed into bed. She closed her eyes and pretended to be asleep when Brian crawled in.

Lying there, feigning the steady breathing rhythms of sleep, her mind raced. She wouldn't go on the tour tomorrow. She'd tell Michael that she and Brian had to meet with someone or do something, maybe go see the Tea & Scones again. The Tea & Scones. Her dream house in this perfect town, everything she'd ever wanted, until a few hours ago. How did this happen? She had to get back some control.

She'd simply never see Michael again. A painful sadness overtook her. A bottomless sadness.

CHAPTER 10

When Joanna woke up, there was a note on her pillow. *"You tossed all night. Let you sleep. I'm at breakfast. B."*

She moved her body slowly, worried that something might come apart. The coffee and food smells that got her going yesterday were too much today. As she walked to the bathroom, images from the night before flooded her mind. Her face flushed remembering the kiss. The beveled mirror hung over the sink but she wouldn't look into it as she brushed her teeth, unwilling to meet her guilty face. Resolved not to think about anything, she dressed and went down to have breakfast with her husband.

She grasped the banister hard going down the stairs. Once in the dining room, the noise of the conversations and the smells of the food were overpowering. The chair next to Brian was empty and waiting. She sat, grateful to be off unsteady legs.

Brian said, "I'm relaxed, for a change. You getting food? This frittata is great."

She couldn't face eating. "In a minute or two."

The kitchen door swung open. A woman holding a carafe offered "Coffee?" How long ago was Joanna sitting at this B&B dining room table, talking like a normal person, sitting like a normal person, able to function? It was twenty-four hours ago but seemed like weeks.

"Jo?" Brian said. "Coffee?"

"Oh, yes! Sorry. Still asleep. Need the caffeine, huh?" she said, trying to smile at the woman.

"We haven't met. I'm Claire Masterson, co-owner of the inn. I'm sorry I wasn't here to greet you when you arrived yesterday. Are you enjoying your stay?"

"Yes, it's peaceful." Joanna reached for the sugar.

Brian whispered to her, "You okay? You're shaking."

"I'm just…" should she say *sick* or *scared* or *having feelings for someone who isn't you*? The words swam around her head.

"Hmm?" Brian touched her hand.

"Tired. Can't wake up. Maybe that was a migraine last night. I can still feel it." She rose to get some food, not hungry but not wanting to be under Brian's gaze. When she sat down again, she attempted to be social and eat and drink and act normally. But she had the feeling that her life would never be normal again. What was wrong with her? One kiss with a stranger, was that it? No, she was guilty, that was it. Talk to Brian. He's the one that could be hurt by the weirdness.

She turned to him. "You like the food?"

"Are you kidding? This is great."

She looked at her watch. It was almost nine. "Brian, let's skip the tour today."

Brian stopped mid-forkful. "Why? The lady with the coffee said the house is really worth seeing. And didn't what's-his-name go out of his way to arrange it for us?"

"It's probably no big deal."

"Well, now I want to go. Why don't you?"

"It's so nice outside. Why be stuck in a house?"

"It's only an hour and a half, tops."

"I don't feel like it," she said.

"Oh, come on. Come with me. Us. He's your new friend."

"Why don't you and I go play miniature golf or something."

"Is this what my future holds? The excitement of miniature golf and skee ball? No wonder you want to leave Manhattan for all this."

"That was mean." A few people at the table turned towards them. She realized she was too loud.

"I'm teasing. Lighten up. What's wrong with you today?"

"Nothing," she whispered this time. "Stress. I don't know."

He paused. "You said on the phone you were all relaxed but you've been acting weird since I got here. What's going on?"

There was an uncomfortable pause. "I wasn't going to tell you, but Susan, my assistant, called from work yesterday. One of our doctors didn't send in his presentation. It may mess up my deadlines, and my boss is already fed up with me," she said, hoping this little white lie would cover her behavior.

"You hate that dumb job anyway." They paused as Claire poured more coffee for them.

Joanna stalled. "Claire, this breakfast is wonderful."

"Oh, I'm glad you like it."

"Yes, the eggs were perfect. I could eat three servings."

"I'll tell our cook. Would you like anything else?"

Joanna shook her head, and Claire retreated into the kitchen.

Brian continued, "Well, I think we should go on the tour. Also, your new friend would be disappointed if we canceled." He took a sip of coffee. "He likes you."

Joanna's head snapped in Brian's direction. "Why do you say that?"

"Well, it's obvious. He wants to help. Not everyone would house hunt with a stranger. I barely want to help you."

"So I've noticed."

He put sugar in his coffee and stirred. "Is he married?"

"Divorced."

"He lives in Manhattan?"

"Yup."

"You think he'd like your sister?"

"Cynthia?"

"We could set them up."

"Let's not."

"She's still attractive. And Michael's handsome, much better than some of those old guys she's jumped into bed with. You think he likes sleeping with pushy, obnoxious women?"

She looked at her watch. "If we're going, I'd better get ready."

"I'm all ready. I'll stay here and read until we leave." He grabbed a newspaper off a nearby table. "What a luxury not to be staring at spreadsheets." Joanna started to walk away and he took her hand. "Jo, I kinda like it here. The air's nice. The vibe." She tried to smile at the good news.

Joanna escaped breakfast and walked up the stairs to their room. Once inside, she felt trapped. Trapped and terrified. Terrified of seeing Michael again in minutes. She sat on the chair and breathed deeply, with her eyes closed. About ten years ago she had attended a meditation class and now was trying to remember all the steps to centering herself, to stop thinking about Michael's blue eyes, and how good it felt in his arms. Sitting in her room alone her whole body was buzzing. What was going on? Brian was lucky if he "got any" once a month. Clearly she needed to be physical with her husband more often. Breathe, Joanna, breathe. Deeply. Be. Quiet. She was disciplined and stayed with her clear mind and deep breathing and in a few minutes felt better able to face what was ahead.

At 9:35, she was on the stairs leading down to the parlor, killing time looking at each picture on the wall. One picture was a family portrait: father, mother with a baby in her arms, and six children of various ages and heights standing around them. Joanna whispered, "I love your house. Were you happy here? Were you happy?" At the turn in the landing there was a little window overlooking the street. A vase of fresh flowers sat on the sill. As she moved in closer to smell the orange, yellow, and red blossoms, she glanced outside.

There he was, coming down the street, with his baseball cap, and sunglasses. He wasn't whistling this time, and his walk no longer had a lightness to it. Even from here she could see his second day's growth of beard. Her entire body was suddenly aroused, remembering the feel of his stubble against her face and fingers. Why did stubble on Brian make him look like a homicidal wino—which was one of the reasons he always shaved—and on Michael it was so sexy. And why had she never experienced these feelings when Brian, or anyone else, was walking towards her. She watched until he disappeared inside the gate, heading to the front door. She'd be face to face with him in a moment.

The little bell over the front door tinkled, followed by Claire's footsteps. Joanna stood frozen on the steps, listening to him reminiscing with his old friend. His voice was sad, he was talking slower than usual. Joanna wondered if Claire sensed anything different as she glanced down the stairs to watch them interact. It was obvious Claire was charmed by Michael's polite attention. He was very charming. Behind Joanna, a guest came out of a bedroom and was headed for the stairs, so she was forced to move.

Claire was saying to Michael, "If you have any free time, let's have coffee."

Michael sensed Joanna's presence and looked up to her on the staircase. "Sure. That would be nice," he said to Claire with no conviction, his eyes locked on Joanna.

Claire looked from one to the other and said, "Uh, well, I'd better clean off the breakfast table before it's already time for lunch." She rushed into the other room.

Michael's eyes were pained. "Joanna," he said.

Brian came in from the parlor. "Hey. I'll be ready in a minute. I forgot something." He bounded up the stairs.

Joanna walked outside and put on her sunglasses, glad for the barrier between the windows to her soul and Michael's perceptive eyes. She said, with no emotion at all, "It's a nice day."

"Yes, nice." They walked halfway down the block. He had to say something. "Look, last night…"

"Please, let's forget it."

"I don't want to, Joanna." The hurt look in his eyes both surprised and flattered her. "And I couldn't even if I wanted to."

Her breath caught. "I'm married…" she said, hating how stupid it sounded, pointing behind her in Brian's general direction.

"And I'd bet a lot of money that you don't usually go around kissing men on beaches."

She shook her head.

He continued: "I thought we…"

She continued shaking her head. "No we." She knew he was hurting, because she was hurting too. "Maybe our lemonade was spiked? Or we were high on salt?" She tried to smile, but couldn't.

The metal-against-metal sound of the gate warned them someone was coming. Brian arrived before they were ready and said, "Okay, let's go."

The three of them walked. Joanna gazed at and studied every house they passed. She wondered if Brian suspected anything, but she couldn't risk making eye contact with him. From inside it, her face felt like an open, guilt-radiating book. She had to admire Michael. She couldn't form a sentence, but Michael must have seemed, to Brian's outside eye, fine. Brian asked questions, and Michael answered. Joanna knew he was struggling as much as she was, but he chatted with Brian about Cape May and history, and weather and Manhattan. In fact, Brian was much more chatty than usual. Interesting.

They reached the estate, and walked to the designated "good weather" waiting area under a tree. Two couples were already there, and an attractive, elegant older woman soon joined them. She smiled at everyone, especially Michael, and said, "Hi, I'm Madeleine, your tour guide."

Joanna stared at the woman as she spoke, glad to focus on anything other than her own racing thoughts. Madeleine was average height, slim, neatly dressed in a smart beige suit, with an apricot scarf the perfect accent. Her face was expertly made-up, and Joanna instantly felt unfeminine in her casual vacation attire and bare face. Madeleine turned her head, and her silver gray China doll hair swung like a commercial model's. "Actually you have two tour guides today. Michael here knows almost as much about this house as I do."

He bowed a little to her and said, "Not true, but thanks." To the other guests, "This woman is brilliant about this estate and others in Cape May. Ask her anything."

"*They're outright flirting,*" thought Joanna. Madeleine's green eyes sparkled as she talked to Michael. But none of the other guests seemed to mind the flirting, or even appear to notice.

Madeleine said, "We're expecting three other people, so let's wait a few minutes before we start." As visitors checked their phones for messages or chatted, Madeleine and her haircut, perfectly framing her delicate face, turned toward Michael. She said quietly, "Are you ever going to shave?" her hand reached up and playfully pinched his cheek.

"Madeleine, this is Joanna, the woman I told you about, and her husband, Brian. From Manhattan."

Joanna's brain fogged over, due to a combination of embarrassment—what had Michael told Madeleine?—and a vision that flashed on the screen in her head, of Madeleine horizontal under Michael in a four-poster bed. Or was

Madeleine more the riding-on-top type? Joanna blinked hard and forced the evil visions out of her head. It shouldn't matter to her at all. So why did it hurt so much.

She hid her irrational dislike of Madeleine and shook her outstretched hand. "Hi." Brian did the same.

"Nice to meet you, Joanna, Brian."

Joanna knew Madeleine was storing their names in her tour guide brain and would use them later. She heard Madeleine quietly say to Michael, "You staying over tonight?" Michael nodded, then two women and a teenager joined the group under the tree. Madeleine addressed the group: "Now that we're all here: I'm Madeleine Friedhoffer, Executive Director of the Woodline estate. I think you'll find this a fascinating tour. This house was built in 1870 by famed architect Frederick Schmidt for Mr. Alfred Louis Woodline and his wife Adele and their five sons. In today's dollars it cost seventeen million to build. The estate originally was twelve acres, but now is half that size. Let's enter through the front door, right into the main hallway of the house, as a visitor would've been shown in over a century ago."

A tourist in ugly Bermuda shorts asked, "What happened to the other six acres?"

Madeleine said, "In 1980 the property was divided and half sold off. The estate needed the money for renovations and back taxes." As Madeleine ushered the group to the front door, she continued, "There is no smoking, eating, or gum chewing on this tour. There is a gift shop on your way out, so please browse, buy, or make a donation to the care and preservation of Woodline House."

She turned her head again, and again her hair swooshed perfectly.

Joanna's resentment grew.

The tour began, as promised, in the hallway of the house, with its heavy woodwork, ornate patterned wallpaper, and high ceilings. A few original chairs lined the hall, the rope across the seats barring anyone from sitting on the antiques. Joanna attempted to concentrate on Madeleine's narration, but as her resolve dwindled, she'd glance in Michael's direction. When she did, his sad eyes were on her. When she could, she stayed next to Brian, keeping a human wall between her and Michael.

The tour went on without incident, until the group began an exploration of the bedrooms on the second floor. When Joanna was examining a shelf of first editions behind the glass of a Harvey Ellis bookcase, Brian walked into the next room. With some distance between the two of them and the rest of the group, Michael approached and said, "Any Stephen King?"

Joanna saw the real question in his eyes but couldn't reply. She shook her head, and walked away, joining Brian. A little later, Madeleine herded the group into another room. As Michael passed her, she touched his back and then her hand slipped lower. Brian saw the movement and whispered to Joanna, "Hmm, maybe Michael doesn't need to meet Cynthia after all, huh?"

The rest of the group moved ahead, and Michael and Joanna were momentarily alone again. She started to walk away and he gently took hold of her upper arm. From his innocent touch, Joanna's body became alive and tense. Everything in her yearned to touch him back. He whispered in her ear, "Joanna, we have to talk."

She said, "No!" much louder than she meant to.

The few people near the door turned to look at them, Brian and Madeleine included. Madeleine said, "Do you have a question, Joanna?"

After a beat, Michael said, "We can't imagine having to clean a house this size."

Everyone giggled, and Madeleine said, "This house, in its heyday, would have employed at the very least a butler, housekeeper, cook, lady's maid, valet, footman, and chamber maid."

Brian went over to Joanna. "I have to leave for my meeting."

"I forgot. Where are you going?"

"I told you: to see an accountant. He's old and wants to hand off some of his local clients to me. He's going away for the weekend but fit me in. My reputation working wonders again."

She nodded.

"You okay?" he touched her face and she brushed his hand away.

"It's stuffy. Why don't I go with you?"

"This is business, not a social call. Where should I meet you for lunch?"

"I don't know."

"I'll call," he said, waving goodbye and leaving her alone in the room.

Madeleine directed Brian to the acceptable exit route, clearly not pleased that he was leaving the tour early. Madeleine escorted the remaining people. Joanna brought up the rear and, when going up the stairs to the third floor servants' quarters, she almost tripped. The burgundy carpeting under her feet felt rough through her shoes, but of course that wasn't possible. At the turn in the landing, Joanna stopped to catch her breath. The air was still and hot and she felt light-headed.

As Madeleine described various servants' duties to the rapt group, Michael said to Joanna, "You okay?" She nodded and walked away.

In the third floor hallway, Madeleine pointed to a deep frame on the wall. "Here's something I think you'll find interesting: the Victorians framed women's hair." The ornately arranged light brown hair and flowers were creepy enough to make Joanna want to throw up. She redirected her gaze to a calmer country landscape hanging by wire from the picture moldings. Madeleine stated: "Actually, the owners of the house would not have decorated a floor only servants would use. But the estate had some extra pieces worth displaying and we ran out of space on the main floors."

As the group headed to the next area of the tour, Joanna stayed a moment then suddenly realized she couldn't stand being inside any longer.

She snuck back down the main staircase to the front hall, rules be damned. As oppressive as it had been crowded with the tour group, somehow it was worse empty. She ran to the front door and was startled by a glimpse of a stranger running beside her. It was her reflection in the large mirror. The front door opened easily, much to her surprise, as she felt trapped, and she didn't stop running until she was at the front gate of the estate.

She rested against the gate, trying to catch her breath. Her face was damp, her heart was pounding. There were footsteps behind her. "Joanna!" In a moment Michael was by her side. She walked away from him. He followed. "Are we in a race?"

"No," she said coldly.

He reached for her shoulder. "Joanna, talk to me."

"No. And please don't touch me."

He dropped his hands. His attempted levity—"I've never seen this kind of reaction to a tour before"—failed. She turned toward him. Her eyes were blazing, her face flushed. He said, "Can we sit someplace and talk?"

"No." The dizziness hadn't passed, and she supported herself on a tree. Michael rushed over to assist her. She said "No" again but minus the venom. They walked slowly to a bench half a block away in a little sequestered area of the estate.

Joanna said, "She was very touchy-feely, wasn't she?"

"Who?"

"Madeleine."

"Oh, I've known her for years."

"She's beautiful."

"Yes, even more now than when I met her, I think. She's a resourceful Executive Director. Managed to keep the house intact when many others were being torn down."

She glared at him.

"What?" he asked.

"I didn't notice her touching the other tourists, or inviting them to sleep at her house."

"Oh. I understand. About a year after her husband died, Madeleine and I dated for about four months. It was good for both of us and I enjoyed it very much. She's been happily married to Dan, husband number two, a cardiologist who adores her, for years. I was best man at their wedding here in Cape May. I play Scrabble with her and poker with him. I love them both. They had nieces visiting and no room for me. But the girls have left and tonight I'm staying at their tiny house. They have a blow-up mattress with my name on it. They feed me. Madeleine's like a sister to me."

"Sister, huh?"

He paused. "You know, you almost sound jealous."

"I am jealous, and I shouldn't be jealous…"

Two people walked past and stared, or was it just her imagination? Michael made a move towards her, about to say something, and she jumped in with "Michael, this has to end here." She immediately could see the affect of her words. She had to look away.

"Oh, please don't say that, Joanna," he said.

They didn't talk. The little park was serene, with perfectly manicured lawns and shrubs. Michael started to say something, but stopped. They were both still, and the only movement around them was some birds flying in and out of a feeder hanging on a tree limb nearby. Michael tried again to talk, and stopped again. Then, weighing his words carefully, "All I can say is, I haven't felt this way…the way I feel about you…in a very long time. Actually, honestly? Never." His pointer finger lightly stroked her hand resting on her thigh. "You and I have a connection. Something special. You feel it, too, or you wouldn't be so upset." He paused. "I can't walk away from this without a fight."

She shook her head, and slowly stood up.

He took her hand. "Was I wrong? Is it just me who feels it?"

"Michael," her voice caught, and tears slid down her hot cheeks. She squeezed his hand, and whispered, "I feel it, but I can't."

And she walked out of the park and turned toward her B&B. Out of the corner of her eye, she saw him still sitting slumped on the bench. She wanted desperately to run back to him but didn't. She made a left at the corner, and didn't look back.

CHAPTER 11

A safe distance away from Woodline, and the garden, and Michael's dejected face, Joanna stopped to call Brian. Trying her best to sound casual, she told him Michael canceled lunch so he could spend time with Madeleine. When Brian made a comment about "lucky Michael getting laid tonight," she almost lost it.

She sat on a bench. Even with the sun baking on her back she felt cold and lifeless. Lifeless. But what had happened? It was just a kiss. After twenty years of marriage, one kiss with a stranger was hardly adulterous. She'd never see Michael again, and she'd be buried with this semi-sinful memory. No need to confess all to her trusting husband just to make herself feel better.

As she sat there, the pain began to sink in. Would she really never see him again? Couldn't they put aside their overblown, exaggerated romantic feelings—which couldn't possibly be real after knowing each other such a short time—and just be friends? She really liked him. His positivity, his humor, and warmth.

Still she sat, unable to move. Eventually she looked at her watch. Over an hour had passed, and she was due to meet Brian. She stood up slowly and shakily, and began walking to the bed and breakfast. The sun hurt her eyes. She fished in her purse for sunglasses.

Where was she? She'd lost her bearings. A young couple, laughing and walking arm-in-arm, strolled past. "Excuse me," Joanna said.

"Yes?" the man turned around.

"Which way is Ocean Avenue?"

He pointed. "It's three blocks that way."

"And then which way to Columbia?"

The woman said, "Follow Ocean for a few blocks. Um, are you all right?"

Joanna was about to say, "I'm fine," when tears trickled down her face. She said, "Thanks," and walked in the direction they'd pointed.

Before turning the corner towards the Manor Rose, she stopped and cleaned herself up for Brian. She blew her nose and wiped the tears away, put on lip balm, and brushed her hair.

The last half block, Joanna breathed deeply and kept telling herself everything worked out for the best. She was going back to her husband, and things would get better and better between them.

The Manor Rose looked picture perfect with its windows open, the curtains flapping in the breeze. Marie was serving tea on the porch. Brian sat reading at one of the tiny wrought iron round tables. As soon as he saw her walking up the steps, he said, "You're late."

Joanna put on her happy face and said, "I got a little lost." She was grateful to be sitting outside, so she had an excuse to keep the sunglasses on.

"Have some tea."

What she wanted was a great big scotch, or some other drink she usually wouldn't have touched. No. What she really wanted was to curl up into a ball and go to sleep, with the covers over her head.

After a pause during which he looked at her with some scrutiny, Brian said, "What's wrong with you?"

"Nothing."

"How was the tour?" The question sounded more like an accusation.

"Interesting."

"And Michael?"

Just hearing Brian say his name made Joanna ache even more. She did her best to answer naturally, but the voice hitting her ears sounded forced. "Fine. I thanked him for both of us."

"It's miraculous you 'discovered' him, isn't it?" Brian said, his voice forced, too.

"Miraculous? Hardly." She couldn't read his mood, and she usually could. "Too bad you left before the ghost."

"What?"

"The guy who kept asking questions, the guy in the Bermuda shorts, swore he saw a ghost in one of the bedrooms." A tear slid under the frame of her sunglasses. She wiped it, her hand knocking against the china plate in front of her.

Brian put his hand on hers, and she jumped. "Your hands are cold."

"How was your meeting?"

"I liked the old guy. He's me in ten years. Still happily working."

"But he's retiring?"

"Partly. I'll tell you about it later. You don't look good."

"I feel a little sick."

"You want to go inside?"

"No. The air feels good. I should eat something."

What was Michael doing, right now? Was he eating? Would he go back to Madeleine's house? Were they really just good friends? She hoped they were, so he wouldn't be alone. Or would the attractive Madeleine comfort him? He'd said they were like siblings. Was that true? Or would she invite him back into her bed? They play Scrabble together, my ass.

"Jo?"

"What?" Joanna replied, a little too brightly.

"I thought maybe we could walk on the boardwalk."

Marie brought out a three-tiered tray of tea sandwiches and desserts. "Here's something I think you'll enjoy!" She put the tray down and pointed to each as she spoke: "This is cucumber and cream cheese on white. This is salmon and dill with butter." Her bright and sunny attitude made Joanna want to scream. "Here's my personal favorite: egg salad on walnut bread with watercress. And last but certainly not least," and here she lowered her voice conspiratorially, "and you don't have to save them for dessert—my homemade scones, with either cranberries or chocolate chips. Savory or sweet!"

Brian said, "Great."

Marie said to Joanna, "Are you all right, honey?"

"Yes," Joanna said, attempting to smile.

"You don't look too well. Can I get you some aspirin?"

"No, thank you."

"Maybe you're not used to being out in the sun. You have such pale skin."

"I'm fine!" Joanna snapped back.

Marie got the message and walked away.

Brian paused before saying, "Wow. I've never seen you do that."

"I feel sick because I haven't eaten. And she's probably right about the sun."

They ate quietly for a few moments. Brian tried again, "Oh, I was saying, we could walk on the boardwalk at dusk. See the sun set."

Joanna couldn't bear the thought of covering the same territory with Brian that she and Michael shared. "Maybe. I don't know. Do we have to talk about it now?"

He paused before saying, "What's going on? You know you're acting weird."

She shrugged and picked up a sandwich and nibbled on it. Apparently her taste buds had stopped working, too.

"Does this have anything to do with Michael?"

"No!" Her head snapped up at him, her face unguarded.

Seeing the hurt look in Brian's eyes made her gasp. "Something's going on, Joanna. I know it's Michael. Is he why you had to take the bus, instead of driving down with me? To be with him?"

"No, of course not. I never saw him before in my life." She had to lessen the pressure. "Brian, I was...kind of attracted to him. But it's nothing."

"Nothing?"

"Nothing," she said, remembering the feel of Michael's lips on hers. It was awful denying something that meant so much—everything—to her, but Brian's feelings mattered more right now. She put her hand on his.

He sniffed. "Was he attracted to you, too?"

"No." Joanna felt like her brain was pushing against her skull. "It was all silly and nothing happened."

He was quiet, then said, "I suppose this is partly my fault." "No!"

"I'm getting dull maybe."

"Stop it. I was just stupid. Let's forget it, okay?" She selected a tiny sandwich for him. "Here. Eat this. You love salmon."

He took a bite. "It's good."

"See?" The little sandwiches, although probably delicious, held no appeal. But if they disappeared, and the plate was empty, lunch would be over and they could leave. She could go upstairs, get in bed, and try to stop the pain. She felt hopeless and lonely. All she could think about was Michael, and how sad he looked when she left. Was he missing her as much as she was already missing him? Yes. She knew for certain.

Forcing down another little sandwich and drinking the rest of her tea, she said, "I'm going upstairs. I think I need a nap." She stood up and Brian did, too.

They walked up the stairs to their room and Joanna sat on the bed, filled with apprehension, and more tired than she had ever been in her life. Brian paced, then said, "How worried should I be?"

"Brian!"

"You sure there's nothing more about Michael I should know?"

"I said there's nothing more."

"You seem pretty rattled over *nothing*."

She stood up, wanting to get away. In the doorway of

the bathroom, she turned to him, her eyes finally meeting his. She calmed herself. "I'm a married woman who for one day after twenty years imagined what it would be like to be single and attracted to someone for the first time. That was it." Her eyes dared him to disagree.

"Was he imagining too?"

"He'd have no idea what we're talking about. He's been a perfect gentleman. And he probably dates thirty-five year olds."

He stood up and said, "Jo," and took a step toward her. She walked over to him and hugged him.

She said, "I'm sorry if I've hurt you."

Brian said, as if reading from a script: "You're human. It's that old *you're married, not dead* thing. You didn't act on it." After a pause, he continued, "Let's go to Fisherman's Grill. That restaurant I told you about. Four stars, just ten minutes from here. Frank the foodie said it was great."

Joanna couldn't face an evening at a table for two in a romantic restaurant. "Couldn't we just bring something in here? Watch a movie in bed? We never do that at home."

He said, his voice colorless, "Okay."

She walked towards the bathroom.

"Hey, aren't we supposed to see that house you liked?"

The Tea & Scones flashed into her mind, with Michael gazing at her from the porch. "Tomorrow. I'm exhausted." She went into the bathroom and shut the door. When she stripped off her damp shirt, pulling it over her head, her eyes met their dead reflection in the mirror. The spark she had seen, the spark brought on Michael, was gone. Her face was older and grayer. She turned away, her throat tight.

As she finished undressing, she heard Brian knock. "Do you want me to get some DVDs from downstairs?"

"Sure."

"And I'll bring up some take-out menus."

He left their room. With him out of earshot, she let go and cried over her loss, knowing she didn't have a lot of time before he came back. She kept trying to convince herself that she barely knew Michael, and he couldn't mean that much to her, but she just kept crying. Finally, she splashed cold water on her face and shocked herself out of it. She and Michael had touched something in each other; strangers passing in the night. Saying goodbye was hard, but she had done the right thing. You can't throw away twenty years of marriage over a kiss.

Knowing she probably had ten minutes before Brian came back to the room—he was a methodical DVD chooser—she poured herself a large glass of wine from a bottle Brian had bought on the trip down. Even as she sipped the wine, trying to numb her pain and stop thinking about Michael, she wondered if Brian had bought the bottle at the liquor store Michael pointed out on the bus ride.

All too soon Brian came back with a selection of DVDs. Joanna was standing by the window, gazing out. The room was uncomfortably quiet, especially in contrast with the noises from outside of people laughing and talking. Joanna felt a million miles away from everything, lonely and sad, and old.

Brian stood in back of her and embraced her. "You know, being in a place like this gives me ideas." He not-so-subtly pressed his erection into her hip. Joanna's body decided this had to happen, right now. Anything to stop her brain from thinking. Anything to feel connected and alive again. She faced him and they kissed gently. When she closed her eyes, Michael's face appeared. She gasped, and forced her eyes open.

"You okay?" he asked. She nodded and embraced Brian again, trying to push away her memories of the beach.

They made love, or rather he made love to her, and she tried not to think about another man. She tried to get into it, to really feel something, but couldn't. At least Brian was happy, as they hadn't had sex in so long. It was very quick, and when he was done, he yawned and said, "You?"

She shook her head.

"Y'sure?"

"I'm fine, really."

"Okay. Just a little nap then, before dinner. I want to go to that restaurant. Frank said good things about the food. We can watch something when we get back," and he turned over and fell sound asleep.

With the distraction of sex over, the grief began to overwhelm her again. Fortunately she was so exhausted, she conked out. They slept for almost two hours, woke up, and were silent for the next half hour while they got ready for dinner.

The ten minute drive to the restaurant was quiet, too. Neither of them had anything to say. Joanna caught friezes of Cape May life framed in the windows. She longed to see women in elegant dresses with their hair up, men with mustaches and ties, life a hundred years ago. It all seemed idyllic. On the outside. Beautiful. Elegant. Life was no picnic back then, of course, but she wasn't finding the twenty-first century very easy either.

The Fisherman's Grill was a chic, understated restaurant. They sat at a small table and shared red wine, salads, mushroom risotto, coconut shrimp, and grilled chicken. Luckily Brian didn't like to talk much at dinner, and what little was said was about his possible new accounting gig. The food was good, but Joanna couldn't eat much. She somehow got through dinner. They drove back to the inn in silence.

She put on her pajamas in the bathroom, not wanting to undress in front of Brian. She fixed herself a cup of herbal tea and ate some homemade cookies that were left for them in the mini-kitchen, while they watched a not very passionate or funny romantic comedy Brian thought she'd enjoy. Why were most romantic comedies about twenty- and thirty-somethings? Probably because most people in their fifties or sixties were settled and boring. Who'd want to see a sixty year old woman fall in love with a sixty year old man? At this very moment, Joanna wished she had seen cinematic examples of how to behave if you're an over-the-hill married woman who is brought to life by a complete stranger. But no one else would care, would they.

At last the movie was over and they went to bed. Luckily Brian was exhausted, because Joanna couldn't face cuddling with him. It was one thing to lie there while they had sex, when he was obviously otherwise occupied. Having to cuddle, which she couldn't fake, would be too awkward. He fell asleep and she stayed awake, for what felt like all night.

The pseudo gaslight from the street filtered into the

bedroom through the lace curtains. All the events of the past two days montaged in her mind. Walking on the boardwalk with Michael. Laughing at that ridiculous owl made of shells. Just talking. Experiencing a strange and miraculous combination of pure comfort and physical excitement. Feeling like she'd known him forever. But it hadn't been enough. She wanted to know more. She wanted to hear about his novel. She wanted to see pictures of him on his first bicycle. She wanted years with him. The rest of her life. She wanted to touch him and her body ached to be touched by him. Right now.

When she turned over, tears fell onto the hand she placed under her cheek. Eventually, she fell asleep.

When she woke up, Brian was in a Manor Rose robe, sitting at the little table, reading the *Wall Street Journal*, already showered and shaved. She watched him. He was still cute, and she did love him, didn't she. It took only a second for her brain to conjure Michael. She felt so guilty now. Brian was such a good man. Oh, Joanna, stop thinking, just stop. "Good morning."

"I was going to wake you in ten minutes, for breakfast. I'm hungry." He modeled his B&B robe. "You like it?"

"Very attractive. You should buy one. They sell them downstairs." Getting out of bed she said, "I'll take a quick shower and I'll be ready soon. I don't want you to starve."

She was half in the bathroom when she had an idea. "Brian, would you think I was crazy if I said I wanted to go home after breakfast?"

"We're supposed to be here another night."

"I know," think fast, Joanna, and lie convincingly, "but if

we leave today I'll be fresh for work tomorrow. We have status meetings on Mondays, and I can clear up the mess with the presentation. If I don't do it one of my coworkers might get stuck with it. Also, I know you have a lot of work to do. And you're taking your mom to see places on Wednesday, losing another work day."

"What about looking at houses?"

"I found a house I adore. I can't imagine ever liking another one more. We can drive past it on the way home, so you can see the outside at least. I have a lot of figuring out to do. I've got enough info for now."

"I'm always ready to go home. You know me. Practically a hermit."

"Great. After breakfast, we'll hit the road." Joanna's smile faded as soon as the bathroom door was shut. She missed Michael. It was as simple—and as highly complicated —as that.

Joanna somehow got through breakfast. Packing took only a few minutes. As they walked to their car, her eyes scanned the streets for a glimpse of Michael. The car stopped in front of the Tea & Scones. Brian didn't even get out as he declared it "okay" and "livable." He turned to her. She was barely looking at the house. He said, "You don't seem that thrilled with it either."

"I love the house," she said. And she did. But to find what she'd dreamt of finding, and for it to no longer be her driving goal in life, and so intertwined with Michael, was all too confusing, and depressing. "I do. I have a lot of thinking to do."

As they drove, she was no longer captivated by the Victorians, or the flowers, or the quaintness of Cape May.

She just wanted to see him again, even for a split second. Brian made the right onto Lafayette. On the left, the Visitors Center, where—could it really be only a few days earlier?—she had arrived with Michael.

In the car, whenever Brian attempted conversation, Joanna couldn't think of a thing to say. If she started saying something, she'd lose track of the subject before she got to the end of the sentence. Her brain hadn't been this addled since menopause. She eventually asked if he'd mind if she closed her eyes. Brian put on the radio for company. Reclining in the car seat, Joanna tried desperately to think of anything other than her time in Cape May. But Michael's face kept appearing before her. It was as if they had known each other for decades, for all the memories that were popping up. Michael's newly-washed face, and how she'd brushed the wet lock off his forehead. Looking back, wasn't it forward to touch this man she'd just met? It didn't seem that way then. It didn't seem to mean anything at the time, and now it was a beloved, and painful, and guilt-inducing recollection.

"My head is killing me. Do you mind if I sleep in the back?" she said to Brian, her voice raspy. "Maybe I'm getting sick. Summer colds, they're the worst." She fetal-positioned herself on the back seat, using Brian's sweat jacket as a pillow.

He didn't volunteer to turn off the radio, and she was grateful for the music, which overpowered some of the noise in her head. Eventually, exhausted, she fell asleep, and didn't dream at all.

They cruised home, not even stopping for a bathroom break. The next thing she knew Brian was waking her as they pulled into the garage under their building. She had slept for two solid hours.

They were home. That word certainly didn't have the warm and welcoming connotations it used to.

***

Earlier that morning at Madeleine and Dan's breakfast table, Michael tried to write. His hosts knew something was wrong but couldn't get him to talk. He leafed through his research books, some from the library with dozens of stickies poking out, and his own books filled with highlighted text, underlinings, and notes in the margins. Trying to envision his detective walking through the streets of Cape May, he instead saw Joanna. She *got* Cape May, in a way that even he had trouble verbalizing. The look of awe on her face as she gazed up at a house. Back to reality, he looked down at his notebook. His fountain pen had leaked, making a big splotch on the page.

It couldn't be over, could it? How could he feel so much now, after feeling so little for such a long time? If she were single, he'd pursue her with everything he had. You don't let someone get away, not when they make you feel that vital, alive, and simply happy.

Keep busy, don't think.

Do what you came here to do. Move forward.

He wanted to visit the lighthouse. Madeleine was using their one car so Michael called another Cape May friend and asked to borrow his. This friend, who he'd known for years, would've listened to his troubles. Madeleine and Dan would've listened. Madeleine, no fool, knew something was up with Michael and Joanna, and knew Brian was in the picture. Michael knew Madeleine was on to him. Still, when she let him know she'd be there if he wanted to talk, Michael couldn't imagine himself uttering the necessary words. If they came out of his mouth—*I've met someone, someone I could adore.* Really? *Yes!* How long have you known her? *Days.* Days? *Oh, also, she's married and may never want to see me again*—how inane and unreal it would all sound. And what an idiot he'd seem.

Michael walked to his friend's house, smiled, chatted, and borrowed the car, as if nothing were wrong. The car smelled of cigarette smoke, so he opened all the windows. And put the radio on. Loud. Even so, the wind rushing in and the music blasting didn't stop his brain from producing images of her lovely face. All the houses he drove past made him think of Joanna, and how much she would enjoy them.

Stop.

The lighthouse.

Think about the lighthouse. Built in 1859. Outside wall three feet ten inches at the bottom, one foot six inches at the top. Inside cylinder eight and a half inches thick. Designed to withstand hurricanes.

How could this information be used in his book? Maybe in a vision the psychic sees the lighthouse being sabotaged. Maybe the detective risks his reputation believing her, because he's fallen in love. Perhaps the politician is going to tour the landmark and…Michael tried to plot and analyze the relationships and emotions of the people in his book, but his thoughts filled with Joanna instead. Joanna, whom he might never see or hear from again.

He drove to the Cape May Point State Park and stopped the car. In front of him was the lighthouse, painstakingly restored, painted white with a red top. The sky behind it was so blue it looked unreal. The temperature was in the mid-seventies. A perfect day.

A newspaper in 1897 said that "one of the interesting features to Cape May summer visitors is a journey to the top of the lighthouse" but Michael couldn't even get out of the car.

CHAPTER 12

After an uncomfortable Sunday evening unpacking, pretending to read, making pasta for dinner, and going to bed early, Joanna left for work at seven the next morning. Brian thought it was due to work problems, but the real reason would've broken his heart. She missed Michael so much it was making her hate her husband. Everything he said and did irritated her.

And it wasn't just Brian. She couldn't concentrate, and kept dropping things. Manhattan, too, was annoying and unpleasant. The train took too long to arrive and was overly air-conditioned when it did. When her assistant Susan arrived at the office and said, "Welcome back! How was your trip?" Joanna barked, "Fine," hoping her tone would discourage further conversation. But young and sweet Susan said, "Did you take a lot of pictures?"

"No, come to think of it. Anything I need to know about Dr. Harvey?"

"Yes, there's been a bunch of emails. You were copied on everything. I updated the slide decks based on his changes. You don't look good, Joanna. Is everything..."

"I'm fine. Thanks for your help."

Susan tried one more time. "Can I get you a cup of tea or something?"

"No, thank you." Joanna's head bent over the research materials on her desk. "Can you shut the door, please?"

The instant Susan was gone, Joanna plunged into work, trying to ignore her very real pain. An awful combination of emotional and physical pain. She'd never been in this much pain in her life. Never. Not even after the abortion. Not when her parents screamed at her or each other. Or when they divorced. Or when her mother died or she had to watch her father die slowly of alcoholism. The pain from those events stopped, eventually. This would have to stop, too. She'd just have to wait a few more days and it would stop. She was married to a man who loved her. Their future was promising. None of this lessened the longing of wanting to see Michael again. To look into his blue eyes. To touch the stubble on his jaw. To feel his soft lips on hers. More than anything she wanted to hear his voice and his laugh.

STOP. This wasn't the way to get over him. She worked, and worked, and worked. Somehow, that first day ended and she left the office. Once outside in the fresh air, it all came crashing in on her again. She couldn't go home yet, and called Brian and left a message: "I've been sitting all day and I need to walk. I'll see you when I get home. Pizza for dinner? Bye."

She walked slowly, killing time and getting home as late as possible. She still got there too early to go to bed, which was all she wanted to do. Fortunately she'd planned ahead and had taken out some documentaries from the library to watch with Brian. Anything so she wouldn't have to talk to him. She felt guilty for being distant with him, and angry at him for keeping her from Michael. Pain, guilt, anger. Repeat.

When she did go to bed, she slept poorly. The inside of her eyelids became a screen for her brain's projections of Michael. Her memories of him were even more vivid at night.

On Tuesday morning, Joanna again left at seven. She didn't leave the office that night until eight, digging up extra things to do. When she got home, she retreated to her computer to do research about real estate and running an inn. At least that's what she told Brian. What she was actually doing was embarrassing. She was looking for information about Michael. She read reviews of his mysteries and found a skimpy paragraph about him in a magazine. When a picture of him popped up after she clicked on a link, tears pricked her eyes. Brian walked in and she switched to her email with the speed of a teen getting off a porn site.

Brian accepted her level of busy the first few days without asking too many questions. She did catch him studying her out of the corner of his eye. Fortunately, he had a lot of things on his mind. Not only projects with deadlines, but also family matters. That Wednesday he was up early, preparing to leave for New Jersey to have breakfast with his sister and mother before visiting assisted living facilities. While he was shaving, Joanna pretended to get ready for work. The minute he left she went back to bed. From there, she left her boss a message that she'd be in by noon.

She slept for another two hours, which she needed after spending nights staring at the bedroom ceiling. Having some time in the apartment alone took pressure off. It was a luxury to be in bed and not worry what she'd do if Brian got playful. When it was time to get ready for work, she showered. In the stream of hot water she masturbated, trying to quiet her body. It had been screaming at her, begging all night to be touched. It wasn't erotic, it was more like finally getting out a sneeze.

After another long, break-free day at the office, she went home. Brian was on the couch reading brochures from the assisted living places he'd visited with his mom. It had been a hard day for him, and Joanna hated herself for not being able to do more than pretend to comfort him. She tried to participate in Brian's "What should we do when we're old?" discussion. She listened and nodded but wished he would just shut up so she could collapse into bed. Pain, guilt, anger, and now self-loathing.

Thursday was a dull blur. By Friday morning, Joanna was dreading the upcoming weekend, knowing she wouldn't have work as a fallback excuse for her antisocial behavior. They had a few plans but would be alone together a lot of the weekend.

At work she opened an email from Ruth, the realtor in Cape May: Was Joanna still interested in any of the houses she had seen, including the Tea & Scones? Joanna wondered the same thing. The phone rang.

"This is Joanna Matthews."

"Joanna."

She knew instantly who it was. How could she not? His voice had been in her head all week. If she were stronger she would've hung up. "Michael."

"How are you?" he said, wishing he'd been stronger and not called.

"Fine. How are you?"

"Not fine. I'm in the neighborhood. Any chance you're free for lunch?"

"No, I can't," she said.

"Please. We need to talk."

Susan walked past the open door. Joanna said, "I'm working."

He didn't say anything. Then, "I know you like your food. You gotta eat, right? That's why God invented lunchtime."

Her heart was pounding. "I'll meet you in the lobby at noon."

Emails needed answering, but she was filling them with typos and gave up trying. She grabbed her purse and went to the ladies room. In the mirror she looked alive. Miserable yes, but excited and alive. Her heart was still pounding, and she couldn't wait to see him. It was only 11:45, but she was useless now anyway. On the way to the elevator she told Susan, "I'm going to lunch. Might be awhile."

To any observer, she probably looked like every other office worker heading out to lunch. They couldn't feel her legs longing to run, or hear her breath coming too fast. A second after pushing the down button for the elevator, she pushed it again. When the elevator did come she entered it sideways, like a crab, before the doors were fully open. As the doors were closing, she saw Susan smiling a little smile at her, not knowing what she had done to make Joanna distant. Joanna waved. As the elevator inched its way down to the lobby, Joanna's body was so full of adrenaline she wondered if she was damaging herself somehow.

The elevator doors opened and she was in the lobby. He wasn't there yet. Wait, pacing just outside the glass doors, there he was. She watched him a moment, her heart aching. He suddenly stopped and turned towards her, and he gave her a little smile. Had things been even slightly different, they would've run into each other's arms. He opened a big glass door and walked towards her as she walked towards him. They stood for a moment a foot apart, smiling goofily at each other, the yearning palpable between them.

"Hi," she said, holding out her hand, needing to touch him.

He took it and held it longer than socially necessary, obviously feeling the same way. "Joanna."

Her face was hot. "Lunch?"

"Sure," he said. "Is there anywhere quiet where we can talk?"

"Hard to find midtown. Wait, what about the Excelsior? They have a pretty quiet restaurant."

They walked, slowly and closely together. She said, "How are you?"

"Honestly?"

"Maybe not."

"Then I'm fine. Great. Dandy."

"Me, too."

"I wasn't sure you'd even see me."

"I didn't want to, I mean, I know I shouldn't. I've missed you, though." She stopped walking and looked at him. "A lot." People streamed past them, some jostling them but they didn't care.

He said, "There's so much I wanted to talk with you about, and now none of it seems worth it." They continued walking.

"No," she said. "Please. Talk about anything." She wanted more of his voice, live and in-person, instead of in her constantly replayed scenes of Cape May.

"Well," he said, trying to make it light, "this has been the worst week of my life."

"Me, too."

They arrived at the Excelsior in the mid-Forties off Sixth Avenue. The popular hotel also had a restaurant and a bar. Joanna and Michael were sat a table for two and the waiter welcomed them.

Michael said, "Coffee please," and Joanna nodded in agreement. They fleetingly looked over the menu while they talked.

She said, "When did you leave Cape May?"

"I took the bus on Sunday. I was supposed to stay a few more days but couldn't face being there after you, after..."

"I'm sorry about the way I left things, but I didn't know how to...what else to do. I still don't."

"I know."

"We don't even really know each other."

"You don't really mean that, do you?" he said. She shook her head. The waiter brought coffees and they ordered, although neither was hungry. "How's work?"

"I'm spending all my time there, and now my boss is starting to like me. He's got an obsessed employee, mornings and evenings."

He paused. "Things hard at home?"

She nodded. "It's...yes. Hard."

"Brian seems like an okay guy. I wish he wasn't."

After a long, painful pause, Joanna tried making small talk. "Did you finish *Time and Again*?"

"Yes, on the bus home from Cape May, although my thoughts might've been elsewhere."

"You have to read the sequel now."

"Sure. Will do. And you? Are you still thinking of moving?"

"Well," and she looked at him wistfully, "my life is a little confusing at the moment."

The waiter brought their salads, and they settled in to eat. They talked of movies, politics, even the weather. Conversation flowed easily, comfortably, perhaps because it helped them avoid discussing what was uppermost in their minds.

She said, "How are things with your son?"

"Not great."

"Want to talk about it?"

"Yes, actually. I'd like to talk to you about him, or anything else, really. Rob lives in San Francisco and works with computers. I don't understand half of what he does, but he makes a lot of money and is happy. We have a… tenuous relationship. Even though his mother left me, I somehow became the bad guy. No, that's not fair, there's a lot more to the story, and I'm not proud of my behavior."

"I've heard rumors that parenting can be hard."

"Not like you think. He's a great guy, but, I mean *and* he's gay. Donna accepted it with no hesitation and it took me a while. Is taking me a while, still."

"I see."

"In December he and his partner are getting married, and he wants me to fly out there. And I don't know what to do. You think I'm wrong?"

"It's not for me to say."

"Look, I have, and love, my gay friends, but it hit me differently when my one and only kid turned out to be gay, like I had failed in some way as a male influence or some-thing. That, because of me, he had a tougher time in life."

She didn't say anything.

He said, "Say something. Really, go ahead."

"I don't have children but…"

"You can just say it."

"It's not about anything you did. It's not about you. Kids should be loved unconditionally. And go to his wed-ding and be proud he found someone to love who loves him back."

He stared at her. "You're wonderful, you know."

"I don't know how you jumped to that conclusion."

A busboy refilled their water glasses.

"That house," Michael said, "the Tea & Scones. It would be a good investment, you know. It's a good price, and I could see you running it."

"Me, too. I felt right at home there, but…"

"What?"

"Well, how can I plan anything when I can't stop think-ing about you. It's awful."

"Thanks," he said, moving the salad around with his fork.

"I didn't mean…" she put her hand on his wrist.

"I know what you meant. It is awful. For me, too. It's not like I want the moon moved an inch to the left, I just want to be with you without feeling like a criminal. But those two things now seem equally unlikely."

It was time to go. They each left money on the table and stood up to leave. The tension increased as they walked to the exit through the hotel lobby. They looked at each other, thinking the same thing. Joanna willed herself away from the pull of the registration desk and the possibility of taking the next step. She walked outside, and he followed.

Waving her hand toward the hotel she said, "It's not that I don't...I do, but..."

"In degrees of difficulty I know this is a thousand times harder for you, because of him. It's up to me to be understanding."

"Thank you," she said, dropping her head.

He put his hand on her upper arm, and moved closer to her. He whispered, "Let's get you back to work."

They walked east and all too quickly they were in front of her office building. They lingered, making up things to talk about, reluctant to separate.

She said, "How's your book coming along?"

"Not bad. I'm channeling my misery into my art."

"Don't cut off any body parts."

"No, I'd like to stay whole. Just in case."

She smiled, about to reply, when her smile widened suddenly. "Hi," she said, to a coworker entering the building. Then to Michael, "I can't stand here with you. I feel like I'm wearing a blinking neon sign."

"A scarlet 'A'?" She nodded. He said, "Listen. Would you like to go out for coffee later, after work." She shook her head. He whispered, "We need to talk, without whispering, without interruptions."

"I can't." She looked at her watch. "I have to get back to work. I have a meeting in a few minutes."

"Joanna..."

"I have to go," and she opened the glass door into the lobby.

He followed. "When can I see you again?" She couldn't answer. "Will you call me?"

"Maybe, I don't know." He looked so hurt. She whispered, leaning in closer to him, wishing she could touch him. "I'm sorry."

He nodded.

"I've got to go." And she walked away from him. Again.

***

Michael walked through the door of his apartment, and just stood there, keys dangling from his hand. Although he'd always known that any control he had over his life was merely an illusion, this obvious, painful, total lack of control was unbearable. He didn't try to or mean to but he fell in love—if not at first sight, then at second day. And he had even less control of the outcome. Joanna knew how he felt, and everything was in her hands now.

He changed into sweatpants and an old T-shirt and sat down to work on his book. Every word was like pulling teeth, every completed sentence inadequate. Why bother. Instead, he put on a Miles Davis CD, made some tea, and returned to a recently started project: cleaning out the junk in his apartment. Living alone, he'd let things get out of hand. Piles of newspapers and magazines stood atop his tiny kitchen table. Books were in swaying stacks on the floor. Now he was thinning out his library. The massive job was keeping him sane, and keeping his mind off the guilt. It clawed at his insides—the thought of possibly being responsible for breaking up someone's marriage, and at the same time praying for it. His parents had been married forever. True, they didn't like each other much, but due to their vows and inertia, they stuck it out until death did them part. His own marriage fell painfully apart, and he was at least half to blame.

Meeting Joanna, even this late in life, was akin to a miracle. Admittedly, the real woman of his dreams would be *available*, wouldn't she? He loved Joanna. That was the miracle. Parts of him that had been closed and cynical even to the concept were suddenly, uncomfortably, wide open. The funny thing was, if he and Joanna had been set up, this all might not have happened. But as strangers without expectations, they were unguarded, and just themselves, and discovered each other. He knew she had strong feelings for him, but what she'd do with those feelings he really didn't know. He found her, and it was more than likely he would lose her. She was a woman who wouldn't want to hurt her husband. Michael needed to protect himself from further damage to his heart. But how? It was too late to shut back down.

Back in Cape May when she walked away from the Woodline estate and out of his life, he'd sat on the bench in the little park for what seemed like an eternity. Since then, he'd examined his feelings for her many times. Could he really be in love with her? Perhaps if she were available the excitement wouldn't be there? But Michael wasn't that kind of man. He never had been. As unsatisfying as his marriage had been, he would probably still be married to Donna if she hadn't left him. (The realization of that unhealthy little fact landed him in therapy for a few years after the divorce.) He should've wanted a divorce as much as she did. But he was loyal and liked being in a relationship. Even an unsatisfying one.

Since leaving Cape May, he realized he'd never felt anything for any woman the way he did for Joanna. It made him contemplate calling his ex-wife and apologizing. How good a husband could he have been, never truly, fully loving her. Donna must've sensed it, and resented him all those years and been thrilled when she found someone who truly loved her...the way Michael now loved Joanna.

He couldn't let himself think about Joanna's husband. Brian. Why couldn't Brian be an idiot or nasty? He seemed like a regular guy. And the pain Michael went through as a dumped husband, he might inflict on Brian.

That afternoon he made many trips to his building's basement, filling the recycling bins with newspapers and magazines. He purged his desk drawers, throwing dried up pens, and pictures of his ex-wife, down the garbage chute. He found empty boxes in the laundry room and brought them upstairs to load for the thrift store. The living room seemed twice the size. Misery properly channeled was productive. His New Agey friends would say he was making room for Joanna in his life, spiritually and physically. That may have been true. Another truth was, if the worst happened, if he never saw Joanna again—an unbearable thought he could not dwell on—he would still have to find a way to live the rest of his life.

The clock on one of his bookshelves read 6:00. It was three hours earlier in San Francisco. He picked up the phone and called his son.

***

After leaving Michael in the lobby, Joanna walked back into her office, pining for privacy and time to think. But sitting there behind the desk, typing on the computer, was her sister Cynthia.

"What are you doing here?"

Cynthia continued typing. "Two weeks ago, we made a date for lunch today, which you obviously forgot. And I've been checking my email while deciding if I should forgive you for standing me up." She looked up. "What's wrong? Why are you all flushed and out of breath?"

"I-I guess in the back of my mind I knew you were here and I rushed."

"You always were a lousy liar."

Joanna shook her head, and she started crying, unable to move.

"Shush!" Cynthia shut the office door. "What's going on?" She grabbed a tissue from the box on the desk and handed it to Joanna, while maneuvering her down into a chair. "What?" Joanna just shook her head. "Okay, just cry. Do what you need to do." Cynthia paused for a second, thinking. "Is this work-related?" Joanna shook her head. "You're too old to be pregnant. Our parents are already dead. If you were fired you'd be happier." Cynthia paused, going over every possible reason for her sister's emotional outburst. "Archie has some cat disease."

"No!"

"You have cancer?"

"No."

"Brian has cancer?"

"No!"

"Neither of you is dying of anything?" Joanna shook her head. "Well that's good news at least." She kneeled next to the chair, her hand on her sister's. "Uh, oh. Brian is having an affair."

Joanna reacted as if Cynthia had slapped her. "No. Stop!"

Cynthia paused, examining her sister's guilty face, and gasped: "No. It's *you*! You're having an affair."

Joanna was still as a stone.

"Well, are you?" Joanna shook her head a millimeter. Cynthia stated: "But you want to." Joanna nodded. "Who is he?"

"I met him on the bus to Cape May."

"Oh, my baby baby sister. What are you going to do?"

"Right now, nothing. I have to work."

"But I want to know more. Tell me about him."

"Cynthia, I'm holding on by a thread, not even a string, and I can't talk about it."

Cynthia stood up, and smoothed down the front of her expertly tailored beige pants. "Okay. If and when you need to talk, I'll be here. I promise not to judge you, or I promise to try not to judge you, which is the best I can do."

"You won't say anything to Brian, right? Even though you've grown to think of him as a brother, I'm your actual sister and I need you to be quiet right now."

"Yes, I'll be quiet, which isn't easy for me, as you know. Wow, this is big, Jo. Honestly, I would've bet a lot of money you would never stray. What's his name?"

"Michael."

"Tell me about him." Joanna shook her head another

millimeter. "Well, tell me why you're about to cheat on Brian, then."

"I'm not *about* to cheat on Brian."

"What attracted you to Michael? Why him?"

"Why him? Because I can't stop thinking about him. Because he makes me feel special and pretty and young. And when I'm with him the world spins. And he's tender and handsome and so interesting, and funny, and smart. I feel like he knows me, the real me, and he needs me, too. And every moment away from him feels wasted."

Cynthia slumped on the edge of the desk. "Oh, this is bad, Jo. I thought this was only a late-midlife crisis, making-up-for-lost-time, sex thing." Joanna shook her head. "You sound like you're in love."

Joanna continued shaking her head and said, "No. I'm not. I can't be."

"Good luck having that much control over your emotions, honey." Cynthia stood up straight, the three-inch heels of her Manolo Blahniks adding to her already imposing figure. "Well, think at least twice before you wreck everything. I've been through a divorce and it's not fun." She opened the door, and the sounds of a busy office floated in. "Brian may not be Mr. Excitement, but he does love you and he's been good to you. Be careful, Jo."

Joanna wiped away the tears still on her cheeks, and nodded as Cynthia walked out of the office.

CHAPTER 13

After Cynthia left, Joanna couldn't think, sit still, or work for more than a minute at a time. She left at 5:30, and walked home, stopping whenever she could. Never a shopper, she now browsed any store that caught her eye, to delay having to walk through her own front door. If only she could be in the apartment alone, with some time to think, but Brian was there working. At a bookshop she bought a magazine, got a coffee and biscotti, and sat for an hour. Finally she couldn't kill any more time and went home.

That weekend was unbearable. She didn't want to be with Brian, who seemed to be watching her all the time, but didn't want to see people or be alone either. In a way, alone was worst of all, because time went especially slowly even though she read, cleaned, cooked meals for the week, went for walks, anything to keep her mind busy. Still, he was in every thought.

Saturday night she and Brian went to dinner with Fred and his boyfriend. When one of them asked how Cape May was, Joanna talked about the Manor Rose and the Tea & Scones, and how much she loved the town. They asked questions, she answered. Was she such a good actress that they couldn't tell she was dying inside?

On Sunday Brian asked if she wanted to play Scrabble. They played for half an hour and she pretended to get sick, because she couldn't stand it any more. She thanked heaven that tomorrow started another week of work, and she could throw herself into something other than her life.

***

Monday morning it all began again. That week at work, every day felt like two, perhaps because she got there so early and left so late. Occasionally she'd go online to see if the Tea & Scones was officially listed yet. She couldn't bear to lose that house, truly her dream house. She didn't want to lose sight of her goals, but couldn't help it right now.

Then, somehow, another Friday arrived, when she wished he'd call her again. He didn't. At the end of a long day, she had no choice but to go home. She had to be with Brian. She had to put her life back on track.

"Hi," she said, walking through the door of their apartment with a bag of groceries they didn't really need.

"Another long day, huh?" Brian said, walking out of his tiny office holding his now ever-present cup of coffee.

She attempted a smile. "I hope that's decaf or you'll never sleep tonight."

He walked over to her. She could see he'd been jangled by exposure to her, this stranger he'd been living with for two weeks. He took the bag from her.

"I bought rolls and eggs. Thought I'd make an omelet."

They spent the evening together in awkward silence. She tried to think of things to say to him, but they all got stuck in her throat.

He tried also: "How're you feeling about moving to Cape May?"

"I'm not sure."

"Do you want to go see a movie?"

"If you want to."

"Or watch one we DVR'd?"

"Sure."

After what felt like 50 hours, it was a legitimate time to go to bed and Joanna did, without even saying goodnight to Brian. When he crawled into bed an hour later, she was still awake, but pretending to be sleep, her back turned to him.

Saturday rolled around and Brian was up at his usual 7:30, making coffee and expecting Joanna to join him by 8:30 at the latest. By 9:30 he checked in on her. Even in sleep she looked troubled. He didn't wake her. She slept until 10:30, something she hadn't done in a decade, but still had trouble getting out of bed. A shower helped a little. Wearing her oversized blue terry cloth robe, her hair wet, she entered the kitchen.

Brian said, "Morning."

"Morning."

He watched her as she made coffee, then couldn't keep quiet any longer. "We need to talk."

"About what?" she snapped, and immediately sat down at the table, as if her legs wouldn't hold her any more. The apartment was deadly quiet. Archie rubbed against her legs but she didn't pick him up.

"Joanna, even the cat knows something's wrong." Silence. "You come home late every night. And then you're not really here." More uncomfortable silence. "This has nothing to do with work."

"I have been working late. I swear. You can call my boss and ask him."

"You've never cared about any job this much. You're acting weird. At dinner last week, when you went to the bathroom, Fred asked me what was wrong with you, what was going on."

"He did?"

"You're having an affair, aren't you?"

She was silent.

"Joanna, I'm not blind or stupid." The tension grew as he paused. "You've been like this since Cape May." He paused again. "What's going on with you? Is it Michael?" She tried to leave the kitchen but he caught her arm. "It is Michael, isn't it. You're sleeping with him."

"No!"

"Oh, come on Jo! At least be honest."

"I am! I mean I'm not…having an affair."

"Then tell me what the hell is going on," he said. She shook her head. "Jo, you owe me this much."

Somehow she managed to push out the words: "In Cape May, on the beach. Michael and I…kissed."

Silence.

He said, "And…"

More silence.

He tried to hold in his anger. "Have you been seeing him every night? When you were supposedly working late?"

She couldn't look at him. "No, I hadn't seen him since Cape May. Then last Friday he called me at work. We had lunch."

"Lunch? Just lunch. I'm supposed to believe that?"

"We went out to lunch. That was it. I swear."

Brian paused. "Are you going to see him again?"

She shrugged.

"You want to see him again?"

She met his eyes and said, "Please don't ask me." He stared at her, unblinking. With the oppressive quiet in their apartment, sounds of Manhattan came in through the open window. Cars driving by, a distant siren, a dog barking. She said, "I miss you being my best friend, like in the old days. You're the person I'd most want to talk to, about something like this."

He took a deep breath. "So tell me. Like when I was your best friend."

"What?"

"Pretend I'm still your best friend. For the next couple of minutes. Talk to me."

"I couldn't."

"I give you full permission to tell me what's going on."

"Are you a masochist?"

"At least I'd be in some control of my pain. I can't stand not knowing what's going on, or where you are, or what you're doing."

"I..."

"So, Joanna," he said. "How was your trip to Cape May?"

"Brian, this is ridiculous!"

"For the next two minutes I'm willing to forget I'm your husband and just be your friend. What happened in Cape May?" She couldn't reply. "Jo, two minutes. That's it. Start talking."

"I keep thinking about him. I try not to, but I can't help it."

"Did you sleep with him?" She shook her head. "Do you want to?" She didn't answer or move but Brian paced, then looked out the window, then poured himself a glass of water in the kitchen. He drank it, thought a minute, and spat out: "You didn't sow many wild oats in your youth, you know."

"You mean, maybe this is my body saying, *hey, honey, you're not getting any younger?*"

"Maybe."

"Brian, before last weekend I never even looked at another man. Well, I had the occasional fantasy about that guy in the bookstore with the great beard. But I'm old enough to be his mother."

He attempted a smile. It came out a grimace. "Like me with the gorgeous Shaniqua at Dunkin' Donuts."

"She knows you like her. She always gives you free Munchkins."

"Joanna, what are you going to do?"

"Nothing, of course."

"You gonna get back to normal?" She shrugged. "I can't live like this. These two weeks have been hell."

"I'm not sure how…or what…"

He suddenly spat out, "You know, you're right. I can't do this. I don't want to know anything more. Figure things out. Get this out of your system. One way or another." He got up, went into the bedroom and slammed the door.

***

Joanna kept busy over the next few hours. One benefit from all this inner turmoil: the apartment had never been cleaner. She changed the sheets, did two loads of laundry, emptied the wastebaskets, cleaned the kitchen, brushed the cat, and watered the plants.

Brian sequestered himself in the bedroom or office. In the few seconds he spent going from one room to the other, she said, "Chicken okay for tonight?" and he said, "Sure."

Getting more than two syllables out of him was impossible. She could hardly blame him.

By 2:00 she needed to leave the apartment and the oppression. When Brian was in the kitchen with the radio on she went into their bedroom and called Michael. When he answered the phone she couldn't talk, her throat was so dry.

"Hello?" he said again.

She sipped some water from a bottle on her night table. "It's Joanna."

"Joanna. Hello."

"Michael, I want to see you."

"Yes. You tell me when and where."

"Want to take a walk in the park?"

"Yes."

"Want to meet on the northeast corner of Amsterdam and Eightieth?"

"Yes."

Even his monosyllables made her skin tingle. She couldn't help but smile. "What if I'd said the southwest corner of Columbus and Seventy-Ninth?"

"Oh, no. That would've been out of the question."

"Are you always going to be this difficult?" she said.

"I'll try not to be," he said, and she could hear that he was smiling.

"In an hour?"

"I'll be there. And Joanna?"

"Yes?"

"I'm glad you called."

After forty minutes, during which she changed her shirt four times and almost canceled on Michael three times (even picking up the phone once), she walked into the living room on her way out. Brian was napping on the couch with the TV on and Archie on his lap. Her heart wrenched, and she felt like both a horrible human being and a fool for possibly jeopardizing this version of a happy home.

She wrote Brian a note: *"Out for a walk. See you later. J,"* and because the omission would be noticed, she drew a heart as she always did on her notes to him. Tiptoeing, she left the apartment, shut the door, and headed for Michael.

CHAPTER 14

Michael waited on the corner of Amsterdam and Eightieth, trying not to search for her face in the crowd. He attempted a cool New Yorker stance, but when he saw her halfway up the block just seconds before she saw him, he wanted to run to her. When she saw him, and her plain street face lit up with a smile she couldn't suppress, his nonchalance vanished. She walked a little quicker, too, and they met in the middle of the block.

Puffing, they stopped just short of embracing in the street. She said, "Hi!"

"Hello, Joanna."

What was it about his voice that affected her so? They stood for a moment, smiling at each other. She said, "Want to walk? Looks like rain though."

"I brought my umbrella."

"I didn't."

"I'll share."

They walked without talking, happy simply to be together, and entered Central Park. They felt some rain drops. He said, "Anyplace in particular?" as he opened the umbrella.

"East?"

They walked, slightly awkwardly. Although the umbrella necessitated closeness, she didn't want to appear "together" in an area so near to where friends and neighbors might see them. And being so close to each other but not close enough was a form of torture.

He said, "How was your week? The Excelsior seems months ago."

"Yes," she said, happy to make conversation. "My big project is done. I met all my deadlines. That's a first. I'll be able to catch up on emails and get through some of the journals stacked on my desk. My next assignment is a diabetes drug, so I have to read up, learn everything I can."

The park was pleasantly crowded, despite the rain, which was getting heavier. Her shoulder was getting wet so she moved closer to him and linked her arm through his elbow. They watched kids run around, smelled vendors' foods, and heard snatches of conversations, music from boom boxes, and street performers.

He said, "I imagine you'd get a sense of fulfillment knowing you're educating people. Your work could help save lives."

"Not really, but you are putting a positive spin on me helping pharmaceutical companies make money." She paused. "This last project did save one life, mine. Or rather my sanity." Inside, under the dome of his umbrella, it was almost private. Intimate.

They strolled without looking at each other. He said, "I'm sorry meeting me made your life harder. That's pretty much the opposite of what I'd want, you know."

"I know."

His hand, warm and soft, covered hers, his fingers lightly stroking her. They came to more secluded pathways in the park. She held onto him tighter. The rain, and the need for the umbrella, somehow legitimizing their closeness. On an empty path, he drew her off to the side of a large rock and lowered the umbrella over them. They were instantly in each other's arms. She nuzzled his neck, loving his smell and the feel of his skin. He kissed her head, inching his way towards her lips, longing to put an end to their separation. They were about to kiss when a large group of laughing and chatting teenagers walked past them and they broke apart. When alone again, Joanna buried her face again in Michael's neck. She stayed in the safety and privacy of his arms and he rocked her slowly. "It'll be okay, it's okay," he whispered, his lips grazing her hair, until her tense body relaxed.

They walked. After awhile he said, "Hey, did I ever tell you, in the years and years we've known each other, that I wanted to be an artist, during my enforced years in med school and before writing took over my life?"

The rain had stopped and as much as he didn't want to, he closed the umbrella and they walked a little farther apart.

"You're a regular Renaissance man."

"Unfortunately I was as skilled an artist as I was a pre-med student."

"At least you gave your dreams a try."

"I like that. Thank you. My ex-wife used to say I was unfocused and fickle. She liked the *eff eff* sound of it I think."

More comfortable quiet followed. "I'm getting hungry," she said. "I forgot to have breakfast."

"Well, there's hot dogs from a cart, if you're feeling adventurous, or we can dine like sophisticated New Yorkers at the Met."

"I'm feeling very sophisticated right now."

"The Met it is. Feel like seeing some art first? I'm a member, and…"

"Ooh, a member are you?"

"Mock me and I won't let you use my ten percent discount at the gift shop."

They walked across the park, pointing out an especially interesting tree, or cute dog, to Fifth Avenue and headed north to the Metropolitan Museum of Art. After having their bags indifferently searched for explosives by tired security guards, they walked to the admissions booth. Holding his membership card up for all to see, Michael puffed his chest out with pride: "I'm a member," he said to the pretty girl behind the counter. Joanna couldn't help but laugh. "Where to?"

"You pick."

They headed south and up a few flights in the huge museum and found the room full of Toulouse-Lautrec's work. It was dark and moody in there. Joanna walked over to one, "This is one of my favorites. Although I think I love his posters even more. Jane Avril or La Goulue. Don't look so shocked. My favorite class ever was art history. The other students were falling asleep as soon as the lights were turned off for the slides, but I was enthralled."

His eyes took her in. "You are perfect for me."

Her eyes filled with tears but she stopped herself, saying, "Of course, I was probably the only kid in the class who hadn't stayed up partying the night before."

Later, after he showed her his favorite works in the Impressionism wing, she showed him two Walter Sickert paintings in the modern collection. Sickert was suspected by some of being Jack the Ripper. Joanna hadn't believed the evidence she'd read, but had to admit his work was eerie. Seeing those paintings led to discussions about Sherlock Holmes, serial killers, and their mutual appreciation of London.

She said, "My art appreciation meter is full, and my stomach is empty."

"The Petrie is this way, if you'd like. It's nicer than the cafeteria. Or we can walk somewhere?"

"I like eating in the museum. Like I'm taking in culture along with the food."

As they walked there, Joanna wondered what she'd say if they ran into anyone she knew. As Cynthia correctly pointed out, she was a terrible liar.

There was only a short wait. They were seated at a small table and he ordered grilled chicken salad, she the tuna nicoise. He raised his water glass to her and said, "You know, if things were only entirely different, this would've qualified as a nice, regular date. A walk through the park, some culture at a museum, an early dinner. We've already covered about seventy-four topics. We skipped right over the light, getting-to-know-you type questions."

"It's never too late. How's *What sign are you?*"

"Ouch, that's an oldie. It's obvious you've been out of circulation a long time."

"What about *Do you come here often?*"

"That's a little better, so I'll deign to answer. Yes, sometimes I bring my notebook and write in a quiet gallery. Get myself out of my apartment. I haven't been to this café for over a year, though, I'd say."

"Were you on a date?"

"Yes, as a matter of fact."

"Anyone promising?"

"Are you asking about my love life?"

She nodded. "Is your past filled with hundreds of women?"

"Hundreds?"

"In Cape May there was Madeleine, and Claire was certainly interested. Oh, and the waitress' mother."

"Were you keeping notes? I haven't lived in a vacuum. I meet women on my own. Or used to. And couples do enjoy matching up their single friends. Like Concentration with humans."

She put her hand on top of his on the table. "Maybe I'm hoping you're a serial dater with piles of used women littered around you. I'm trying to find a fault. You occasionally seem too good to be true."

"Wow, I've never heard that before. Quite the opposite. If I compiled a list of my faults, as told to me by women I've dated, including Madeleine and Claire and Sophie's mom, I'd have a very long list indeed."

"How'd you like them?"

"You know how I feel about Madeleine."

"Yes, like a sister, I know."

"Claire's a nice person, but I'm not interested. Many of the women I dated I didn't like much, but I tried. Some broke up with me. My ego got hurt. Hey, I'm human."

"I guess you weren't the lid for their pot, or whatever that tasteless phrase is. Have there been lots of pots?"

"You really want to know?"

"I'm partly jealous and partly mad at them for damaging your ego. Mostly I'm interested in the sixty years of your life before I met you."

"I was born in a log cabin in Illinois."

"Maybe skip to after your divorce."

"Okay, I've dated maybe fifteen women since then, although just a few in the past two years. Didn't make it to a second date with a bunch of them. Dated some awhile. Not long. Went to bed with a few of them."

"A few as in three?"

He didn't answer. He took a sip of water and said, "Enough to have learned what really matters to me." After another sip, he said, quietly, "Am I allowed to ask about your love life?"

"I guess it's only fair."

"How long have you been married?"

"Twenty years."

"Happily?"

"Mostly. Sort of. I was settled. Happy not to be alone? I thought I was…content?" The words caught in her throat, and she reached for her glass, downing the rest of the water.

"Has this"—he waved his hand between the two of them—"ever happened before?"

"Never. Never even tempted."

"I thought so. I'm glad."

After paying the bill and exiting, they returned to Central Park, heading west. She asked him, "Did you want to be a painter?"

"I wanted to paint, and write, and be an architect, and possibly a doctor, too. And of course an astronaut. I was interested in everything when I was younger. It distilled down to 'writer' because I could write about artists and builders and doctors.

"Maybe you should've been an actor."

"Or that criminal who pretended to be all those things. You know, Leo DiCaprio. Writing won. It's what I enjoy the most, and I seem to be good at it. Although it is solitary."

"Brian says…do you mind me talking about him?"

He said, "I can stifle my jealousy."

"No, never mind."

"What about you? What made you want to change your life and run a bed and breakfast?"

They talked and talked, as if they'd known each other for years. A block from the park exit a man in a tuxedo stood playing the violin. The case was open in front of him for donations. As they listened and stood side by side, Michael linked his pinkie with Joanna's. The simple touch of the pad of his finger upon hers stirred her whole body. She pulled away from him to find a dollar to throw in the violin case. They exited at Seventy-Seventh Street and stood awhile, not wanting to say goodbye.

He said, "Oh, I've got some good news. I called my son. We talked. It went really well. I chatted with his soon-to-be husband, too. My future son-in-law."

"That's wonderful! Were you apprehensive about talking with him?"

"I think things will be less difficult. I should say *I'll* be less difficult. I understand more now, about having absolutely no control over who you fall in love with."

Those words filled Joanna with warmth and happiness, followed immediately by an ache so powerful she physically reacted, turning away from him and clutching her abdomen.

"Joanna, you all right?"

She knew words wouldn't come out so she didn't try. She just nodded.

"Want to walk me to my apartment?"

Again she couldn't answer. She shook her head.

"Well then, Ms. Matthews, thank you for the date." He held out his hand. She took it and they stood there for another moment. Hands still holding, eyes still locked, he whispered, "Will I see you again?"

She nodded. And this time he turned and walked away first, knowing he couldn't endure watching her leave him again, and headed south towards his apartment.

CHAPTER 15

Joanna watched Michael walk away, and didn't notice the annoyed faces of the people having to walk around her. When she could move, she meant to walk straight home, but couldn't. She sat in a deli with an untouched glass of iced tea for half an hour, then paid and left. She truly meant to turn right, north, home, but she couldn't. She turned left instead, and headed south towards Michael's apartment. She forced herself to amble for a block, hoping will power or guilt would kick in and stop her, but then practically sprinted and in few minutes, she was standing in front of his building.

It was a doormanless apartment building. She stood in the outside lobby for many long seconds, until she lifted a finger and rang his bell, hoping that he wouldn't be home, praying that he would. He asked who it was and she squeaked out, "Joanna." He said, "Second floor. G." She walked up because there was no way she could stand still to wait for the elevator. His apartment was at the end of the hall, and he was there holding his door open for her. The hairs on her arms were spiking. Neither spoke.

She was inside, Michael shut the door, they were alone. She walked down the short hall, feeling his eyes on her. The air was heavy. The tension needed breaking and she turned to him to say something chatty, but the look of adoration and desire in his eyes silenced her. No one had ever looked at her like that. Overwhelmed by her own desires, she stalled for time, putting her purse and jacket on a chair. Her back was to him. Neither of them moved. Then suddenly he was behind her, his hands heavy on her shoulders, his lips on her hair. She turned into his arms and they embraced, fitting together like intricately cut puzzle pieces. Then they kissed, and kissed, heads tilted in opposite directions then switching and noses clashing, pelvises pressing into each other.

She turned away from him and walked over to a shelf, examining the spines of some books. He realized how nervous she was when she said, "I think you have even more books than we do," and her voice quavered. "And you're so neat."

"Only recently," he said, his hands caressing her shoulders again, needing the contact, and wanting to calm her. "My life is either finally coming together or about to permanently fall apart. Either way, I've needed to keep busy."

"I've been cleaning a lot lately, too. It's like a therapy." Needing a moment, she said, "Can I have some water?"

He stepped into the tiny kitchen, and she tinkled the keys of a scratched upright piano. "Do you play?"

"Chopsticks, badly. It was my grandfather's. He always wanted me to learn, but I was too busy reading." He was talking too fast and too much. "It's in my 'stave off dementia by learning something new' plan. I started Italian lessons when I was fifty. Not that I learned enough to actually speak Italian. Perhaps because I quit within the year."

"There's so much about you I don't know," and she sipped the water.

He finally said what he had to say: "Maybe all you need to know about me is that I love you."

He took the glass from her and put it on the table. His hands cupped her face, his pinkies tickling her neck and sending shivers down her spine. Then he kissed her, softly, just grazing her lips, sympathetic about her skittishness. Her arms encircled his waist. They stood, holding each other, her head against his chest.

She tilted her head up to him, asking to be kissed, desperate to be kissed. They kissed again, for a long time, lightly, then deeply, parting only to gasp for air. His lips were on her neck, her fingers kneaded his shoulders. Together they stumbled over to the couch and fell on it, laughing.

They sat, cuddling, quiet in their own thoughts, each fully aware of the magnitude of what might happen next. He turned to her, and kissed her, and it was different, slow and sacred. He left her lips and kissed her cheek, then neck, his fingers moving aside her collar to kiss her clavicles. He unbuttoned the top of her blouse, pushing the material off one shoulder to kiss what he uncovered. His hand slid down to her breast and caressed it through her shirt, his thumb rubbing against the hardened nipple. Deep moans came out of her, sounds that she hardly recognized as coming from herself. She reclined into the couch, pulling him with her, her hands roaming from his head to his waist, pulling his shirt up so she could feel his bare back with her bare hands.

Suddenly her whole body tensed.

"You okay?" he said, holding her. She nodded, not meeting his eyes. "We going too fast?" She shook her head. "Tell me. Is it Brian?" She nodded. "I want this, Joanna, *you*...but only when it's right. I want you thinking about me, not him." Her eyes were still downcast. He lifted her chin. "I may look remarkably youthful, but I'm not a teenager any more. I can wait."

He sat up, bringing her gently with him, and redressed her—slowly pulling her blouse up over her shoulder, rebuttoning the button, perhaps letting his gentle fingers linger longer than necessary. Then he turned her back to him and massaged her shoulders. It took awhile but he felt her begin to relax. He ran his fingertips up and down her bare arms and then returned to the massage. She leaned back into him and he wrapped his arms around her, kissed her cheek, and whispered "Joanna" in her ear. There was a sudden flush of warmth between her legs, so intense it hurt. Her libido, which had been at "practically nonexistent" for a decade was making up for lost time.

She moved away from him, whispering, but he couldn't understand. "Hmm?" he said.

"I *can't* wait."

"Oh?" he said, a simultaneously sexy and goofy smile appearing on his face. "Well, it's my duty to be an obliging host, isn't it?" He stood up, and pointed. "Right through that door is my bedroom and bed, with fresh sheets put on this morning." He reached for her hand, and she gave it to him. When she stood up he put his arm around her waist, to lead her to the bedroom, and her entire body trembled. "If this were ten years ago, I'd carry you."

She said, "As long as I can still walk, I don't mind."

"You're shaking."

"I'm nervous."

"I'd say don't be, but I am, too." As they walked into the dimly lit bedroom (the window faced the brick wall of a taller building) he flipped on a light.

"Oh," she said, "please don't."

He switched off the light.

She said, "I promise I'll try to be less shy next time."

As he drew her close, he said, "Shy's nice. And you said *next time.* I'll hold you to that."

The warm breeze whooshed the curtain and Michael reached over to lower the blind before joining her on the bed. They kissed, and helped each other remove various pieces of outer clothing, and touched, awkwardly, shyly, but quickly learning.

Perhaps it should've felt odd being in someone else's bed. Not the bed she'd been sharing with Brian for the past twenty years. But it didn't. Everything about Michael, and his surroundings, made her feel safe, and comfortable, and at this very moment, more alive than she'd ever been. Their heads were both on his pillow, and they looked into each other's eyes for a few moments. Then they held each other, every inch of them touching from foreheads to feet. They kissed, his tongue tasted her lips, entering her mouth just the right amount, softly, as she met it with hers. Hands slid up and down as far as their reach would allow. After a few minutes she backed away just enough to reach down to fondle him. It made them both gasp, then smile because they both gasped. He pulled off his boxers so fast it made her smile again. He pushed down the material of her white lace bra and ran his fingertips lightly over her nipples. She froze, paralyzed with pleasure. Then his hand rode her body, stopping between her legs, over her underwear. Her breathing became labored as his finger rubbed her through the cotton, and she lowered the pink garment. His finger returned to the same spot, taunting her.

She gasped, then whispered, "Now. Please."

He sat up and fished around in his nightstand drawer and grabbed a condom from underneath a notebook. He rolled it on as she watched, lying there about to burst with anticipation. When he was on top of her, she reached down and guided him inside.

Had she ever had sex before? If so, it certainly wasn't like this, with her entire body vibrating. Her four limbs hugged him closer, her feet tickled by the hair on his legs. Her pelvis rocked up to meet him, hands cupping his rear end. He looked down into her eyes and smiled, and kissed her. "You're lovely," he said, and it was the most wonderful thing she'd ever had said to her. His thrusting slowed, then sped up until, eventually, he climaxed and collapsed on top of her. "Oh, Joanna!" She cradled him, his weight somehow familiar, protective. His heart pounded against her ribs, almost another part of him inside her. She stroked his hair, her fingers weaving into the curls on his neck.

When he could move, he gently rolled off her and onto his side, his leg over hers. While his breathing slowed, he fondled her breasts and delicately pinched her nipples. He kissed his way down to one of them, covering the hard nub with his mouth, licking and sucking on it until she was squirming, her breathing shorter and shorter. Sensing she couldn't stand it another second, he put his hand between her legs. His fingers slid into and around her, making her back arch, her body straining for release. The room began to spin and she closed her eyes. It wasn't long before she surprised then delighted him by producing an unexpectedly deep and guttural scream. Her fingers dug into his shoulder, her head tilting and heart pounding. He watched her face, her eyes closed in ecstasy. It lasted a long time, her hips bucking uncontrollably. It filled him with pride, to do this for her. As she came down from her high, she began to cry softly, and he held her. He didn't question her, just held her tighter, and she turned on her side into his arms. When her body finally, fully relaxed, he drew the sheet over the two of them, and they drifted off to sleep, with their arms and legs entwined.

Michael woke up first and ran his fingertips lightly over her skin under the sheet, his hand exploring everywhere until stopping at her thighs, inching its way higher. He said, "What? What's that?"

"Hmm?" she said.

"Shush, I'm not talking to you. I'm talking to your cunny. She says she wants more." His fingers stroked her, entered her, toyed with her, until many minutes later she screamed again, her arm around his neck in a chokehold.

BANG! BANG! BANG! Someone in the apartment next door pounded on the wall above the bed. "Shut the fuck up!"

At first they were startled, then Joanna began to laugh, and Michael joined in. Tears rolled out of her eyes, as she and Michael held each other. He managed to say, "My neighbors haven't heard anything like that from this apartment, believe me!"

She wiped some tears away, "Am I ruining or making your reputation?"

"Time will tell," he said. They lay there together, perfectly content. He said, "Do you, uh, can you, if I had had some staying power, would you have finished with me, uh, in there?"

"No, I've never had one that way."

"Well, that would be a fun biology project for us, don't you think?"

She nodded, "Although how I get there doesn't really matter."

He rubbed his shoulder. "I think you carved your name into my shoulder with your nails. I'm branded: Property of Joanna Matthews."

"I'm sorry," she laughed and kissed the crescent-moon wounds. "Think of it as a badge of honor for a job well done." She pulled his face to her and kissed him. "Very very well done."

"Other than this service I offer, free of charge, I might add," he said, giving her breast a loving squeeze, "can I do anything for you? Get you anything?"

"I don't think a trip to Paris would top the last hour. And from me that's high praise."

"Speaking of praise, may I say you have incredible breasts?" he said, cupping one.

"You should've seem them at their peak, no pun intended."

"Well, they're beautiful now. As for peak, I've found it necessary to invest in those little blue pills now and then."

"I guess we're not twenty anymore."

"We're not forty anymore, and I don't mind at all right now." He kissed her delicately.

She grinned and nodded, her fingers touching his chin. She said, "These past two weeks at work I could feel your stubble on my face. Sort of a phantom prickling."

He rubbed his chin against hers. "I'll never shave again."

They cuddled quietly a long time, listening to the sounds coming in from the city. Then she sighed, "I suppose at some point I'll have to get up. And face my life."

He paused before saying, "You know I want you to leave him."

"I know."

He waited but she didn't continue. He said, "Tell me what you're thinking."

"I don't want to talk about it now."

"But I do. I need to know what's going on. Where I stand. How you feel."

She paused. "How could I do that to him? Hurt him like that? How could I leave him? He's been my friend for thirty years."

"You said *friend*. Not husband or lover."

"But that's not his fault. I'm the one who's been...withholding. It's funny. I'm just now realizing it."

"How much does he know?"

"He guessed about us, because I've been hell to live with. He told me I'd better see you and figure things out. That's why I called you today."

"You came here because of him? Because he told you to?" he said, his voice heavy on the pronouns. He tensed, and she felt it.

"No. Well, sort of. I came here because I couldn't *not* come here. I fall asleep thinking about you. I wake up thinking about you." She sat up, pulling the sheet with her. "Even as, as unaware as he can be, he figured things out. Said he can't live like this."

"But you could?"

"No." She could feel him starting to slip away. The reality of the situation was sinking in, and making her more frazzled and upset. "It's just, Brian thinks he knows me, and my history. I have a terrible track record with men, back to high school. I'm sure he thinks this is something that will go away."

"So to prove him wrong you came here to take me out for a test drive?" He sat up, and pulled on his underwear.

"No! It's not like that. Oh, I'm messing this up. Michael, this happened so fast and is so big. I don't know what's happening or what I'm doing. I don't know if I can toss away everything I've known for decades for..."

"*Just* me?" He stood up, put on the rest of his clothes, and left the bedroom, leaving the door open. She quickly dressed, keeping an eye on him in the kitchen. The way he opened the refrigerator door and pulled out a bottle of water, his shoulders hunched, was breaking her heart. She was hurting him, and it was killing her.

She walked over to him, and put her hand on his back, saying gently, "Michael, don't turn around, so I can say this: you...arouse me so much I'm afraid I'm thinking with my vagina instead of my head and it might not be the best judge of how I should run my life."

He turned around. "Stop it, Joanna. You know this isn't just about sex."

"Don't you see that if it isn't...my life is going to blow up. Michael, I can't...I care about...I feel more for you than I've ever felt for anyone. But I don't want to say anything or do anything without being one-hundred percent sure. I've had, *have*, the emotional maturity of an awkward teenager, and it has to end here. I have to figure things out. I don't have the right to ask you, but I'm going to. Can you please, please be patient? Just give me some time."

He nodded, and stood up straight. "I'll try. But it's not easy. I don't need to make excuses, because I have no doubts. I love you and want to spend the rest of my life with you."

"Oh, Michael."

"But I'll keep my mouth shut now."

"Thank you," she said, reaching for her purse and jacket. "I have to go."

He walked her to the door. He sounded testy when he asked, "Am I allowed to call you? I don't know the rules."

"Yes call."

"This isn't going to be easy," he said, opening the door, "knowing you're sleeping in the same bed as Brian."

She shook her head. "No. I'll be on the couch." She passed by him, exiting.

"Good." He whispered in her ear, "Meet me for lunch on Monday?" She nodded. "The Excelsior? At noon." She nodded again. "Tomorrow is going to be a very long day," he said.

And she left, walking down the hall as he watched her. She pushed for the elevator and they looked at each other until it came. When it did, she waved to him and got in, and started her journey home.

CHAPTER 16

Joanna walked home from Michael's with scrambled emotions. She might not have the courage to say it out loud, but she was in love. For the first time in her life. At almost sixty years of age. What did it say about her that she had married and spent twenty years with someone she wasn't in love with. Now she saw clearly she'd been stunted emotionally. She married Brian to avoid being alone, to try to be like everyone else, and thought Brian felt the same way. She finally admitted to herself what she'd ignored for years, possibly decades: Brian loved her. And now she was in love with someone else.

All too soon she was in front of her apartment building. Dreading entering, she stood there. The doorman did his duty, so her inertia was short-lived. Once inside the lobby, her nerves got the better of her. Would Brian question her? If he did, what could she say? There was a bench in the lobby and she sat for a few minutes before heading upstairs.

"Brian?" The place was silent. Archie greeted her with a meow, and rubbed against her leg. She bent down to pick him up. "Hello, darling. Where's daddy?" Brian wasn't home and she breathed a sigh of relief.

She took a shower and stayed in, cocooned in the warmth. As the bar of soap traced the paths of Michael's hands, she felt such an overpowering, dizzying rush of happiness and love that she had to sit on the edge of the tub. It was a fine line to try and walk—treasuring this awakening, but not hoping too much, and not feeling too guilty—and she wasn't doing a good job of it at all. When she got out and was drying off, she heard movement in the apartment. He was home. She wrapped herself in her robe, and left the bathroom. Brian was in the kitchen, unpacking grocery bags. She wondered if he'd be able to tell where she'd been and what she'd been doing. She was reminded of being a teen and returning home after her first make-out session, wondering if her mother could see the tell-tale signs. After an afternoon with Michael, would Brian? How could she not look and seem different?

"Hi," she said.

He stopped, with cans of tomato sauce in his hands, and faced her. "Hi. I...obviously went shopping. Couldn't just sit here, waiting. Thought I'd make turkey meat sauce for dinner. You hungry?"

She nodded. "A little. I had lunch at the Met. Saw some paintings."

"Yeah?"

"Did you work?"

"A little. It was hard to concentrate, you know?"

She nodded. He stood there awkwardly, looking at her for so long she had to do something and grabbed items from the grocery bag to put away. He seemed about to say something, so she detoured, "Can I help with dinner? Cut up something?"

He handed her two onions and some garlic. "Parsley's in the fridge."

While she cut up onions (relieved to be shedding tears only because of the vegetable), he cleaned off the table. When she sniffled, he was beside her, again his eyes searching hers. She couldn't look into them for more than a second, nauseated by guilt.

He said, "Wanna listen to *Prairie Home Companion*?"

"Sure, whatever."

He clicked on the radio. "Oh, my mother called after... after you went out."

"How is she?"

"She's decided on an assisted living place. Even made a deposit."

"How's she feeling about moving?"

"Mixed," he said. "She'd rather live at home, of course, but she's eighty-four and her eyesight is getting worse."

"Eighty-four and still going strong. Do you realize only a century ago, you and I at our age would practically be dead?"

With painfully penetrating eyes he pinned her and stated: "Joanna, we've got a lot of years ahead of us. Let's make them good ones, okay?"

Joanna saw tears in his eyes and went over to give him a hug. She meant it in a sympathetic, apologetic way, but Brian took it as more. He held her tight, his hands wandering, and she jerked away.

Brian grabbed the cutting board and threw the diced onions into pot. The sizzling as they hit the hot oil startled Joanna and she winced. He stirred them once, then threw the wooden spoon down on the stove and stormed into his office, slamming the door behind him. Even with the radio on, and the sounds of cooking, the kitchen became oppressively still.

When the pasta was al dente, she knocked on the office

door to tell Brian dinner was ready. They dished out plates for themselves. Brian sat at the tiny table and spread a newspaper out to read, essentially uninviting her to dinner. She sat on the couch with a magazine, reading the same paragraph over and over.

Her cell phone buzzed indicating a text message: "Looking forward to lunch on Monday." Her heart jumped, and her face flushed. She also admired Michael's diplomacy.

Somehow they made it to bedtime, after she loaded the dishwasher and they tiptoed around one another, the small apartment never feeling smaller. Then came the moment she was dreading: she went to the closet and pulled out sheets and a blanket. Brian stared at her. She said, "I'm... I thought I'd...sleep on the couch."

He went into their bedroom and closed the door, as close as he could get to a slam without actually slamming it.

Later, on the couch, Joanna tried to get comfortable. Her pillow was in the bedroom and she couldn't face Brian again, so she made do with a not very comfortable couch pillow. She tried to sleep but her mind kept racing. Part of her wanted to comfort Brian but knew he wouldn't let her, and knew she shouldn't try. She wanted to be his friend. He wanted her to be his wife. He wouldn't want to be comforted by the person who just inflicted the biggest pain he'd ever experienced, not if the comfort was a bandage soon to be ripped off. She wanted to call Michael but felt too guilty to allow herself the luxury of his voice. She needed to experience this pain, as if somehow it would lessen Brian's.

Eventually she passed out, with Archie curled asleep in back of her knees. She didn't hear Brian leave the apartment early the next morning. He left her a note: *"I'll be back late afternoon."*

Waking up, her first thought was to call Michael, which made her already soaring level of self-hatred even higher. Maybe a bath would lessen how skuzzy she felt. Soaking in the hot water did make her feel a little better. When she got out, and glimpsed the clock, she was shocked to see almost an hour had passed. First thing she did was check her cell phone. There was a text message from Michael: "I miss you already." She missed him, too, with all her heart and soul, but she didn't text or call him back. She called her sister.

***

They met at a coffee shop around the corner from Joanna's apartment. Cynthia walked in to see her sister nursing a cup of coffee, hands cradling it as if for warmth even though it was a hot day. Joanna looked up, so pathetic and forlorn, Cynthia bent down to give her a hug. "God. You look awful, Jo." Cynthia ordered an iced coffee at the counter and brought it over to the table. "What's going on?"

"Brian...knows about Michael. He's so hurt and angry and it's all my fault."

"Wow. What are you going to do?"

Joanna snapped, "I don't know!" and a few patrons turned towards them. More gently then, "I'm sorry. I just don't know."

After a pause during which they both sipped their drinks, Cynthia said, "Have you entered the fully unfaithful stage?" Joanna nodded. "And?"

"And what?"

"How was it?" Joanna couldn't answer, but color filled her cheeks. Cynthia said, "I see. I'm happy for you, sort of. But are you sure this isn't just about being with someone new?" Joanna nodded. "You've been married to Brian a long time. You can't maintain that early excitement forever. That *if I don't see him soon I'll die* feeling like at the beginning of a relationship."

"I never felt that way with Brian."

"I know! I told you not to marry him, remember?"

"I've never felt that way about anyone before."

"Never? Are you talking about love or sex? "

Joanna shook her head. "I'm not sure I can split those things apart."

"Don't kid yourself that you need love for great sex. In fact sometimes it's just the opposite."

"Well, they came wrapped together in a package for me."

"I guess you've made your decision then."

"No! I haven't. I can't. Brian and I have been together so long. We went into this whole thing as a team. We knew what we were getting into. We made a pact."

"They say one out of two pacts end in divorce."

"He used to go to the store and buy tampons for me, for Christ's sake!" Joanna said, standing up to bring her cup to the counter.

Cynthia rose, too, and followed her sister. Outside they walked slowly. "But you don't need tampons any more, Jo."

Joanna smiled despite everything. Her sister was nothing if not practical. "You know what I mean."

"What if Brian had fallen in love with someone and wanted to leave you."

"I can't play the What If game right now."

"The important thing is being happy. You just get one life. And it's pretty short."

"But isn't that selfish?"

"If you don't think of you, who will?" Cynthia thought for a few moments. "Can't you keep seeing Michael and live with Brian, and give it all some time? You might change your mind."

"No, we're not French or in the Bloomsbury group. Oh, this is so ridiculous! Me dealing with two men. I couldn't get a date for the high school prom. You had boys practically killing themselves over you and I couldn't give my virginity away."

"You coulda been a great nun."

"I almost wish I could move to Cape May and forget about Brian and Michael. It's too much, to have two hearts in my hands, knowing I'm going to drop one."

"What about your heart?"

"It's already broken, either way."

**

The apartment was once again empty. Even though nothing had been resolved, Joanna felt a little better after talking with her sister. As the younger sister of a pushy know-it-all, Joanna secretly wished Cynthia would simply take control. Then she wouldn't have to think any more.

She looked around the apartment. There was nothing left for her to put away, dust, vacuum, clean out, or bring to a donation center. All her official work had been completed in overtime the week before. It was too early to put chicken in the oven for dinner. After standing motionless for a long minute trying to remember how to spend a Sunday at home, she gave up and went into the bedroom to take a nap. Seeing the bed, with her side untouched and Brian's pillow all the way on the left side, it hit her again how hard this must be for him. No, they had never had a deeply physical relationship, but they were a couple. Until Michael came along, she would've said that she was satisfied enough. Now it seemed like the past forty years were just a waste of time until she met him. How could she give that up?

Unable to sleep in that bed, she grabbed her pillow and sat on the couch with one of her books about managing a bed and breakfast. Maybe if she could move on with other frontiers, this broken part of her life would magically fix itself.

The phone rang. Joanna didn't recognize the caller ID so she let the machine answer it. "Hi, Ms. Matthews this is Ruth Halemayer from Cape May Realty. I wanted to talk to you about one of the houses you saw."

The Tea & Scones. It all seemed a lifetime ago. Astonishing how much things can change in such a short time. Joanna blanked out and missed some of the message. "…eager to sell and has an offer I think you'd like to hear."

Knowing she wouldn't be able to sleep or read anyway, Joanna returned the phone call. "Hi, Ruth, I just got your message. What's happening?"

"Remember the Tea & Scones? With the stained glass in the front door? The owners are cutting the price by $25,000. And they're willing to include most of the furniture, minus a handful of family pieces, in the selling price."

"Really? Do you know why?"

"They're older and want to move closer to their grandchildren on the west coast. I know you had some reservations about the place." Joanna smiled, remembering Michael advising her to curb her enthusiasm. She instantly saw him in the Tea & Scones surrounded by Victoriana, the color of his shirt, his eyes, everything. Even sitting here in her own living room she could smell him, hear his voice, feel the touch of his hand. A lump formed in her throat, as painful as if real thumbs were pressing against her esophagus. "Ms. Matthews?" she heard. "Ms. Matthews, are you still there?"

Joanna swallowed painfully. "Yes."

"I was saying, I wondered if you and your husband are still interested."

"I am, but things are kind of up in the air right now." Joanna rolled her eyes at her own understatement. "Can I call you in the next few days?"

"Of course. But I should tell you someone else is seeing the house on Wednesday. Call me sooner rather than later, if you're really interested, okay?"

"Thanks. Bye."

The apartment was quiet again. Joanna closed her eyes and pictured herself walking through the front door of the Tea & Scones. Dropping the mail onto the small table by the window. Reaching out to adjust a knickknack. Straightening a picture hanging on the wall. Removing a dead leaf from a plant. Her sandaled foot smoothing a bump in the rug. Both hands sliding a chair back two inches. Michael sitting in one of the other chairs. He put his book down, looked up at her with a sad smile and reached out his hand. She took it and he pulled her onto his lap. She unbuttoned her blouse, feeling she'd die if he didn't touch her. They kissed and fondled until Archie jumped on her lap and woke her up.

The clock read 2:45. Brian would be coming home, probably hoping to put an end to the torture of not knowing what was happening in his life. He was an accountant, a plan-ahead kind of man. It was bad enough she was thinking of uprooting him from his beloved Manhattan to the wilds of southern New Jersey. Now instead she might leave him for a man she'd known how many days?

All too soon, Brian's key was in the door. Joanna's heart beat faster out of a sort of fear, not for the romantic excitement she'd felt so recently with Michael. The thought of dropping dead from a heart attack wasn't so unpleasant at this very moment. Her thoughts quickly returned to Michael, not Brian, as she imagined herself dying in his arms, Camille-style, looking up into his captivating blue eyes. The ridiculously dramatic vision made her smile, which is what Brian saw when he walked in.

"A smile. That's been rare," he said in a quiet, tired voice.

"Hi." She paused. "You okay?"

"No. I've been wandering around all day."

"Oh?"

"I swam at the gym. Bought two tax deductible books at Barnes & Noble, looked at new jazz CDs. Went to lunch with Frank. To talk."

"How is he?"

"Helpful. Gave me some perspective. About us."

"Wow. I didn't know you two talked about real stuff."

"Not usually. Had to though. Don't want an ulcer." He pulled off his sweaty T-shirt, threw it onto a chair, and walked into the kitchen for a glass of water. She wanted to say something, but couldn't face hearing his reply to any of her possible sentences. Brian continued. "Bottom line, he said you were worth forgiving, and waiting for."

"He did?"

"Yes. You can do no wrong in his eyes. He's always had a crush on you."

"Really?"

"God, Jo, you are the least self-aware woman I've ever met." He paused. "And as I've had a crush on you since the day we met, I agree with him."

Joanna was stunned into silence.

He continued, "After twenty years of marriage, anyone could get bored. Need a change." When she didn't answer he continued. "I know you didn't go looking for this or anything."

She shook her head.

"Things happen."

She nodded.

"Do you…have any idea when things might…get back to normal? I may be able to get through this if I know…a decision is…there's…"

"I understand."

"Just…soon, Jo, okay? Maybe our marriage started in an unconventional way, but I love you. And I'd do anything to make you happy again."

"Please stop, Brian. You're making me feel even worse."

"Good. I'd hate to feel this rotten alone. Just, please, end this soon. I don't think I can stand it much longer, okay?"

They ate dinner together, trying to make polite conversation. It was awkward, but they got through it. Her hands shook, and he noticed, but didn't say anything. After dinner he said, "Let's watch a movie or something."

"I'll put on my pajamas." She went into their bedroom and changed. She heard a strange voice in the living room and opened the door. Brian was going through the messages on the answering machine.

"Hey, Jo, what about this house?"

She walked out of the bedroom. "The Tea & Scones. You saw the outside of it, remember?"

"You interested?"

"Yes."

He walked over to her and lightly caressed her arm. "Maybe we need to do this? Maybe you need this change?"

"Maybe."

"Listen. I'll do whatever's best for you, now." He gulped, "I can't lose you."

There was no way to reply to that.

Later that night, Joanna sat on the couch with Brian and managed to stay awake during some of the movie they watched. If she were asked the next day what that movie was, she wouldn't have been able to answer. It was just time-filler until she could close her eyes and put an end to an awful day.

She did fall asleep on the couch, about halfway into the film. Brian watched the rest of the movie alone, numbing his pain with soda and potato chips. Then he went into their bedroom to sleep, alone.

When she heard the bedroom door shut, she was suddenly wide awake. It was the start of the longest night of her life. Every molecule in her missed Michael, and wanted him. She'd see him tomorrow at lunch. They had made the date. But if she saw Michael tomorrow she might not be able to leave him again. But if she stayed with Brian right now she'd end up resenting and hating him. She needed to get away, to try and think without their influence.

***

She was awake and resigned the next morning. If her personal life was a disaster and seemingly beyond her control—or more realistically too much in her control—at least she could continue to move forward with her Cape May dreams.

The bedroom door opened and Brian emerged, with puffy eyes, looking as if he hadn't slept at all. She shoved down the guilt and said: "How would you feel if I called Cynthia today and drove with her to Cape May, and got her opinion of the house?"

Brian saw a glimpse of light at the end of his dark tunnel. "That's a good idea. You want me to come?"

"No. I've stopped you from working enough already. And I need some time away from things. You know?"

"Yeah."

"Brian, I'm still…I haven't…"

He put his hands on her waist, "I know."

"I'll call my boss and see if I can take a few days off." He made a move to kiss her and she gave him a peck. "I haven't brushed my teeth."

Joanna called her boss, asked for, and got, the week off. Her haggard voice undoubtedly fed her bosses' belief that she needed vacation time, even on such short notice.

Her possibly skewed thinking was that if she didn't go to work, she wouldn't take a lunch hour, and if she didn't have a lunch hour, she couldn't go to Excelsiors. If she stayed away from Michael, she could try to figure things out logically.

After a quick call to the realtor, and then Cynthia, everything was in motion. Joanna picked up the phone again to call Michael, but Brian came in the room and she quickly put it away.

She began packing for a few days in Cape May. Keep moving. Make plans. If she kept moving maybe she wouldn't get caught.

Brian went back in his office. Joanna took out her phone. Again. She tried to push the numbers, but just couldn't move. She couldn't bear hearing Michael's voice. How unforgivable would it be to send a text message? By the time she punched a few feeble words, and then deleted them, and then tried again, Brian came back into the bedroom. He sat on the bed next to the open suitcase. "How's it going?"

She continued packing. "Good. I'm picking Cynthia up at 11:30. Her assistant will run the shop while we're away. We're looking at the house sometime after four. Ruth—the realtor—said she'd be free anytime after that. I'll call her when we get there."

"Um, where are you staying?"

"There's a little place not far outside Cape May." Tops, pajamas, and underwear went into her small suitcase. "It's less expensive than right in town."

They were quiet. "Jo," he started.

"Hmm?"

"He's not in Cape May now, is he?"

Joanna winced. "No. He's not." She didn't add he's here in Manhattan, and that he'd soon be hating her, waiting in Excelsiors realizing she wasn't showing up for lunch.

"Good," he said, and stood up. "I'm going back to work now. And Jo? I can't do this much longer. I don't know what's happening in my own life. Like I have no control over anything. I love you enough to give you some time to figure things out, but have a heart." And he left the room.

Joanna felt a horrible pang in her guts, because of Brian, and because she couldn't face calling Michael to tell him she wouldn't be meeting him. If she spoke to him, she'd have to see him, and if she saw him, her life as it was now would shatter into a million pieces. She wasn't ready for that.

She quickly thumbed in a text message to Michael. It wasn't enough, but nothing would be.

***

Michael woke up Monday feeling something wasn't right.

As was now his M.O., he woke up thinking of Joanna. As his eyes focused on the room around him, he tried to see it through her eyes. It was sparsely decorated, maybe too bare. He'd put more effort into the living room, which had tons of personality. The bedroom was just that: a room for a bed. The walls were white, the antique dresser was falling apart, and the carpet threadbare. He couldn't stop his hopeful mind from thinking of the future. If Joanna left Brian, she might move in. That was the main reason he was cleaning and thinning out the bookshelves, no matter how he lied to himself about other reasons. He was making room for

Joanna and her things. Just in case. He'd like her to decorate the bedroom any way she wanted. Whatever would make her happy. It struck him suddenly that he didn't know what type of furniture she liked, or how she lived in her apartment with Brian. Twenty years of living with her husband uptown. He wanted to imagine what she was doing right now, but couldn't place her in a bedroom or living room.

He imagined her standing on a chair, putting up curtains. The thought made him smile, and filled him with warmth, and not a small amount of lust. Later on, they could look for another, bigger apartment in Manhattan (if they could afford it) or, if she bought a bed and breakfast, he'd move to Cape May to be with her. Luckily, he loved Cape May and his work could be done anywhere, but he had to admit that if she wanted to move to the moon, he'd willingly go with her.

So why did he feel something was wrong? Because this was all so fast and so intense? The past few weeks were surreal, yet he'd never felt more centered and purposeful. Except for that possibility of having his heart broken permanently. That very real possibility. The potential loneliness ahead of him was too cavernous to even glance into.

He tried to dismiss his negative feelings, got ready, and arrived at the Excelsior at 11:45. There were knots in his stomach. Maybe he was just excited about seeing her again, but this felt different. Unpleasant. He found a comfortable seat in the hotel lobby and checked his watch frequently. By noon, when she wasn't walking through the doors, he got up and went outside, searching for her in the crowd. By 12:10

he took out his cell phone to call her. He'd forgotten to turn it on. He did, and called her at the office.

"Joanna Matthews's office," said a woman.

"Is she there?"

"No she's not coming in."

His phone buzzed, indicating he had a text message. "I'm a freelancer. She told me to call, about potential work."

"Oh, well, she's taking off the rest of the week. Do you want her voice mail?"

"No. No thank you." He hit the "End" button, and warily clicked all the necessary buttons to get to the waiting message.

Five words from the woman he loved: "I cant come. Im sorry."

CHAPTER 17

When Joanna pulled up to her sister's building, Cynthia was waiting with her luggage. Joanna popped the trunk. One of the doormen easily lifted the heavy suitcase into the car. After thanking the man, Cynthia got in and the sisters headed south.

"Are you ready to do this?" Cynthia said.

"I brought water bottles and fruit, and CDs. I think you'll love the house in person. You liked all the pictures on the website, right?"

"Yes, I think you've found a good one," Cynthia nodded. "I really meant are you ready to move?"

"Sure. I love Cape May."

"You don't sound excited."

"I brought some CDs," Joanna repeated, "in case there's nothing on NPR worth listening to."

Cynthia paused, then said, "Do you want to talk, Jo?"

"No. But thank you."

"You can't hold it in forever."

"Right now I have to. Can we just drive?" Joanna turned on the radio.

The one stop they made was for a bathroom break and a quick cup of coffee. While Cynthia browsed the magazine rack of the convenience shop, Joanna walked around, suddenly unable to sit still. Michael would've read her horrible text by now. Why hadn't she called and talked to him? She should've called him. Still striding around, she took out her cell, pushed the numbers of his cell phone and hit "Send," just as Cynthia walked up to her.

"Are you wearing a FitBit?"

Joanna terminated the call. "What?"

"You're pacing like you've got to reach 10,000 steps or die trying."

"Oh. No. Just antsy. You ready?"

She held up her purchases: "Mints and *Vogue*. Let's go. You drive."

***

Back in Manhattan, as Michael walked uptown, he tried to convince himself that this wasn't the end of everything. She just got scared, or maybe a relative died, or her cat was sick. Obviously she was going through her own hell, but she should've called him. He was angry.

His phone rang, but by the time he got to it the call was disconnected. He checked: it was from her. Should he call her back? No. The ball was in her court now. He'd give her some space, and try somehow not to let the hurt hobble him. Was it anger or hurt? Either way, it felt awful.

***

Cynthia thumbed through her magazine in the too quiet car. The vibes coming from the driver seat were spiky and uninviting. For Joanna, the drive was torture. It was as if her psyche had permanently recorded every single minute of her time with Michael. She saw herself on the bus with him, thought about him when she saw signs for the Atlantic City bus terminal, heard his voice talking about the court house, and the Lobster Hideaway. It was almost unbearable. She must've gasped or something because Cynthia said seemingly out of the blue, "Are you all right?"

They drove past the Welcome Center, and the store with the balloon-penis cards, and Captain Mey's Inn. When she saw Henry's, and the arcade, she began having trouble breathing. She had to pull over to the side of the road into a handicapped parking space.

"Jo! What's the matter? Are you sick?" Cynthia undid her seat belt so she could lean over and feel Joanna's head.

Joanna couldn't talk, so she just kept shaking her head.

"Breathe, honey, just breathe."

Some words came out: "I'm fine. I'll be fine."

Cynthia uncapped a water bottle. Joanna took a few gulps and slowly calmed down. Cynthia wet a paper towel and held it to her sister's head. "You feeling better?" Letting out a deep sigh and sinking back into the car seat, Cynthia said, "Ohmygosh, I thought you were having a heart attack. Don't do that again, okay?"

"I'll try not to."

"I was really scared."

"I'm sorry I scared you."

"I'll drive the rest of the way." Cynthia got out of the passenger seat and walked around to the driver's side while Joanna climbed over the gearshift column.

When Cynthia buckled herself in, Joanna told her, "I suddenly thought about you seeing the house and hating it, and yelling at me for dragging you down here." It was semi-true anyway.

"I'm not really that scary, am I?"

"Everything's a little scary right now. If you love the house, that's scary, too. There goes most of the money I have in the world."

"And Brian's money."

"See? That scares me, too."

"Let's go see the house. No matter what I think, it's your decision, and Brian's, if...if...Well, I don't know what the hell is going on inside you, and you won't talk to me, so, whatever."

Joanna answered by buckling her seatbelt.

"That's all I'm gonna get from you, huh?"

"Cynthia, drive. It's the next left."

Cynthia drove the few moments more to the Tea & Scones while Joanna tried to turn off her emotions. It didn't work. The physical pain of missing Michael grew when the car pulled into the driveway. The house once again was inviting, gorgeous, and Joanna's dream come to life. But he was there, everywhere, standing on the porch telling her to stop being enthusiastic, his warm breath hitting her ear and disturbing her. God, she had been in love with him already, and she hadn't even known.

Cynthia was out of the car and up the front steps before Joanna even managed to unbuckle her seat belt. Joanna took a deep breath, and got out to face the future. As she walked up the path, she said to Cynthia, "Do you want some time alone with the house or should I call Ruth the realtor. She's in town, waiting for our call."

"Give me some time and then call her." Cynthia checked out the roof with binoculars she'd brought. If she were buying the house herself she couldn't have been more thorough. She walked the perimeter, examining the windows, landscaping possibilities, backyard, parking area, everything outside the house. Then Joanna called Ruth.

While waiting, the sisters sat on the porch steps and talked. "It's a great house, Jo. Perfect location. Close enough to walk to the shops and beach, but a little off the beaten track. It offers people quiet, if they want quiet. I think if you're ready to handle everything, you should buy it."

"I think so, too," Joanna said, trying to sound enthused. She did adore the house and did want to buy it, but life in general was bleaker than it had ever been. Throwing herself into planning, seeing the house again, meeting with Ruth, it all was supposed to drown out her yearning for Michael and her guilt about Brian. But sitting on the porch, where she had stood with Michael, she was mourning his loss. It was as if he had died. But he wasn't dead. He was back there in Manhattan, probably in his apartment by now, wondering what the hell was going on.

"Joanna?"

Joanna jumped. "What?"

"Where are you? I've never seen you like this. Is it all because of him?"

Joanna nodded, stood up, and walked down the path, pretending to look for Ruth's car. While Cynthia remained on the porch, Joanna took out her cell phone and called Michael again.

He answered after two rings. "Hello."

"I...I'm sorry," was all she could manage.

"That's all I get?" She couldn't say anything. He continued, "What's going on?"

"I don't know." Joanna felt the tears coming, and the lump in her throat made it hard to talk. To make matters worse, Ruth arrived and was parking. "I beg you to forgive me for…everything. I can't stay on. I'm in Cape May, with my sister. We're looking at the Tea & Scones again. I think I'm going to buy it."

"Is Brian there?"

"No. I needed some distance from both of you. To think."

"You're buying a house with him, so you've made your decision, haven't you."

"Michael…"

Ruth was walking towards her, smiling so much that Joanna wanted to punch her in the face.

"Michael, I have to go," she said, but he had already disconnected the call. "Hello?" She felt paralyzed with grief, but Ruth started talking and selling, and rattling off percents and numbers and dates. Joanna walked into her future house, and something inside her clicked shut.

***

Joanna put a binder on the house. Over the years, Cynthia had bought antiques from and sold antiques to Cape May residents. She knew people who knew people in charge and somehow managed to get the Tea & Scones inspected within the week. It passed. Joanna and Cynthia decided to stay a few more days in rooms at a tiny bed and breakfast just outside town. The separate rooms prevented them from getting on each other's nerves.

One afternoon Cynthia walked into Joanna's room. "Dinner plans. I saw a rustic restaurant, near the water. I can't remember the name. Probably bad but fun food. Wait, I think it's a man's name. Harry's? Henry's?"

Joanna practically yelled, "No not there."

"Ooooookay."

"It's only four o'clock. I practically just finished lunch." She grabbed her sunglasses and headed out, saying, "I'm going for a walk. I'll be back in an hour."

Later they went to a diner. Joanna said, "I hope this place is okay?"

"It's fine. And Jo, I don't know what I said earlier..."

"I'm having breakfast for dinner. You?"

Cynthia nodded and pulled out a magazine to read. Joanna pretended to read. Not another word was uttered by either of them through the whole meal other than "Pass the salt."

When she was alone that night in her room, Joanna went to bed early, hoping to fall asleep quickly. It wasn't to be. Brain called to check on her, and a friend called to chat. The conversations were over quickly yet upset Joanna, probably because both times her cell buzzed she hoped it was Michael, even though she had no right to hope it was Michael.

The next morning, while waiting for various papers to be faxed by the sellers' lawyer, Joanna and Cynthia went for a walk on the beach. Joanna was covered in sunscreen plus long-sleeved white shirt and big hat, and Cynthia was wearing a tank top and absorbing as much sun as she possibly could.

Cynthia said, "You know, it's really nice here. Relaxing. I may come and visit you a lot."

"I'd like that." They continued walking.

Cynthia linked her arm through Joanna's. "You can visit me, too, during your off-season. We'll see some shows, go to exhibits."

"I'm glad to hear you still want to spend time with me. I know I haven't been a joy to be around."

"No, you've been a pain in the ass." Then quickly, "With reason, of course." There was another long pause. "As nice as this is, I don't know how anyone could give up a two-bedroom apartment in Manhattan."

"I don't want to live in New York any more. It's changed, and I've changed."

"What about Brian?"

"He'd stay in Manhattan until death do them part. In that apartment, too. He's lived there over thirty years. I was thinking..."

"What?"

"Brian should keep the apartment. Sublet it or something." Joanna stopped walking. "That's a good idea, Cynthia. I'm going to talk to him about it."

"What about the money you'd get for the apartment? Don't you need it in order to buy the house?"

"Not if I use more of my inheritance, and savings. I've been socking away my paycheck since I started looking at houses. I'm not saying it's a fiscally responsible thing to do, but it's better than making Brian give up his beloved Manhattan after what I've, if I," she stopped, staring off.

Cynthia said, "What?"

Joanna looked around toward the buildings. She saw the back of Morrow's and the wooden walkway and steps. "Michael and I kissed for the first time right here." With that, she turned and walked away, and Cynthia followed.

***

Everything that could be done in Cape May—the first steps on the tall house-buying ladder—was done. Before Joanna was ready, it was time to go home, and she was back in the car with Cynthia heading north to New York.

After an hour of quiet in the car, Cynthia took a chance and said, "This trip must've been painful for you."

"Hmm?"

"You know what I'm talking about, Joanna," she said, not caring if she got yelled at. "Michael."

"It was."

"It must've been romantic, meeting him like that."

"It was."

"Is it possible, Jo, that you got caught up in the drama of it all? Handsome stranger, beach, stars."

"Maybe."

"Any idea what your future entails?"

"No."

"Well, sis, I don't mean to be the cold, hard slap of reality, but you've just put a binder on an expensive house. Are you sure you want to be doing all this right now?"

"Cynthia, the only thing I know for sure is that I have to keep going forward. I want to move. I want that house. It's the only thing I have any control over."

"Okay, sister. I'm on your side, whichever it is."

The usually long ride was much too short this time. She dropped Cynthia off at her apartment.

"Jo, please call if you need me. I meant it: I'm on your side."

Before Joanna was ready, she was pulling into the garage under their building. Brian was upstairs waiting for her.

The elevator stopped at the eleventh floor and she stepped out, slowly heading towards her apartment. She'd only been away a few days, yet the hallway looked and felt different, as if some reality show had swooped in the minute she left, just those few days ago, and smashed walls, relocated doorways, painted, and changed lighting fixtures. She half expected some overly enthusiastic former athlete or C-list actor to jump out with a camera crew to document her flabbergasted reaction to the changes. She stopped, overcome by a memory of being seventeen and visiting a beloved third grade teacher back at the elementary school. She'd felt like a giant next to the kids. It seemed impossible that she had ever physically fit into the building, that it had ever been *her* school. That was how it felt now. That despite having lived on this floor, in this building, almost twenty years, she no longer belonged. Or even worse, she was no longer welcome.

The suddenly alien keys, on a bunch of key chains lovingly collected and added over the years, fell to the floor. When she picked them up they wouldn't stop shaking until she used one hand to steady the other. The door unlocked. Archie meowed, rubbing against her leg, and she was relieved to see him, something familiar, something warm and loving in this now strange atmosphere. At the sound of the door closing, Brian came out of his office. Although it was late afternoon, he was still in his robe. Her normally clean husband looked awful, his robe stained, and himself unwashed. He hadn't shaved. The apartment was a mess, too, with dirty dishes on the coffee table, DVDs out of their cases on the floor, and stuff all over.

She said, "You okay?"

His voice was raspy when he answered, as if he hadn't uttered a word since she left. "That's a stupid question, coming from you."

She just stood there, her throat tightening, her stomach a stormy mess. What could she say? Words couldn't repair this.

He waved his arm, trying to explain. "I shouldn't've said that."

"No. I understand."

"No, you don't. You can't. Jo, this whole time you've been away. I kept thinking of you, picturing you, seeing you with him. I've never done that before. I mean, I've never not trusted you."

She wanted to say she was sorry but those words sounded hollow even in her head. And they wouldn't have scratched the surface of his hurt.

He continued. "Now you're buying a house. But I don't know where we are, together. How we're gonna be. Making me leave New York and everything."

"No," she said, mobilized, taking off her jacket, and putting down her keys. "I had an idea. We should keep this apartment for you."

"How? Why?"

"You love it, and Manhattan, more than I do. This could be your pied-à-terre."

"And I'm supposed to be happy about this? Gee, it makes me feel really secure about our future together, Jo," he said, and went back into the office, but not before she saw he was crying.

***

After another night on the couch, Joanna lied and told Brian she had to go to work. She did plan on quitting in person later that day. First, she needed to go and talk to Michael. She left the apartment and headed toward the subway, in case somehow Brian was hanging out of the living room window watching her. Instead of going into the subway station, she walked downtown. A niche between two buildings offered a quiet place from which to call Michael. It smelled of urine and she didn't care. Would he even answer when he saw her caller ID? If he did answer, would it be to just curse at her and hang up? If he did that, she wouldn't blame him.

"Hi. It's Joanna." He didn't say anything. "Are you there?"

"Yes."

"Can I come see you?"

"Why?"

"Please. I need to talk to you." More silence. "Please."

"If you think you can manage to keep the appointment."

He hung up.

As Joanna walked there, her level of dread climbed. By the time she was in front of Michael's building, she was shaking and felt sick. He buzzed her in without saying a word.

This time he wasn't at his door waiting for her. It broke her heart to think she'd never see that look of love and desire in his eyes again. She walked slowly towards his apartment, swallowed hard, and knocked, wary of how he would greet her after what he'd said on the phone. He opened the door, silently, barely making eye contact at first. He ushered her in, and shut the door. They stood there.

Her eyes scanned his face. He looked older, all the hurt, anger, and rawness showing.

"You bought the house? You and Brian?" She nodded. "Why are you here? To rub salt in my wounds?"

"Please don't hate me," and tears came. "I couldn't take that."

"*You* can't take it?"

She started to talk, trying to say she wanted to explain, but froze. He kept his distance. Finally, "Oh God, I missed you." He said nothing. "Every minute I was in Cape May." Her thoughts were so scrambled. "Monday, about Monday, and everything…now…I'm…"

"That was pretty cruel, you not showing up."

"I didn't know what to do."

"And a text message?"

"I was wrong. I'm sorry."

"That doesn't help much. I didn't know, I still don't know, what the hell is going on with you. Us."

Some tears slid down her cheek, and she wiped them away quickly, embarrassed. He was the one who had the right to be crying. But still he handed her a tissue.

He said, "I've missed you. Even after what happened Monday. And this week of hell. Even while I was hating you, or close to hating you." There was an awkward pause. "Why are you here?"

She needed a moment before continuing. Looking around his spotless apartment, she said, trying to make any kind of conversation, "You must've gotten rid of a hundred books."

"Joanna."

"It looks great. Bigger."

"Joanna. Why are you here?"

"Could I have some tea?"

He put the kettle on, then said, "You look as unhappy as I feel. Go sit down." He brought over the cup and honey and put them on the table in front of her. Seeing the sad, resigned look in her eyes made Michael go cold. For some stupid reason he had still held some hope.

She spoke slowly and carefully, like a drunk trying not to sound drunk. "Meeting you was the most unexpected, wonderful thing that's ever happened to me."

His heart dropped. "But…"

"It's ripped my controlled established world apart." She lowered her eyes, unable to meet his. "At first I thought maybe it was just something physical. I didn't know I could feel so much, or want someone so much."

He quickly wiped away a tear. "If my heart is about to be broken, again, can I get a hug first?" He leaned forward to take her in his arms. That simple embrace, just being touched by him, set her spinning. They kissed. It started out lightly but they couldn't stop. They ended up horizontal on the couch, her leg wrapped around him, his hand sliding up her thigh.

Summoning every ounce of will power, she broke off the kiss, removed her leg, and stopped his hand, saying, "Michael, I can't."

They sat up.

"I can't leave him."

"You mean you don't want to leave him."

"Don't want to. Can't. I don't know. What's the difference. I know I want you. But there's more to it than that."

"Joanna, it's the twenty-first century. People get divorced."

"Other people."

"You're looking at one. Donna's happier. I'm better off for it, too."

"You said your divorce was awful, wasn't it? Donna's rejection was painful wasn't it?"

"Yes, it was painful, but I got over it and moved on. People do."

"But he doesn't deserve to be hurt like this. And I can't stand feeling this guilty. It's making me sick. He hates me. I need him to forgive me."

"I don't want him to forgive you if it means you have to spend the rest of your life with him." He reached for her cup of tea, spilling some of it. He sipped. "I can imagine what you've been going through. This hasn't been easy on me either. The guilt." He drank some more of her tea. "Oh, I'm sorry. Do you want another cup?" She shook her head. He continued: "But I think we're meant to be. From the moment you beat me at Scrabble."

She shook her head. "We didn't finish the game. You might've gotten another seven-letter word. Beaten the pants off me."

"That's incentive right there."

"Michael, I wish things could be different. I swear it. But I can't do it to Brian. I can't."

He sat forward, his clasped hands between his knees. "It's almost comical: all those pointless dates I've been on, thinking maybe by the third date I'll grow to like her, or maybe it's okay that she's not funny or we don't have much in common, or maybe we'll get closer if we sleep together. Then I meet you and bang! no doubts. So simple: I love you and I don't want to waste another second of my life away from you. One slight problem…"

"Brian." They were quiet for a long time. She took his hand and they just sat. Finally she attempted to explain: "You have to understand. To try to understand. He and I… we made a deal, to get married. I know couples fall out of love, but Brian and I weren't in love. It was a partnership. Somehow it feels more sacred and unbreakable. And he does love me now. And he hasn't done anything. He's the same as he was before. Before Cape May. I can't pull the rug out from under him. I can't do it to him."

"But you can do it to me?"

"I'd rather walk through fire. But don't you see I have to put him before you, or me. I owe it to him."

"Do you? I guess you do. You have history. He met you first."

She could barely whisper, "Imagine if you and I had met when we were younger."

"I was very different then. Cocky. Maybe you wouldn't have liked me. Although I was rather handsome."

"You're rather handsome now." She stood up, and picked up her purse. She couldn't cry. She had to be strong.

"I wish we could've gone for another walk in the park," his voice was raspy, "or sat at a restaurant together, just one more time."

She said, "I wish we could've made love one more time."

"I would've said that, but I didn't want you to think I love you just for your body." He tried to smile, so did she, but they failed. "Joanna, isn't there something I can say to make you…can't you…wait…a month…" She shook her head.

"But I can see the wonderful life we could have together. Why can't you?"

"It wouldn't be wonderful. I'd be wracked with guilt. It would spoil what we've had. And that might be even worse than this."

His voice cracked. "Nothing could be worse than this. Not seeing you again? I *like* you. God that sounds stupid. But couldn't we have lunch every once in a while? Just talk?"

She shook her head. "Michael, the truth is, I'm a weakling. I couldn't see you without touching you, and wanting to be with you. And I'm a coward because the pain of missing you is easier for me to face then my conscience. At least it's me hurting and not Brian."

"I'm hurting, too." He was immobilized on the couch.

"I know."

"Please don't leave me, Joanna," Michael said. "Don't end this." He stood up and she ran into his arms. They hugged and kissed goodbye until she pulled away and ran out the door.

***

Joanna walked home. She couldn't face the office. She was quitting anyway, so what difference did it make. What difference did anything make.

When she closed the apartment door, Archie greeted her and she picked him up. He was purring, happy to see her, and it was a small comfort. Brian came out of his office holding some papers and looking even worse than before.

"Why are you here?"

"I didn't go to work," she said.

"Why? Are you sick?"

"No. Not sick. I'll go in tomorrow to talk to my boss."

Brian waited.

Archie jumped out of her arms. "Brian, I'm asking you to forgive me…"

"Are you coming back? Coming home?"

She had prepared a speech of contrition, walking to the apartment from Michael's, but all she could do was nod. He ran over to hug her.

"Oh, Jo," he smiled, and cried, and kissed her. She barely responded, just managing to lift her arms to embrace him. "It's good to have you home. I'll fix things. I'll try harder."

"Brian, I should be saying all this to you. I'm sorry for everything."

"No. Stop…"

"But none of this was your fault."

"Let's just move on from here then. Back to the way things were. No. Better! I'll move to Cape May with you, and try to settle in and help you run the bed and breakfast, and things'll be better. Better."

She nodded. "I may need some time."

"Whatever you need. I understand. I'm so happy you're back."

"I'll make us something to eat."

"No! Let me take you out to lunch. To celebrate."

"Please, Brian. Let me…" she couldn't finish. She walked into the kitchen and began preparations for her chicken salad. She was thinking about Michael but forced herself to stop. She couldn't think about him. Not yet, anyway. That was a luxury she might allow herself later.

CHAPTER 18

In the following weeks, Joanna began her separation from New York. She (happily) quit her job. In reality, she could've continued working, but she hated it and wanted to sever ties as early as possible. Besides, every time the phone rang at work she hoped it was Michael, and was destroyed when it wasn't. She signed documents with her lawyers, with the realtors, with the banks, and made frequent trips to Cape May, some of which weren't absolutely necessary. Anything to keep moving, to keep afloat, to not give her mind time to remember. Brian seemed relieved. Even though Joanna wasn't back one-hundred percent, she was moving forward with their life together.

Nights were especially hard for her, sleeping in the same bed with someone who felt like a stranger. He'd made a few physical overtures—cuddling in bed, hugging her from behind while she washed dishes—and she wasn't receptive to his touch. He didn't push, for which she was grateful, and he just seemed happy to have her home.

One afternoon, lazing in their apartment, she said, "Don't you want to come to Cape May and see the inside of the house you're going to be living in?"

"You say you've done your research, and you say the house is fine, so I'm sure you think it's fine. I'll give up my semi-view of the trees of Central Park for a real view of the ocean. That should be nice."

"It's a great view."

"I do admit I am leery about getting rid of this apartment, after all these years. But I'll just have to satisfy myself with more space, walks on the beach, and sex with you in an antique bed."

"What about my idea, you know, about you holding on to the apartment," she said. "If Cape May ends up boring you, you could use this apartment as an office or weekend retreat. Or if things with the inn don't work out we could move back."

"It's not a bad idea. But don't you need the money from the sale of my apartment for your B&B?"

Joanna ignored Brian's highly specific use of pronouns and said, "We can swing it. It'll take most of my inheritance, but we can have a rental income from subletting at some point. If we need more, there's always our friendly loan-sharking bank."

A week later, they had a quiet dinner during which both of them read. Brian volunteered to clean up the kitchen and living room before they settled in for the evening with some TV, and Joanna went into the bedroom to put on her pajamas. Reaching into her bedside table for some lip balm, the first thing her hand touched was the lighthouse keychain that she and Michael picked out at the arcade in Cape May. All her careful shoring up over the past weeks collapsed. She burst into tears, rocking herself and sobbing into her pillow so that Brian wouldn't hear her. She stopped crying long enough to shout to Brian in the kitchen, "I'm taking a quick shower." She stumbled into the bathroom, climbed into a hot shower and cried. When she couldn't cry any more, she dried off, put on her pajamas, and joined Brian in the living room.

If he noticed how washed out and quiet she was on the couch next to him, he didn't say anything. They drank wine and watched a movie. That became their nightly routine when they were both home.

Hours passed. Days passed. Weeks passed.

Now she was spending too much time at home, and wished she *hadn't* quit her job so early in the moving process. There were constant delays. The previous owners' representative took weeks choosing and removing the pieces of furniture they wanted shipped to them. One of the items in question was a huge sideboard that had been anchored to the wall. When it was removed part of the wall came with it. Joanna's lawyers wanted the owners to pay for the repair. The owners blamed the workers who removed the piece; the workers blamed the owners for doing a bad installation in the first place. The owners said a previous owner had installed the sideboard and that it wasn't their fault. It took weeks, into almost a month's worth of faxes and phone calls back and forth for it all to be worked out.

With no job to go to and still not at ease spending time with Brian in the apartment, exercise became an escape, an excuse to get out of the house. She walked for hours around the city and spent a lot of time in Central Park. She tried not to look at passersby, afraid she'd see Michael. If she saw someone his height or with his hair color, or someone a distance away wearing a blue baseball cap or sunglasses, her heart pounded. She switched from walking in Central Park to taking yoga classes, going two or three times a week.

Another month passed. She kept waiting to return to normal, and at one awful point realized that this was her new normal.

The only thing constant is change.

Although her days and life now revolved around the Tea & Scones, whether she was in New York or Cape May, Brian never asked a single question about the town or the house. He didn't want to talk about Cape May, and all she was involved in had to do with Cape May. The apartment was very quiet.

Brian was different, occasionally snappy, and she felt it was to be expected. She'd cheated on him, he forgave her. That had to come with a price tag. He'd say, "Frank invited us to dinner. I picked that new Thai place on Amsterdam. You'll find something." Or "I'm binge watching *Game of Thrones* this weekend." It was hardly abusive behavior but he frequently left her out of the decision process. If he wanted to go to movies, he picked the movie and the time and she said yes. If he wanted to have friends over, she said yes, and she shopped and cooked dinner and chatted as though things were the same as before.

They watched a lot of documentaries of Brian's choosing, usually about World War II or sports or politics or crime. Joanna didn't care much one way or another. One particular night, Brian brought home a movie from the library. An erotic romance. He opened a bottle of wine and poured her a rather large amount. They settled in to watch. The movie took place during World War II. A beautiful French resistance fighter and wounded American soldier could no longer deny their passion. Every kiss and caress made Joanna think of being in Michael's tiny bedroom, that one time. Before Michael she'd go months without even thinking about sex. Now, her body seemed sex-starved, throbbing and full and aching. The movie wasn't helping.

The foreign film had several fairly graphic sex scenes. They got through the first without incident. The second one was affecting Brian, as evidenced by his erection, visible under his lightweight pajamas. He moved closer, and put his arm around her. A peeping tom would have thought they were nervous teenagers on a first date. With her brain fuzzied by the glass of wine that Brian kept topping off, and her body demanding attention, Joanna figured she might as well let Brian get on with it. They hadn't had sex since that night in the Manor Rose months ago. They'd hardly kissed since she'd returned to him. He kissed her, she tried to kiss him back, but her body shut down, like a switch had been flipped. His hands wandered and her body shrank from his touch. She kept backing away until she was inching up the arm of the couch.

"Joanna, come on. It's been a long time." His hand stroked her arm. "Honey, try." He kissed her again and she tried to respond, but froze. He moved away from her. "Shit."

"I'm sorry, I'm tired," was all she could come up with. There was no way to explain to Brian, to anyone, that it felt like she was cheating on the man she loved.

"You're always tired." A pause. "What's going on?" She shrugged. "Are you still seeing him?"

"No!"

"Then what?"

She shook her head, afraid of saying something hurtful.

He continued, "Was he so much better in bed than me?" When he slurred it, "Wazzhe so muss beddrnbed th'me?" she realized that he'd been drinking too much, too.

"I don't want to talk about this."

"Tough. I do."

Suddenly she felt unpleasantly sober, and it scared her on many levels.

Brian continued, "I've been as understanding as possible."

She just nodded once, blowing her nose and unable to say anything. What was there to say? He was right on all counts.

"I don't wanna sexless marriage. Do you?" It came out "sezlish" but of course she understood. "I can't help being boring, same old me." His voice got louder. "I'm sure it was hot, screwing some stranger you picked up on vacation. Especially after our boring sex life."

"No..."

He paced in the living room, getting more upset, and seemingly more sober, with each turn. "It's your fault, too, you know. Our sex life. Your parents really fucked you up. Maybe if you'd've done it with me more than four times a year..."

She was shaking her head and started to say something but he interrupted, "And I'm such an idiot. I even gave you the go-ahead. I figured if you fucked him you'd get it out of your system."

"Please stop."

"Oh, is that too strong a word for genteel little you? That's all it was, Joanna. Admit it."

"It wasn't about sex, Brian."

"You're such a liar. Of course it was. You don't even know him."

"That's not true."

"And you're full of shit, Jo. It was all about sex. You're just ashamed to admit it."

"No!"

"Well you should be ashamed. I thought it was men who couldn't keep it in their pants. But you think I haven't wanted to bang half the women in this city?" She didn't reply. "You wanted to sleep with someone who wasn't me. You just wanted to get laid."

"That's not true! I love him!"

Brian stopped pacing mid-turn. She hated herself the second the words came out. His face went white, and she knew she had just rebroken his heart, this time permanently. She said, "I didn't mean to throw that at you…"

He yelled, "Just stop! Shut up." He walked into the bedroom and she said, "Oh, Brian, I'm sorry. I'm so sorry," as he slammed the door.

She stood outside the closed door and started shaking. She couldn't move. She was exactly in the same spot when, a few minutes later, he came out of the bedroom with a backpack. "I'm through," he said, wiping his cheeks with the cuff of his shirt. "Be out of here by tomorrow at noon. This is *my* apartment."

And he walked out the front door, slamming it behind him.

Joanna was still. The tears flowed but she didn't wipe them or move. When she could move she picked up her phone. "I need you. Brian's left me. Please come."

***

Cynthia let herself in with the set of keys she had used twice in two decades: once to feed Archie when the cat sitter bailed out, and once when Brian was away on business and

Joanna had food poisoning and couldn't leave the bathroom to open the front door.

Joanna was curled up on the couch, quiet and still, with a blanket around her legs. Cynthia sat and held her. They didn't talk for a long time. When Joanna reached for her glass of wine, Cynthia moved it away. "That won't help anything. And it looks like you've had enough. That's all we need now: you becoming an alcoholic."

"He left me. And I deserve to be left."

"What happened?"

"He wanted to, and I couldn't."

"I'd guess it was about more than just that."

"He's throwing me out. Cynthia, can I stay with you tonight?"

"Yes, of course. Let's get your stuff."

Joanna sat like a statue and watched as Cynthia packed two suitcases for her, and filled Archie's food bowl. Then they left. With Joanna still in her pajamas, they took a cab to Cynthia's apartment. Within half an hour, Joanna was asleep in her sister's guest bedroom.

The next morning, Joanna had every sort of hangover —physical, emotional, spiritual. She couldn't look in the mirror when she brushed her teeth in Cynthia's elegant aubergine bathroom. The world was unfriendly and Joanna wanted to go back to bed, forever. The smell of coffee and toast helped a little, as she brushed her hair and tried to look presentable before entering Cynthia's immaculate kitchen.

Cynthia said, scrambling eggs. "How are you?"

"Breathing," she said, heading towards the coffee machine. "I think that's as good as it'll get today."

"Sit down. The way you're shaking I'd better pour your coffee."

Joanna pulled out and sat on the posh chair. "Smells good."

"I want you alert so we can talk."

"About nothing important, please."

"We have to talk about one thing. Do you still want to move to Cape May and buy the Tea & Scones? I called my lawyer this morning. He can try to get you out of the deal if we act quickly, but it'll cost you."

"No! I have to buy it, and move. I love the house. That I'm sure of. But I'm not sure about the money…I'm not sure…about…"

"And your love life?"

"I don't have one."

"What about Michael?"

"No. It's over. I've hurt him too much. I've ruined Brian's life, too. I'm toxic."

"Oh, stop it, Joanna! Things are bad enough. Don't wallow."

"Cynthia, I just want to get out of here. I hate me here. And I know enough to know I can't live the rest of my life hating myself."

"You're sure about moving. You're not just running away?"

"I'm running *to* something. I've got to make a life for myself, somewhere. Yes, I'm one-hundred percent sure about moving. I'll adjust, rethink. I'll use the rest of my inheritance, and retirement money, if necessary. If I have to, I'll get another loan."

"No. Bad plan. You need to keep something in the bank, for emergencies, and retirement. It's not like a B&B is going to rake in the money. You ready to hear my idea?" Joanna nodded. "I'll make a deal with you: I'll lend you the money, and you'll pay me back with interest. It'll be less than any bank would charge you."

"Cynthia, are you sure?"

"I loved that house, too. If I ever lose my mind and leave New York, I'll have a home."

"Really?" Joanna whimpered.

"Yes. You know I'm loaded. The shop is thriving. We're probably going to expand, or open another one in Tribeca. Maybe in Cape May someday. But even though I'm your sister, we'll treat this as a business deal, and sign papers, and they'll be legal and binding, okay?"

"Yes. I don't know how to thank you."

"Get better, Jo. You're my only family. That'll be enough. You being sane again."

"I can't promise anything. It's not that easy."

"I know. First you'll eat my delicious breakfast, then I'll contact Brian and find out when he won't be there so we can move you out."

"Be nice to him, please. He didn't deserve any of this, you know."

"I know, and I'll continue to be like a sister to him. And honestly? He deserves someone who loves him. I don't think you ever have. I told you not to marry him."

"Please don't kick me when I'm down."

"I don't mean to kick you, honey, but if we're starting a business together..."

"No," Joanna interrupted. "This is my business. You'll be a silent partner with an open wallet, or I'll take my business elsewhere."

Cynthia was surprised and silenced.

Joanna downed her coffee. "I've worked hard towards this, and it's everything now. My whole life. I have to finally do something right."

"I'm impressed." Cynthia smiled, "You deserve more coffee."

CHAPTER 19

In stages, Cynthia and Joanna went to Brian's apartment and packed up Joanna's possessions. They were careful to adhere to the schedule Brian set. Even so, anytime Joanna heard the elevator doors open, she tensed, thinking Brian might walk in any minute. Part of her wanted to see him, to see if he was okay. A larger part was afraid of seeing him, not ready to face his hatred. Would she ever be? Would he ever not hate her? She needn't have worried: he never showed up. And every time he didn't show up, she was sad, and missed him, his friendship, their history. She was mourning the death of their life together. Or perhaps more accurately, her assassination of their life together.

One night, Cynthia said, "Want to go see a play? Before you move away from the theater capital of the world?"

"Maybe not tonight."

"Want to call Michael and invite him over for a glass of wine?"

Joanna paled, and opened and closed her mouth, unable to answer.

"Thought I'd try. Want to play Scrabble?" Joanna flinched and again didn't say anything. Cynthia tilted her head like a quizzical dog, "Okay, there's something I don't understand, but I'm guessing that's a 'no'."

Joanna nodded. "Something else? Boggle? Cards?"

The sisters half-heartedly played Gin Rummy and split a bottle of wine. Cynthia was quiet and tried to ooze receptiveness, kindness, nonjudgmentalness. She basically tried to look like a big pair of ears. That, plus the wine, loosened Joanna's tongue: "Can I tell you something?"

"Sure."

"I don't want to hear what you think. I don't want advice. I just want to get this out in the open, so maybe you'll understand more."

Cynthia nodded.

"Whether you think I am or not, I'm damaged. I feel damaged. For too many reasons for me to ever explain to you. Not good enough. Certainly not good enough for him. I can't ask or expect someone...*him*...to...to love me if I don't love myself. I think part of me couldn't respect Brian when I realized he loved me." She took another sip of wine. "People expect more from someone they love. If we, if Michael and I tried to make a life together, eventually I'd mess it up, and he'd see the real me, and my inner demons, and they'd rip him apart, and I couldn't take that. Ending it now, as awful as it is, is the better way."

Cynthia, true to her word, didn't say anything, and just hugged her sister, for a long time.

***

Too many boxes later, they hired a moving company to haul everything to a storage facility about two miles from the Tea & Scones. Although the boxes could've fit in the inn's large unfinished basement, Joanna wanted the house as empty as possible for ease of renovations and repairs.

In stages, too, the sisters drove more precious or breakable items down to Cape May. Joanna was taking only a few pieces of furniture from the apartment. The house in

Cape May was furnished, and anyway Joanna didn't want to unsettle Brian's apartment any more than necessary—he deserved as little upheaval as possible. Strange: she had lived there twenty years and it was still "Brian's apartment." That said a lot about her, or their marriage.

Life appeared normal from the outside. Joanna woke up, did things during the day, ate, went to sleep, and started the whole process over again. She was on automatic pilot. The immense changes, and losses—her husband, her apartment, her city, even her job—numbed her, but she kept moving forward. It helped that she nurtured the newly discovered businesswoman inside of her. Absolutely determined to make her inn a success, she read about the hospitality industry, subscribing to *Inns Magazine, Business &B&Bs*, and took online courses. She learned about head hunting, interviewing, and managing employees. Studied books on architecture, landscaping, and interior design. She channeled all her energy into the Tea & Scones.

When thoughts of Michael came, and they still did, all the time, she stuffed them down. They hurt too much and if she let them they'd ruin her hard-won progress.

The overall plan was to get Joanna's living space on the top floor of the Tea & Scones in order, so she could move in and supervise the work being done in the rest of the house. Until her space was finished, she rented a room on the outskirts of Cape May, where it was much cheaper. She visited Cynthia every other weekend, staying at her apartment in Manhattan. When in Cape May, she continued her new exercise regime and every morning walked the two miles from her hotel to the Tea & Scones. She got up early, and tried breakfast at a different restaurant, café, or even fast food place. Her "Places to Eat" notebook was coming along. Staying and working in Cape May, she was starting to feel like a new person. The slower pace suited her.

One afternoon, sitting in a coffee shop nursing a latte, Joanna looked up to see a woman walking towards her. "You're Joanna, aren't you?"

"Yes," it took Joanna only a moment to recognize the well-groomed woman. It was the tour guide at the Woodline estate. "Madeleine, how are you?"

"Doing well. You?"

"I live here now. I own..."

Madeleine finished the sentence, "the Tea & Scones. Yes, Michael told me." The walls blocking out thoughts of Michael immediately crumbled. A thousand questions deluged Joanna's mind, but she didn't ask any. She couldn't say anything. There was an awkward pause, then Madeleine continued. "Every time we talk on the phone he asks if I've seen you."

"Oh?" Joanna's face was burning.

"Any message for him? I'll probably be talking to him tonight."

Hadn't Michael told Madeleine that it was over between them? Joanna stood up with her latte and looked at her watch. "No. No message."

Madeleine looked at Joanna as if she had three heads. "Michael did tell you we were finished long ago, didn't he?"

Joanna nodded.

"You seem uncomfortable with me. I thought maybe that was why."

Joanna had no reply.

Madeleine continued, "You know he's a great guy, yes?"

"Yes."

"And they come around as often as unicorns?"

Joanna smiled, despite herself. Her phone buzzed and she read the text. "I've got to go meet with the carpenter."

Madeleine's refined face instantly registered a combination of disappointment and annoyance. "Well, best of luck with the inn."

"Thank you, Madeleine." Joanna exited the café.

***

Joanna researched proper Victorian colors for the outside of the house—she envisioned a pale yellow house, with creamy deep brown tones and cranberry accents—and met with officials to get the colors approved. She had a long list of things to be done, which needed prioritizing. A dividing wall, added to a private area of the house in the 1960s, was scheduled to be torn down. That would need to be done before any painting. Energy efficient but period-specific windows were going to be installed. Molding needed to be replaced. The original oak flooring needed a few new boards, and sanding and finishing.

Everything took longer than she anticipated. A workperson's promise of "I'll be there Monday" turned into a Friday arrival. An "It'll all be done by mid-September" project wasn't even started until the first week of October. Oddly enough, Joanna didn't mind. The work was being done, and being done well. She had done her homework and found the best plumbers, painters, and renovators she could afford. Fortunately, the main kitchen had already been updated with a new stove and appliances, and only needed painting. The sage color she picked, with pale orange trim, filled Joanna with joy every time she walked into the kitchen. It was just what she wanted. She was also doing some sweat-equity projects: removing all the wallpaper from the bedrooms and first floor, even attempting some furniture refinishing in the garage, and other minor improvements. When it came time to choose a color to paint her bedroom upstairs, she went for a deep Victorian iris that fed her soul. Brian would never have allowed that color on the wall of his bedroom. Too girly or too dark. Basically, "It's not white" would've been his complaint. As it was more than likely no one would ever share that bedroom with her, iris it was.

Cynthia visited often, sensing her sister needed her, even though Joanna still was frequently uncommunicative. During one visit, they were having a morning cup of tea at the house when the door bell rang. Joanna opened the door. "Hi, Rich. Thanks for coming."

A handsome middle-aged man walked in carrying his huge toolbox, wearing jeans and a ripped T-shirt. "Starting to look good in here."

"Thanks. There's a few things I'd like you to look at. The crack in the west wall of the Earl Grey room, and a stuck window and closet door in the English Breakfast. Also, I'd like another lock on the basement door. That one's a little iffy."

Rich said, "I'll take a look. Probably can fix some stuff now. I'll come back for the rest, Ms. Matthews." He glanced at Cynthia. "Hi."

"Rich, this is my sister, Cynthia." Cynthia waved. "And I told you, please call me Joanna. You're in my house practically every day."

"Will do," and he headed upstairs, but not before looking admiringly at Cynthia.

Cynthia watched him walk up the stairs. "Nice."

Later the sisters were having lunch in a Chinese restaurant half a mile from the Tea & Scones. "Next time I visit I'll bring Archie."

"Oh yes, please! I miss him more than almost anything else in Manhattan."

"I figure the way you're headed, you're very likely going to be a Cat Lady. Archie is your starter cat."

"There are worse things than being a Cat Lady."

Cynthia decided to risk her life. "You going to call Michael today?"

"These dumplings are good. Light."

"Joanna!"

"I thought you finally understood! How I feel. I thought I explained."

"Jo, he's no saint. He's human. He's not perfect and he'd never expect you to be perfect."

"I don't want to talk about it!"

"Are you punishing yourself for Brian?"

"Probably."

"But why are you punishing Michael?"

"Punishing? I'm doing him a favor. Cynthia, I..." Her sister waited. Joanna thought a long moment, was about to say something, and her eyes filled with tears.

"Don't you still love him? I know you still love him."

Joanna blinked away her tears: "Cynthia, shut up and eat your dumplings or I'll throw them down your $300 silk blouse," and walked out of the restaurant. When Cynthia finished her lunch and exited, her sister was sitting on a bench right outside the restaurant. Joanna stood sheepishly, linked arms with her, and they walked to the Tea & Scones.

**

One day, in an interior design shop, the sisters picked patterns for chairs being reupholstered, and then chose a paint color for the walls that perfectly complimented an inch of burgundy in the fabric. They left the shop and walked to the Tea & Scones…

…to find Michael sitting on the front steps. Joanna saw him first, and froze in her tracks.

Cynthia said, "What?" and looked in the directon of Joanna's gaze. "I take it that's not one of your troupe of handymen?"

Michael looked up, then stood. "Hello," he said, his eyes transfixed on Joanna.

She and Cynthia walked down the path to the steps. Cynthia couldn't stand the silence and immediate tension so she walked to Michael, hand outstretched. "I'm taking a wild guess that you're Michael. I'm Cynthia, Jo's sister. Nice to meet you, finally."

He shook her hand. "You too, Cynthia."

Joanna couldn't talk. Michael took the initiative: "I'm here, helping Madeleine. She hurt her knee, and her husband's in Florida. Thought, since I was already here, I'd come see the house." More silence. "Can I see the inside?"

Relieved to have something active to do, Joanna walked up the steps and opened the unlocked door. "Workmen are coming in all the time, so I don't bother to lock it," she explained, unnecessarily. She moved aside, he walked in and looked around. On the one bare wall there were four squares of paint samples, all perfect for the room.

"You've done a lot already. The floors are perfect, and you've started picking colors? I like the top left, by the way."

"Rookwood terra cotta."

"Nice. Warm."

Cynthia said, "I'll make some tea," and left for the kitchen.

He continued looking around the house, stepping into the dining room. "It's going to be a grand house again."

"Well...the workmen...and I've been at it night and day, too."

"I know. You were so busy you didn't even call me," Michael said. "It's good to see you. I missed you."

"Michael, no. Please don't."

"I rushed you. Was that it?" She didn't answer. "We hadn't known each other long enough? You weren't sure about us, like I was?"

"No. It wasn't any of that. It's me. And I was married."

"But you're not with Brian any more."

About half of the wallpaper had been torn down in the dining room. Unable to face him, Joanna plugged in the steamer, waited for it to get hot, and held it to the wall. He watched her, getting more frustrated with her behavior. Finally he pulled the plug out of the wall and took the steamer out of her hands. He put his hands on her shoulders and turned her toward him. "Joanna, talk to me." She felt his touch everywhere and almost weakened but Cynthia entered, and Joanna jumped away from him.

"Damn my timing," Cynthia said, putting down a tray with three tea cups, saucers, and plates. "Michael. Would you like a piece of Jo's strawberry rhubarb pie? She's become quite the baker."

"Absolutely. Thanks. I'm not leaving until I know what's going on."

Cynthia said, "Good luck with that." Michael nodded and attempted a smile. Cynthia left the room. He walked over to the wall Joanna had returned to and started peeling paper off, too.

They each kept their eyes on the work in front of them. He said, "Joanna, I know you have, *had* strong feelings for me. But it's not…it wasn't just about Brian, was it? There's something else that I'm not getting?" She said nothing, and he was getting mad. "I drove all the way down here, you can at least answer me."

She turned to him, snapping, "You're here for Madeleine."

"I lied. She's fine. I had to see you."

Joanna couldn't bear looking into his hurt, eager face. She turned away from him and walked over to open the window. The breeze brought the smell of flowers, but Joanna didn't notice it. "I'd ruin your life, Michael. I can't be trusted. Every major decision I've ever made has been wrong."

"I don't know if that's true. But *this* decision is wrong."

"I'm sure I'd hurt you."

"Worse than this? Impossible." He walked around the messy room, trying to gather his thoughts, to say the right thing to convince her. Settling on a sheet-covered chair, he tried to speak as rationally and unemotionally as possible, but didn't manage it for long. "You left me to go back to Brian. It killed me, but I understood. You didn't want to break up your marriage. That made a kind of sense. Now we're apart and it hurts like hell and the worst part is I don't understand why."

She sat on a stool. "It's too…it was too much. Too quick. Too late."

"I don't know what that means."

"I'm getting older."

"Me too. And everyone else on earth."

"You're not a woman."

"That's true."

"I'm getting saggier, and more wrinkly, and grayer every day."

"Me too. So what?"

"You'll look boyishly handsome when you're ninety-five."

"Let's see if that turns out to be true, together." He leaned forward in the chair, elbows on his knees, chin in his hands. "Joanna, I'm still obviously not understanding something. Are you worried I'm one of those idiots who'll run off with a twenty-five year old? I wasn't interested in twenty-five year olds when I was twenty-five."

"It doesn't matter. It's too late."

"You said that, but it's not true. It's never too late. Our future could be wonderful."

"But our future will involve illness and doctors and dying," she got up and paced.

"Wow that came out of nowhere. Is climate change your next excuse?"

"Michael you know what I'm talking about. People get older, and their health…"

"You shouldn't run your life like that." Hammering started upstairs, and he looked in the direction of the noise. It took him a moment to refocus. "None of us knows how long we'll be here."

"But to have found you and maybe lose you…"

"That almost sounds like you love me, Joanna."

"Stop."

"You're losing me now, definitely, this way."

"Before we're in too deep."

"Oh it *is* too late for that. We were in too deep probably before we got off that bus." He paused. "What we have is a gift, whether from God or Cape May ghosts, or just a roll of the dice, it's a gift."

She didn't reply. Just shook her head.

"Joanna, this doesn't make sense!"

"It makes sense to me. This is my life now. I can't risk it. I'm not rocking this little boat. I've found a kind of peace here."

"Peace at any price?"

"Anything to help quiet my inner demons."

"Don't appease them. Fight them. For yourself. Fight them for me."

"I'm just not strong enough."

She didn't say anything else, and he slowly turned and started to leave as Cynthia was coming in with the pie and a pot of tea. "Michael? Stay."

It was as if he didn't hear her. He stood shaking his head, glaring at Joanna. "I should be mad at you. Believe me, I was. You really proved to me that the line between love and hate is razor thin. But now I'm only sorry for you. You don't trust us." He ripped a piece of wallpaper down. "I hope you'll be happy here. And I hope it'll be enough." He opened the front door but couldn't leave yet. He cleared his throat and continued, in a low and raspy voice: "Maybe *we* scared you. Stirred up those demons of yours. But I'd fight, risk anything, rock any boat, to kiss you on the beach again, and beat you at Scrabble and skee ball. Go to bed with you every night, and have coffee with you every morning. Whether it's for the next ten months or ten years." There were tears in his eyes. "Maybe I'm just an idiot and you didn't…don't feel about me the way I feel about you. I don't know anything any more."

A tear slid down Joanna's face but she didn't move, or say anything.

Michael held up his hand saying goodbye to Cynthia.

"Michael," Cynthia called to him as he closed the front door behind him.

Joanna's head snapped in the direction of the closed door. She slowly sat down. Both women were silent. Cynthia sipped the tea.

"Joanna, I've kept my mouth shut long enough." Joanna got up to leave but Cynthia said, "I'll be quick, and you'll listen. You owe me that. I've put thousands of miles on my car, and neglected my shop and my own life for you. I've helped you emotionally, financially, everything." Joanna sat down again, the drop cloth billowing underneath her. "You've got this great place, and a new fulfilling life, thanks to your hard work. Your pursuit of your dream. Put some of that effort into your relationship with Michael. He's willing to forgive you and move on with you. Why aren't you?"

The hammering upstairs stopped.

After another sip of tea, Cynthia continued. "I'll tell you something. I've had lots of men in my life. Enough that if I never have another it'll be fine. Even relaxing. There's nothing wrong with being alone. However, if I do get the chance for love or just good old meaningless sex, I'll grab it with both hands."

"Well, that's good to know!" Rich stood at the bottom of the stairs, holding his tool box. Both sisters looked at him. He walked over to Cynthia, handing her one of his business cards. "Maybe I can buy you a cup of coffee?"

She smiled and said, "Why not."

"Half an hour? Joe's Café?"

"I'll be there."

"Ms. Matthews, er, Joanna, I'll be back tomorrow morning by 10," He looked at Cynthia. "Maybe later. Bye."

He left and Joanna was instantly on her way up the stairs. Cynthia said, "Wait, Jo. One more thing. I guess our parents' divorce affected you more than it did me. And our crazy controlling mother. And you were hurt in college, like everyone gets hurt in college, but you put up walls. You married Brian knowing nothing would be demanded of you, so there was no real risk. Now you've been given this miracle, this lovely man who adores you, and you're sabotaging yourself. You're just plain scared."

"No, it's…"

"Shut up! I'm not done! Yes, you hurt Brian, and maybe broke his heart. Breaking Michael's and yours, too, won't make Brian feel any better."

Joanna looked at her sister, to see her crying—something she'd never seen Cynthia do, even as a child when her pet died, or later when they buried their parents. "Cynthia."

"You and Michael? On the steps outside…in here…I've never had that…that chemistry…hell, *I* felt it. And a man willing to open himself like that, to come here for you. Do you think that's gonna ever happen again? You're throwing it away. That feels sinful to me."

Silence from her sister. Cynthia continued. "I'll never say another word about any of this. I'm done. And now I'm going to get treated to a cup of coffee by a hunky guy at least fifteen years younger than I am." She opened the door, turned back to Joanna and said, "I might be home very late…or tomorrow."

***

Michael left the Tea & Scones totally dejected. At some point, in the distant future, he might be proud of himself that he tried, he did everything he could, to get her back. Right now he could barely stand the walk to Henry's. Although he couldn't face a crowded restaurant, he couldn't face being alone more, knowing he'd be alone the rest of his life, missing her.

He sat at a table at Henry's outside in the back. In a few weeks it would be chillier, and the owner would close off this section of the restaurant. A little death. He sat there, the menu a blur in front of him, and he suddenly realized he felt old. For the first time. The coming autumn didn't offer any attractions either. Before everything went wrong, he looked forward to walking amongst Central Park's changing trees, with Joanna. Or going to the village for hot chocolate on MacDougal Street, with Joanna. Or cuddling with her under blankets in front of a fireplace at the Tea & Scones.

It was all his fault. He fell too fast. That had never happened to him before. He loved her, he always would, but her barriers were up, and he couldn't get past them. And maybe she didn't really love him? Could he have been that wrong? Now he felt old and lonely. Even after Donna left him, after his son went to college, after boring dates, he never felt alone. Joanna was perfect for him, but it wasn't going to happen...that made him alone. He also knew he'd never date again. What would be the point?

He wouldn't pursue her any more. He'd done everything he could. It was humiliating and hurt too much. It was over. It was over before when she chose Brian, but he was too stupid to accept it. He already missed her so desperately that he couldn't stand it.

He was an idiot. Allowing himself to go through all this yet again. It wasn't bad enough that she rejected him in New York. He had to come all the way down to Cape May to beg her to hurt him again, to get beaten down again. There are words for people who inflict pain on themselves. Masochist was too elegant. He was a plain old fucking moron.

There were no more buses back to Manhattan that night, and he didn't have a car, so he couldn't escape Cape May until tomorrow. Tonight he'd have dinner with Madeleine and Dan, and this time he would need their friendship, their wisdom, their sympathy. And many glasses of their finest $20 bottle of red wine.

CHAPTER 20

Of the furniture left by the ex-owners of the Tea & Scones, Joanna kept what she felt belonged in the house, Cynthia took some for her shop, and the rest was sold or given away. The owner's quarters were fully painted, a new half-size refrigerator, mini-washer/dryer, and dishwasher delivered, and Joanna moved in.

Cynthia spent the first night in the house, too, to keep her sister company. True to her word she brought the drugged Archie. Joanna was ridiculously happy to see him and waited patiently while his sedative for the long car ride wore off. She petted him, fed him, and showed him his two litter boxes. In no time at all, the enviably adaptable cat set off to explore his large new home. She didn't see him for hours. At 11:30 that night, Joanna almost cried when she heard his pawsteps enter her room. She slept better then she had in a long time, with the warm cat cradled in her arms.

The next morning, it was time for Cynthia to go back to New York. On the porch of the Tea & Scones, Cynthia hugged her sister goodbye, a little too vehemently. "I can't keep visiting this often, but I'm worried about you."

"I'm doing okay. Go back to your regular life. I'm fine, really."

"No, you're not. You don't talk about anything other than this house."

"I love this house and I'm devoting myself to it. That's a good thing."

"And you're okay being alone?"

"Alone? There are workers in and out every day."

"You know what I mean!"

"I'd better get used to it. I may be alone the rest of my life."

"That's your choice, Joanna. Maybe I've coddled you too much."

"If you did, thanks. It helped having you here."

"Will you promise to call if you need me? Anytime, day or night?"

Joanna nodded and Cynthia hugged her again. Halfway down the path to her car, Cynthia turned around and looked up. "It's a great house, Jo, but I wish I could get the image of you as Miss Havisham out of my mind."

"I'm too busy to sit and rot. I'll keep in touch. Go have a life. I need you to keep earning money so I can borrow it."

"It's good to know you need me for something." Cynthia drove off, waving before she turned the corner.

Joanna stood on the street for a few moments. Despite her show of bravado for her sister, she was suddenly engulfed in loneliness. She deserved it, after the pain she'd caused everyone. But life had to go on. She turned around and gazed at her house. She imagined how it would look after the paint job was finished next week—it was going to be warm and welcoming, and she'd have to be, too. A book on B&Bs said, "The owner sets the tone." If she was miserable and bitter, it would be reflected in the house, too, and no one would want to stay there. Luckily, she had some time before the inn would be up and running.

The first few days and nights in the house, alone, felt odd, but she persevered. It became more comfortable, more like her home as time went on. As busy as she was, she was easily derailed by memories of what she now thought of as her "old life." Something silly or minor—like a neon sign for coffee or a pile of newspapers—would remind her of Brian and she'd feel crippling remorse. The little things... she couldn't look at a row of DVD spines without thinking "What would Brian pick?" At the grocery store she had to stop picking out food Brian liked but she didn't. (There might never be a box of Oreos on her kitchen counter again).

She often had trouble sleeping, and lay on her back staring at the ceiling, listening to the old house creak. After all those years of marriage it was strange sleeping in a big bed alone. What she missed, more than the actual Brian, was the sound of another person breathing next to her. And it took her a long time to force herself to move to the center of the bed.

She adopted the European way of food shopping. What do I want for dinner tonight? Almost every day she stopped in the local grocery store. They knew her by name and asked if there was anything special she'd like them to stock for her. One day, half way to that grocery store, to get supplies for dinner, Joanna suddenly stopped, sat down on a bench, took a deep breath and called Brian.

He picked up the phone. "Jo."

"Hi, Brian." The other end was silent. "How are you doing?"

"Surviving," he said.

"How's work?"

"Quiet, this time of year."

"Good." Silence. "Has your mom moved to the assisted living place yet? I've lost track of time."

"Yes."

"I'll visit her when I can. She never liked me much anyway."

"She'd still like a visit, even from you, I'm sure." Seconds passed. "You wanted to say something?"

"Brian, I'm sure it's too soon, but I wanted to call you, to apologize, for everything."

His voice was affectless. "Supposedly it takes two to mess up a marriage. And it doesn't get more messed up than divorced."

"You didn't do anything. I guess there was just something missing in me."

"Or missing in me for you."

"Stop it. I take full blame for this."

His voice was hard. "It's not your fault that you couldn't really commit, that our experiment didn't work. Well, it worked for me…" He paused a long time. She didn't know what to say. When he did talk again he was louder. "If we had kids you probably wouldn't have left me. We would've been more bound together. Forever. I should've let you adopt a kid."

"Having kids doesn't keep people together. Certainly didn't help my parents. Who knows."

"I wasn't enough for you."

"It wasn't that. I was wrong for you."

"No. You weren't, Jo."

"Brian…"

"I suppose you think you're right for *him*?"

She paused. "No. It's over."

Brian shouted, "I thought you left me for him! What's the matter with you?"

"I think I'm better alone."

"Wow, wrong again. I thought he'd last at least six months before it all came crashing down on you."

"Brian…"

"Have you given up on the house yet? Let me guess. Too much work? Town's too small? Too close to the water? The sand is too sandy."

She wanted to scream at him to stop, but felt he, as the injured party, had the right to bitch. She took another deep breath. "Brian, I called you to apologize."

"Fuck you and your apology."

She expected him to hang up. She wished he'd hang up.

"Joanna, you just want to make yourself feel better."

"That's probably true, but I really am truly sorry. I hope someday you can start to forgive me."

He tossed off a "Whatever."

"Just please know I never meant any of this to happen."

"Uh huh."

"And thanks for letting Cynthia bring Archie to me."

"He always liked you more."

"I've discovered, in ways you don't want to hear, that he's a good mouser." There was a pause. She continued, "How's work?"

He said, "You already asked me."

"Oh."

"Joanna?"

"Yes."

"Don't call me again." And he hung up.

Joanna stayed on the bench for half an hour, thinking. Wanting to understand why things had gone so wrong, she self-analyzed. Question number one: "Why did I marry Brian?" Pathetic answer: "He asked me." Brian was nice, and *there*. And she was way past the age of meeting even Mr. Almost Right. She had felt *something* for him, maybe it was some form of love. A need to be needed. Not alone. Looking back, of course it was a mistake. But if she hadn't met Michael, she'd probably still be with Brian, either in Cape May or that cramped apartment, with white walls. They probably would've been married until one of them died.

The grocery shopping would have to wait. She turned around and headed home. Scrambled eggs and toast on her deck, watching the sunset, would do her fine.

***

"I'll be in Cape May by noon on Saturday," said Cynthia over the phone.

Joanna was in the garden pulling weeds. "I'm glad you're coming."

"Jo, you do know what Saturday is, don't you?"

"It's not every day I turn sixty. Thank God."

"No big deal. Been there, done that, moved on. You're so lucky to be the younger sister, and have the advantage of my wisdom."

"I say that to myself every day."

"Pick the nicest restaurant in town and make a reservation. Let's make this very special. Let's dress up."

"That sounds really nice."

"I kind of wanted to throw you a surprise party, there or in Manhattan, but..."

"Thanks for knowing that's exactly what I don't want."

"At my apartment, next time you come for a visit, I'll have a brunch for you."

"I'd love it. Thanks, Cynthia. You've been a rock for me, you know."

"I know."

When Cynthia arrived on Saturday, Joanna showed her all the updates in the house. Some bedrooms upstairs still needed painting, but the main floor was almost finished.

"I'm stunned. Jo, it's all beautiful. Elegant yet comfy. Spotless. Welcoming. Hell I want to stay here."

"You know you are always welcome. I couldn't've bought the house without you. And tell all your rich New York friends that the Tea & Scones is the place to stay when visiting Cape May. That's one of my many rejected tag lines for the inn, by the way."

"Good. It's awful. The house deserves better."

"Seriously, though, take a bunch of cards and brochures and chat up the inn to your patrons. The more money I make the faster I can pay you back."

That night, the sisters put on dresses and heels and took a cab to a restaurant about ten miles outside of town. The May was a sophisticated, quiet restaurant with an excellent wine list (hence the cab) and reportedly the best lobster in the northeast.

The waiter uncorked and poured the wine. Cynthia okayed it, waited until it was fully poured and the waiter gone, then held up the glass: "Joanna Marie Matthews, approximately fifty-nine years and three-hundred and sixty days ago, I wanted to kill you."

"I did not know that."

"It's true. Shari Freilicher, down the street, was my best friend…"

"I remember her."

"…until her mom had another baby. Then Shari became the biggest bitch any single-digit human could aspire to be. One day, when she was smacking me, she paused and told me her life was hell now because her new little baby sister cried too much, and smelled, and their mother didn't read to her at bedtime any more."

"Shari was a very aware seven year old."

"Oh, she was almost nine."

"Well, that explains it."

"She said you would be as annoying, and life wrecking, as her sister was."

"Proper assumption, I'd say. And how long is this toast going to be? Can I take a little sip…"

"Lord knows we've had our differences, and I frequently don't understand you. I was a grown up at twelve and you may be an Olympic level late bloomer, but you have bloomed, beautifully. After those initial death threats, I've loved you every decade of our lives together. But I love you now, *like* you, and admire you more than ever. It's nice when your sister is also your best friend."

Joanna lowered her eyes and her glass. "Don't make me cry here in public."

"I'll just say, then, happy birthday. I hope it's a great year for you and the Tea & Scones!"

They clinked the glasses and sipped the dry wine as the appetizers arrived.

After an incredible, and incredibly expensive meal— which Cynthia waved off with a flourish of her American

Express Gold card and a tossed off "I bought an antique today so it's all tax deductible"—the sisters staggered to their cab for the quick ride back to the inn.

Feeling full and tipsy, Joanna said goodnight to Cynthia, who was staying in an almost finished room on the second floor, and walked upstairs to her haven, with Archie steps in front of her.

Nights were hard, even after full, lovely days like this one had been. In bed, instantly, the quiet and the dark were a terrible combination. When she closed her eyes, Michael was there, across a table, or at the end of the hall at his apartment door, looking at her longingly, making her feel more desirable than Helen of Troy. Her body awoke in a way it never did with Brian, or any other man. Eventually she passed out, but sleep, this night like many before it, was hardly restorative. Her dreams were unsettling, overly sexual, and she'd wake up with clenched thighs.

***

By now Joanna knew every inch of the Tea & Scones, from the low-ceilinged basement to the creepy, claustrophobic attic crawl space. (Months ago she reluctantly gave up watching or reading scary stories.) She learned to kill bugs without screaming for Brian first. She tried hands-on repairs, little things. In Manhattan she would have thrown away a broken lamp and bought one at a thrift store. Now, she attempted rewiring one, and succeeded. When the painters and other workers were in her house she made them coffee and sandwiches, and watched them work, trying to learn. It shocked her to realize, after many many days, that two different guys were flirting with her. When it was obvious that one nice guy was about to ask her out, she made herself scarce. There would never be another love in her life. Of that she was sure.

When she wasn't planning or vacuuming the dirt and dust brought about by the workers and the work, she was baking and trying new recipes. The Cape May library became a second home to her. She read more books to expand her knowledge of Victoriana, and memorized dates of Cape May's history, using homemade flash cards. She started interviewing employees and writing pieces for a blog to publicize the November opening of the house. The website she helped design already had traffic and inquiries.

Joanna appreciated that there was always something to do/learn/fix, knowing she was now officially an inn workaholic. After years of doing work she couldn't care less about, the change was remarkable and welcome. The few moments she allowed herself to relax, she'd sit on her deck, with a partial view of the ocean. The sunsets and sunrises were beautiful and bittersweet.

Occasionally she'd stop in another bed and breakfast and introduce herself to the owners. Although her inn would be competition for the other inns, the innkeepers were unfailingly welcoming and helpful. They'd discuss their own additions, renovations, color choices, and landscaping ideas. She was beginning to make friends.

Waves of longing passed through her when she saw the outside of the arcade, or Morrow's Nut House, neither one of which she'd set foot in since relocating. Life in New York City seemed so long ago. Knowing it was a drive away made it easier. She wanted to remain active in New York culture and also see friends who were still talking to her after what she did to Brian. Through the Internet, she kept in touch with them, ex-coworkers, and former neighbors. In fact, she'd reconnected with both childhood and college friends and used social networking to keep people up-to-date with the progress of the renovations. The Tea & Scones already had one-hundred seventy-five "friends."

She wondered, had Brian begun to hate her less? He'd have to call and tell her because she'd never call him again. Had Michael moved on with his life? She missed him every day, but knew their relationship would never work. He could never trust her again. She did her best to put him out of her thoughts. Most of the time it didn't work.

The next time Cynthia visited, after an outing with Rich she joined Joanna for a cup of coffee on the front porch. "Cape May is starting to feel like my second home. And not just because of my new boyfriend."

"It's entrancing here, isn't it?"

"This house is like my niece or something. I look forward to visiting her and seeing how she's changed. You've done a good job of raising her. I'm glad you're happy here."

"Happy?" Joanna said the word as if she'd never heard it before. "Yes, I guess I am."

Cynthia said, "Is there a 'but' coming?"

Joanna chose her words carefully. "I'm happy with the house. Ridiculously happy. I adore it. I belong here. Cape May is perfect for me."

"But?"

"Not so much *but*. Maybe *and*." Joanna paused. "You know I got my divorce papers a while ago?"

"You told me."

"Took me a week to open the envelope and then three days to sign them."

"You haven't changed your mind about anything, have you?"

"No. I signed them, and mailed them back. I'm officially divorced."

Cynthia said, "We're both happy-go-lucky singles now, huh?"

"I'm certainly not feeling that. I feel guilty. Less than before, but still."

"Life happens, Joanna. If it helps you at all, Brian's not doing too bad. Even had a date last week."

"Wow. Brian on a date. Good for him. Did I tell you I called him, to check in and apologize?"

"How'd he take it?"

"Very well. He told me to fuck myself and never call again."

"Oh, that's a start I guess."

"But somehow I felt a little better. And I'm glad I called. If he's embarking on the dating ship, he should know nothing was his fault."

"Joanna, it wasn't all your fault. Forget *fault* anyway. Brian wasn't perfect. And he sure as hell wasn't right for you. That you made it twenty years is amazing."

"Sister, I think you might be right."

Suddenly Cynthia walked over to Joanna and hugged her.

"What?"

"I'm proud of you, and I like the new and improved you."

"Thank you. That means a lot to me. You know, I've been self-examining, a lot. Seeing a therapist, too."

"Good! I couldn't live without mine."

"I'd love to just blame everything on our parents."

"They're dead. Go ahead."

"I do, partly. But I'm a grown up. It's too late to throw everything at them. I suppose they did their best. I've been thinking, about everything. In the Too Late Department, looking over my whole life, I regret most not having children."

"Oh yeah, that's definitely too late. I'm sorry."

"This house, though, feels like the best of me. It feels like what I've heard mothers say about their children: that I've learned more from this house than this house could ever get from me. I know it's a poor analogy, but I think you get me. Yes?"

Cynthia nodded. "I do get you. And as I've stated I'm proud of you. And I'm hungry." She headed to the kitchen. "I'll make us sandwiches."

Joanna posted some new pictures of the house online, then stared out the window for a few minutes. She loved seeing the Victorians across the street. And the trees. She did love living here. She was, she realized, indeed happy.

Eventually she joined Cynthia in the kitchen. Cynthia said, "You're out of milk. You want me to go?"

"I'd like to get out for some air."

"Great. I'll sit and read."

Joanna walked out of the house and down the path, stopped, turned around and gazed up at her newly painted house. The colors were perfect. Exactly what she wanted, and the repairs inside and out were coming along nicely. It was her house, the realization of her dreams. She felt a surge of pride. The house would be finished soon, if the workers kept to her schedule, and they would.

Her phone buzzed, indicating an email. Joanna touched all the necessary icons to see that the Tea & Scones had its first reservation! Six people checking in the Tuesday before Thanksgiving, checking out on Sunday. Three rooms! She shrieked with joy…and immediately wanted to tell the good news to Michael. The rush of feeling was so overwhelming she rushed to the front steps to sit down before she fell down.

With her head between her knees, somehow, suddenly right there, everything clicked into place for her. She breathed deeply. In. Out. Five full times. She paced on the path a few times, gathering her strength and thoughts for what she knew she had to do. She took out her cell phone and punched in Michael's phone number. Hearing his recorded greeting flustered her and she almost hung up anonymously, but realized her number would appear under his "recent calls." She started talking and then froze and then hung up. "Damn!"

She called again.

"Michael, it's Joanna. I want to drive up to Manhattan to talk to you if, if you're willing to see me. Please call me."

She was filled with such nervous energy she started walking, quickly, down the block, and then back a few times. Her phone buzzed and she attacked it, thinking it was him. It was a text from Cynthia: "r u milking cow im hungry" with a smiley icon.

When Joanna returned to the Tea & Scones, her sister was dozing in a comfortable chair. Cynthia opened her eyes and said, "Something's different. You look glowy."

"I called him. I called Michael, and left a message, and now I'm terrified he won't call me back. Oh, Cynthia," she went over to her sister and hugged her, smiling and crying. "I know what I want." She sat down and stood up again. "I called him." She sat down. "I'm starving."

Cynthia got up, saying, "I'll make us tea and we can eat," and went into the kitchen.

Joanna was left alone with her thoughts. She shook them out of her head and tried to answer some emails, but couldn't concentrate.

After four hours of no phone calls, she tried again. "Michael, I understand if you hate me but please, I have to talk to you. I'm driving up to New York. I should be there by seven or eight, depending on the traffic."

She ran up the stairs to where Cynthia was napping. She knocked on the bedroom door. "Cynthia, I need your help. I'm driving to Manhattan. I need you to stay here to get some deliveries and let the painter in. He's stopping by soon but I can't wait for him. Maybe he'll be cute and you can start dating him, too."

"Oh, aren't we suddenly full of fun."

"Fun? I'm terrified. Michael has every right to never speak to me again."

"Good luck, Jo. Truly. Good luck." They hugged and Joanna ran down the stairs. She was so invigorated she felt she might get to Manhattan faster if she walked. Still, she got in her car, turned the key, and her phone rang.

She answered it and heard, "Don't bother driving to Manhattan." It was Michael.

"Please. I'm in the car. Let me come and see you."

"Then come to Henry's. I'm here."

***

He was in a booth, with three research books open in front of him. The first draft of his book was done and he was editing it. He'd come to Cape May for more research at the historical society. Although he tried to concentrate, every ounce of him wanted to look for her, to scan the patrons arriving at the restaurant. It had taken all his will power not to call her back immediately after her first phone call. But he had to protect himself from further hurt. Suddenly he felt very emotional and tears filled his eyes. Grown men aren't supposed to cry in diners so he propped up the large menu in front of his face.

A moment later, he heard, "Lemonade?"

"No, I didn't order…" he said, and looked up to see Joanna holding a large glass of lemonade with ice and two straws in it.

He didn't offer, so she asked, "Can I sit down?" He didn't reply, and instead slowly closed the books and note-books, wiping his eyes as discreetly as possible.

She quickly put the lemonade down, some of it spilling on the table, and sat opposite him. He stared at her, still too mad at her to speak. Mad at himself, too, that he was excited to see her again. Mad that her frantic phone messages fanned that spark of hope that he couldn't extinguish, as much as he stomped on it. His gaze was so penetrating she had to look away, grabbing some napkins to wipe up the little spill.

She spoke slowly, and carefully, not meeting those angry, hurt eyes again. "I can't even begin to apologize, or explain that I was scared and overwhelmed, by us. Mostly I want to tell you that I'm sorry I hurt you by trying so hard not to hurt you." She knew she was taking too long, and that any second he could jump up and leave her so she tried to hurry. "Michael, I wish...if I could..."

A waitress came over, saying, "What can I get youse?" and plopping down another menu for Joanna.

Joanna squeaked out, "Oh," and picked up the menu. It shook in her hands. "Coffee." The waitress walked away. Joanna looked into Michael's searching eyes and tried to start again, "I wanted to...to..." but the interruption made her lose her nerve. "I...I..." and she froze.

He saw the fear in her eyes, "Go on."

She looked down, and shook her head. "I can't yet."

"I'm not going anywhere. What was so important that you were going to drive to Manhattan for?"

She breathed deeply a few times. When she looked at him, his eyes were softer. It gave her the courage to say, "I'm sorry. I feel like that's all I've been saying for months and that it has no power to actually make anyone feel any better."

The waitress put a cup of coffee on the table. Joanna took a sip, spilling some in the saucer when she put it down. She grabbed a napkin and folded it neatly under the cup. After a moment she said, "You're partly to blame for all this, you know."

"Me? How?"

"You were technically decades late. I gave up on the concept of Mr. Right a very long time ago. Then you show up. But Brian...I couldn't... After that, I felt I...no, I *knew* I didn't deserve you. That I'd ruin it somehow. That maybe

308 | HOLLY CASTER

even somehow I'd begin to think less of you because you loved…because you cared for me."

"Who's to say there's a time schedule for anything in life. And if you think you don't deserve me, that's not real. That's one of your demons talking. You can't listen to it."

"Maybe. But it's been a scary loud demon for so long."

They each took a few seconds. She sipped at the tasteless coffee, and he watched her. He continued, "What about me deserving you? I was willing to fight for you. Over and over again. Humiliating myself."

"No, you didn't. You were brave and wonderful and I admire you." Her eyes were shining. "And I'd fight Satan, Hitler, and Klingons for you. Fighting my demons, though, that's harder."

He was still cautious. "You feeling stronger now? To fight?"

She nodded. "I've grown. Pursuing my dream. Learning. I'm becoming someone I like."

"You should. The house is glowing because of you." She looked at him quizzically. "I drive by it, when I'm down here."

She said, "You know, the Tea & Scones is everything I've ever wanted. I've worked harder on it than all the other things in my life combined. I tried to separate the parts of me. Closed off you, and my failed marriage, and my poor choices, and just concentrate on my dream. But when I found out I'd booked my first reservations…"

"Congratulations! That's wonderful, Joanna."

"…all I wanted to do was tell you."

"Really?"

"That was what mattered. You. I realized if I want all this and you, I have to fight for you."

"How you think you're gonna do?"

"Well, it's really a matter of self-preservation: I either have to fight, or die without you. Because I simply can't live without you any longer."

"Really?"

"Michael, I want to spend the rest of my life with you in the Tea & Scones, making up for how much I hurt you. I want to make you happy. I…want you. I love you."

He excitedly reached out for her hand and knocked over the glass of icy lemonade into her lap. She yelped and leapt up. He grabbed his napkin and blotted her pants. "Oh, Joanna, I'm sorry!"

She shivered out, "I deserve this."

"No. You deserve nothing but happiness," he said, grabbing napkins from the set table behind him, and wiping her wet hands.

"Well, that's in your hands, now. And I think, *think* that I might finally be good enough for you."

"You always were good enough. More than good enough. You're perfect for me."

"Don't make me cry."

"And was it wishful hearing or did you say you love me?"

"Only more than anyone I've ever known. Only for the rest of my life."

He beamed. "I love you, too." They held each other, so tightly that he realized first-hand that "Oh, that really is cold. How can I help?"

"Walk me back to the Tea & Scones, so I can get out of these pants?"

"I'll walk you back to the Tea & Scones, I'll help you off with your pants, I'll go into the shower with you, and I'll never leave your side again...if that's what you want."

"Yes, that's exactly what I want," she said.

"Then let's go home." Michael threw a $20 bill on the table, took Joanna's hand and they walked out of Henry's into the Cape May sunshine.

© DARRYL FOSSA

HOLLY CASTER writes an entertainment column for *The Nyack Villager*, has written dozens of articles for employee assistance websites, and is the Editor of two journals devoted to pain management education. She is hard at work on her next novel *Anne/Island/Whales*. Ms. Caster lives in the lower Hudson Valley Region with her playwright husband Tom Dudzick and their two cats Alfie and Bill.

169 River Road

Unorthodox.